THE PERFECT MOTHER

CLAIRE ALLAN

Best wishes

B

Boldw**oo**d

First published in Great Britain in 2025 by Boldwood Books Ltd.

Copyright © Claire Allan, 2025

Cover Design by Lisa Horton

Cover Images: Shutterstock and Magdalena Russocka / Trevillion Images

A CIP catalogue record for this book is available from the British Library.

Paperback ISBN 978-1-83533-430-0

Large Print ISBN 978-1-83533-431-7

Hardback ISBN 978-1-83533-429-4

Ebook ISBN 978-1-83533-432-4

Kindle ISBN 978-1-83533-433-1

Audio CD ISBN 978-1-83533-424-9

MP3 CD ISBN 978-1-83533-425-6

Digital audio download ISBN 978-1-83533-427-0

This book is printed on certified sustainable paper. Boldwood Books is dedicated to putting sustainability at the heart of our business. For more information please visit https://www.boldwoodbooks.com/about-us/sustainability/

Boldwood Books Ltd, 23 Bowerdean Street, London, SW6 3TN

www.boldwoodbooks.com

For Joe & Luka
whose mother is far from perfect
but tries her best.

PROLOGUE
DECEMBER 2023

'There's been an incident with Tilly,' the woman on the other end of the line says. Mel feels the breath leave her body. Through the ringing in her ears, she hears the quick follow-up of 'She's fine. She's not hurt. But we thought it best to let you know. Given everything.'

So much is implied in those words. 'Given everything.' Mel feels blame settle on her shoulders. She feels as if the soft-voiced woman she is now speaking to is joining the long list of people who look at her with judgement – who tilt their heads with mock sympathy and an unsaid, 'Well, you have to expect such things will happen now'.

Given everything.

'What's happened?' Mel snaps, a hundred different scenarios – none of them good – racing through her mind. 'What do you mean by "incident"?'

'There was a lady... at the fence. She was calling to Tilly – using her name. She didn't gain access to our site. Tilly was perfectly safe; one of our staff spotted her talking to the woman and intervened.'

Without needing to hear any further details or watch the CCTV the nursery offers to show her, Mel knows who the woman is. She *knows that when she asks, three-year-old Tilly will tell her it was Alice.*

It is always Alice. It has been for months now. She has been chipping away at everything important to Mel. Breaking her life down bit by bit by bit. But this is different. The thought of her getting close to Tilly makes Mel's blood run cold.

Immediately she knows that this escalation of behaviour means she can never, ever send her child back to that nursery. Or any nursery in Carrickfergus, the town on the banks of Belfast Lough where she was born and raised. The town she's always thought she'd live in her entire life. The town that no longer feels like a safe home.

Over the course of the last eight months, her feelings of belonging have been stripped away – her very sense of identity flayed from her in excruciating strips. The life she wanted – the life she'd thought she had sewn up – has been taken from her. Her job. Her business. Her reputation. Her ability to walk down the street without whispers and examining looks. Her self-belief annihilated in the process. Rumours spread like wildfire – each crazier than the last. Versions of her life and what happened have been invented and reinvented, and spread like the gospel to anyone with ears, or a functioning Wi-Fi connection.

She'd hoped if she just kept her head down, the rawness of what had happened would pass – Alice would come to accept the truth. Mel is not to blame.

But this? This 'incident'? No. This is not something Mel can ignore in the hope it will just go away.

She is scared now. Terrified, even. Turning up at Tilly's day care like that. It's a message to her that Alice can get close to her beautiful girl whenever she wants and there is nothing Mel can do about it. It's a message that Alice is unravelling further, becoming increasingly unhinged.

And God only knows how she will react when she learns about the baby. The tiny little person growing in Mel's womb. This tiny person, currently no bigger than a lime, according to the diagram Mel has pinned to the wall of the room that had been her home office. Almost six centimetres and just forming fingernails and bones. Something so precious to Mel, but which will feel horribly cruel and unfair to Alice.

Mel isn't showing yet and has kept the news quiet – her parents and Ed's sister Emma being the only people who know, apart from medical professionals. They haven't even told Tilly she is going to be a big sister. Mel dreads the news becoming public – dreads the reactions of strangers, the way it will inevitably set tongues wagging again.

What will it drive Alice to do next?

'Play it cool,' Ed tells her before she leaves to pick Tilly up and have a proper chat with the nursery staff. 'You don't want to scare Tilly.'

'Maybe I do,' Mel cries. 'Maybe I want her to know it's not only strangers you need to stay away from. Maybe I need her to know that people we thought were friends aren't always safe.'

She doesn't really want her child to be scared, but she has to think of a way to let a three-year-old know that Alice – who has made hot chocolate with her, and put her hair in soft curls – is no longer her friend and never will be again. That she is now one of the 'baddies'.

'She wanted me to go with her,' Tilly says, sitting on the swivel-chair in the nursery office, swinging her legs as her eyes dart all around the room, taking in the sights of the space that is normally out of bounds for the children. Tilly is drinking in every detail. She seems completely unfazed by her chance meeting with Alice at the fence.

Mel has to remind her to focus instead on the questions she is being asked.

'She said she was going to take me as a surprise to see you and Daddy,' Tilly says, 'but Miss Rachel said I had to come back inside for story time. Mummy, Alice looked all messy. I think she might have a wee bug or something.'

Mel nods, forcing a few words of agreement and reassurance out of *her mouth before Miss Rachel tells Tilly she can have five more minutes at the sand-tray. Not one to ever turn down the opportunity to play with sand, Tilly doesn't need telling twice. She hops off the seat and runs out of the room to start playing.*

'I didn't speak to her myself,' Miss Rachel says. 'When I called Tilly back, she left pretty quickly. We normally don't let the children play on the grass by the fence.'

'So where were you? Or the other staff? How did she get over there without anyone spotting her?' Mel asks, as she digs her nails into the palms of her hands inside her pockets. It's the only way she can stop herself from screaming.

Miss Rachel blushes – her already toned and bronzed face taking on a distinctly pink glow. 'We were there in the play area too. Tilly wouldn't have been more than a couple of metres from us at any stage but you know, we have twenty children in her group and as much as we try, we can't have eyes on them all at all times.'

'But you should!' Mel snaps, the crack in her voice too harsh, too obvious to try and hide. She knows the nursery is a good nursery. She knows their safety policies are watertight. She knows Tilly is safe and well.

For now.

But she can't shake the dread in the pit of her stomach. Alice is becoming increasingly unpredictable. She isn't stable. And clearly, she is nowhere near done with blaming Mel.

Mel could go to the police, she supposes, but she can't bring herself to set the cops on a grieving woman. Once news like that got out – and it would get out in a town as small as Carrickfergus – it would only give people another reason to paint her as the villain of the piece. It would just feed the narrative Alice has been painting to every single person who will listen.

No, she has to take drastic action, she thinks as she drives home. She has had enough.

1

MARCH 2024

33 weeks + 5 days

It doesn't feel like home yet, but she didn't expect that it would. Not when it is little more than a building site. Their belongings are split between a storage unit, the front room of this decaying farmhouse, and boxes scattered in the rooms they are using as temporary accommodation until a mobile home arrives to house them during the renovation.

They'd originally hoped to be able to work and live around the building works they have planned for their new home, but just a couple of nights shared with the dust, spiders, dodgy pipes and rotted floorboards of this once beautiful home had put paid to that notion.

When the builders started trudging through in muddy boots, before lifting flooring in the unused rooms and drilling into decades-old plaster, the decision was made.

Now, two weeks later, they are just waiting for the second-hand mobile home to arrive, be wired up and plumbed to allow them to move in so the builders can carry on at pace with their work.

The house has potential. Bags of it. Mel can picture it all now – a perfect mix of period features and mod cons. It will be beautiful. Warm and cosy. Surrounded by wildflowers and hedgerows, all with the soundtrack of birds in the trees and the bleating of sheep in the nearby fields. It will be an idyllic location to raise their two children. Tilly, now four, has already decided that this is 'the bestest house she has ever seen in her whole life'. Her inquisitive nature has had her sneaking into rooms with peeling wallpaper, cracked plaster, and mould creeping around the window frames. Mel needs eyes on the back on her head to stop Tilly disappearing altogether into a discarded box or the unused outbuildings to the rear of the yard. Her imagination is already running wild and Mel finds it's a joy to watch her explore her new surroundings.

The fear that her daughter could disappear one day and simply not come back has not left, however. Not even now. Ed has done – and continues to do – his very best to reassure her that they are all safe here. Two weeks ago they packed their belongings into a lorry and shipped their lives to this idyllic fixer-upper just outside of Derry. It's just over eighty miles from Carrickfergus. Eighty miles from the awful, ever-present fear and sadness. Eighty miles from fearing the judgemental looks she expects every time she leaves the house.

Eighty miles from Alice.

Mel's life had become very small in Carrickfergus and so had Tilly's. No carefree strolls around the marina. No lunches out or coffees in quiet cafes. She didn't want to be visible any more. She couldn't take the chance she may bump into Alice, or any one of the scores of people who believed her version of what happened as if it were the gospel truth.

Alice had been prolific in her campaign to derail Mel's life. She posted all over social media, and in parenting forums, about her deep regret at choosing a doula 'like Mel' and how she had thought her birth would be safe in Mel's hands.

Mel, she said, had failed to read warning signs in pregnancy, or notice when things were going wrong 'despite her claims she was a birthing expert'. That this was a complete misrepresentation of what had happened didn't seem to matter to Alice. All she seemed to be interested in was some distorted form of justice or revenge.

Mel's hypnobirthing classes, which had once had a waiting list, emptied over the course of a few weeks.

The interview Alice did with a local newspaper, in which she urged mothers to avoid alternative approaches to birth, had been the final nail in the coffin. Even though there was no way in any reality that hypnobirthing had contributed to Jacob's death.

Perhaps inevitably, the story was picked up by a national newspaper prompting phone-ins on morning radio and TV shows about alternative approaches to healthcare and the state of the NHS. Mothers were warned by hysterical talking heads of the risks they were putting their children under.

No one asked Mel to talk on air. Not that she would've agreed anyway. She knew people believed Alice. People love a good tragedy. A good bit of gossip. They love to spread half-truths, then sit back and watch as they disseminate into the world, twisting and morphing as they go. She started to hear versions of what had happened that were so detached from reality as to make them almost laughable. Except no one was laughing, least of all Mel.

The day she'd got the phone call from Tilly's day care had been the last straw. Mel had told Ed – her beloved, supportive Ed

– that she wanted to move. Not only away from their current home but away from Carrickfergus altogether.

Ed had been delighted at her suggestion – hoping she would finally agree to shipping them all to Australia, where his twin sister Emma and her family have built a perfect life for themselves. His parents both dead, Emma is the only member of his immediate family still living and Mel knows he misses her desperately.

But as much as Mel knows how Ed longs to be close to his twin again, she can't bear the thought of leaving her ageing parents and being so far from them. It's selfish, maybe, but she knows that if his parents were still alive, he would want to be close to them too.

This house, complete with its list of projects a mile and a half long, had been their compromise. Ed, tired of transforming other people's homes, was desperate for his own project. So they'd found this house, complete with an outbuilding large enough to be converted into an office space for Ed – and his construction project manager business.

And this house does hold a certain appeal beyond that, Mel thinks as she lies awake watching dawn break through the crack in the threadbare curtains. She can definitely see it as being their forever home – where they can not only heal from their past experiences but also grow, maybe even start to embrace life again.

The nightmares didn't come last night. That's a positive. But neither did a decent amount of sleep. Each unfamiliar creak and groan of their new home had her extra vigilant. She's annoyed at herself for letting it get to her still. Things are meant to be easier here. She dare not tell Ed how she feels – not when he's still smarting that she didn't go for his Australian dream. Yes, this house is a compromise but she can't help but feel it's a reluctant one.

He understood why she wanted to move, of course, and he says he understands why she didn't want to leave Northern Ireland. But still, he mentions Emma's 'perfect life' outside of Melbourne. How she has a pool in her garden, and how they could have that too for their children. All they have here are a series of puddles and potholes pitted around their muddy yard. She feels incredibly guilty that she has stood her ground on this when she knows he longs for that completely fresh new start, so she feels even more intense pressure to not complain about the mess, or the noise, or the prospect of living in a mobile home for up to six months while the work carries on around them.

He's asleep now, but stirs in the bed beside her, rolling onto his side so that he faces her. Mel has seen that face every morning for the last ten years and she loves it. She loves him. Even when his face is slack and creased with sleep, and his mouth hangs open, he is still the most beautiful man she knows. She can't help but wonder what she has done to deserve him – this man who has told her, time and time again, that things will be okay. They will be happy again.

The baby kicks, as if to remind her not to give into the feelings of sadness that so often threaten to overcome her. Putting her hand to her tummy, Mel revels in the undulations of her skin as her unborn child stretches and wriggles. It's impossible to tell whether it's a hand or a foot, an elbow or a knee that prods forward, brushing under her skin. Not that it matters. The movement itself is reassurance enough, she thinks. *He is here. He is moving. All is well and all will be well.* She reminds herself that she has no real reason to doubt herself. There is nothing about this that is the same as her last, awful, experience of birth.

Just like the new house, this new baby – her beautiful baby

boy – will mark a fresh chapter for them all. There will still be challenges, but they can overcome challenges.

Rubbing her swollen stomach once more, she feels the baby shift inside her, thrusting an unknown limb towards her bladder. She has no choice now but to get up and make her way to the grimmest WC known to mankind. Just a loo in a room no bigger than a cupboard, with not even a sink to wash her hands, it is dank and smells of too-strong disinfectant. Mel takes a deep breath and tries not to think about what horrors the smell is masking, or how much bleach the cleaners had to use. This loo will be ripped out, along with the wall dividing it from the small, dank and mouldy-smelling bathroom. They have plans to make one large family space, with a roll-top bath, rainfall shower and underfloor heating. The cracked linoleum that feels just a little sticky under her feet will be a thing of the past too. Thankfully.

Now fully awake, Mel waddles back to the bedroom and grabs her oversized cardigan and slippers, compelled to go downstairs by a sudden need for some toast and her one permitted cup of coffee of the day.

But first, she peeks into Tilly's room. Even though this room is unfamiliar and rough around the edges, her fiercely independent little girl has insisted on sleeping there until the mobile home arrives.

'I'm a big girl, Mummy,' she'd said when bedtime came around on their first night in the house. 'I want to sleep in my own big bed.' Having just turned four years old, Mel had wanted to tell Tilly it was okay to be a little girl for a while longer. Life's less complicated when you're four. She'd wanted to pull her daughter into bed with her and Ed so she could be sure to keep her safe and warm. There is a comfort in being able to reach her hand out to her at a moment's notice and find her daughter easily. But Tilly has, as Mel has learned, inherited her mother's stubborn streak. She is infused with the belief that she is always right. As Ed says, karma's a four-year-old with an attitude.

Tilly is sound asleep, a mass of skinny limbs and wild curls. Her duvet has long since been kicked off and her pyjama top has ridden up to show off her tummy. Asleep, she still looks so baby-like. Mel feels her heart contract.

She has heard a thousand times that when a second child is born, the heart just expands to grow more love for them both. She has seen that expansion of love countless times. Seen precious firstborns blossom into proud big brothers and sisters without losing so much as an ounce of the love their mothers feel for them. But still, Mel is nervous.

Her new baby is already so precious to her – even more so after the events of the last year – but, here and now, Tilly is her world. Mel takes in her daughter's soft, long lashes and how they rest on her rosy cheeks, and remembers how Tilly kept her going when everything was falling apart, just by being her wonderful, beautiful self.

Tilly sighs in her sleep and rolls onto her side. Mel resists the urge to reach out and stroke her cheek. The pull of an undisturbed cup of coffee is too strong to risk a sleepy, grumpy child getting in on the action. The baby kicks again as if demanding a much-needed caffeine injection and Mel smiles. Of course she will be able to love them both. She'd do anything – endure anything – just to keep them happy and safe. And God help anyone who would try and get in her way.

2

The kitchen hums with the buzz of wiring in its terminal phase. The occasional rattle of Mel and Ed's old fridge as it protests being moved to a new home adds a percussive rhythm to the otherwise silent house. Mel revels in the quiet. In a few hours she will be wishing for it as the builders set to work and Tilly asks her endless questions.

From the kitchen window, Mel can see Binevenagh rise up to the sky in the distance. She knows there's a statue at the top of the mountain, facing out over the Atlantic, of Manannán mac Lir, the Celtic sea god. His hands raised towards the water as if commanding it. If only life were that simple, Mel thinks, as the sound of the bubbling kettle joins in the gentle buzz and rattle in the room. She spoons some coffee into her mug and wonders if it would be a blessing or a curse to be able to command all in the natural world to bend to her will. So much heartache could've been prevented, she thinks, feeling the familiar pull of guilt and sorrow on her heart.

The kettle clicks off, jolting Mel from the flashes of memories that haunt her from those days, and she's grateful for it. 'It's time to focus on the future,' she mutters to herself, parroting what her mother told her as they hugged at the door of Mel and Ed's old house just over a fortnight ago before closing it for the last time.

As she starts to pour milk into her coffee, Mel questions whether or not there is a slightly sour smell coming off it. She eyes the rattling fridge before opening the door to an absence of a rush of cool air from it. It's not quite warm, but it's definitely not fridge-level cold. This is only confirmed when she opens the freezer door to see soggy boxes indicating thawed-out contents. 'Fuck!' she swears, and sniffs her coffee again. She can't be sure, but she doesn't dare taste it – she'll have to go to the shops and get more. At least there is a fridge fitted in the caravan already. She won't have to go to the expense of buying a new one.

Her back aching, she sits down at the battered wooden table the previous owners of Braeside Cottage left behind, and grabs her to-do list and a pen. This pregnancy is making her increasingly forgetful and she finds she's having to write even the simplest of tasks down lest she forget them. Reading down her to-do list to distract herself from her thoughts, she circles 'Call midwife!' in red pen twice. That's one thing she needs to do urgently. She should have done it two weeks ago, but she has been so tired and so busy she hasn't quite got round to it. Or at least that's what she tells herself – the truth being more that she dreads the inevitable conversation that she will have at her first visit with them.

She knows though that she can't put this off any longer. She needs to be checked over and get registered under a consultant at the local hospital.

This will be a hospital birth – she's taking no chances, even though she once had dreams of a beautiful water birth at home. She'd imagined feeling at ease in her own surroundings and

managing her labour using her beloved hypnobirthing techniques. But that was before she truly understood just how wrong
it could all go. Both she and Ed had agreed they are taking no
chances this time.

Mel is scrolling through her phone to find the health centre
number when a loud rap on the door breaks through the peace
and quiet, making her jump in fright.

'Jesus, Mary and Saint Joseph,' she swears, her hand curling
in front of her chest as her heart thuds in fright.

She can see a shadow through the glass panel of the front
door and quickly she assesses its size and shape, unable to
remember the last time she opened her front door without
feeling scared. There had been all sorts of visitors, and all kinds
of deliveries to her old house this past year. Her door splattered
in paint. A woman in her sixties screaming at her – calling her a
'baby killer'. Eggs flung at her windows. Once there was a
delivery of a box containing what looked – and smelled – very
much like human excrement.

Her chest tight, Mel hopes Ed will have heard and will
already be on his way to answer the—

Thump, thump, thump – the banging on the door is repeated.
The palms of Mel's hands are clammy as she covers her ears to
try and block out the noise and to settle herself.

It's probably the builders, she tells herself, trying to switch
her brain back into rational thinking mode. It could be the
postman or any number of deliveries of materials they need for
the renovation. The most logical explanation is usually the
correct one, she reminds herself, running through the script her
therapist taught her to use in situations just like this.

'*I do not have to be scared all the time. I do not need to be scared
now. We are safe,*' she tells herself, remembering that very few
people know where she has moved. The chances of this being

someone with malicious intent are slim. The shadow at the door does not look familiar. It does not look like Alice, she rationalises, although even thinking of Alice's name makes her stomach tighten and threaten to turn.

There's no sound from upstairs. No sign that Ed is coming to her rescue, and the shadow isn't moving. Telling herself to be brave, Mel pulls her cardigan tight and makes her way towards the door. She does not want to let the fear win. Not here and not now. She knows if she gives into it and stays hidden it will only grow bigger and bigger and threaten to fell her and her new start before it has even properly begun.

The sound of feet shuffling on the gravel outside sets her entire nervous system on edge but she is determined not to be defeated by her fears. Offering up a silent prayer to the universe for everything to be okay, she presses her cheek against the cracked gloss paint of the door beside the Yale lock, and peers through the cloudy, grubby peephole. The person outside is not anyone she knows and she doesn't look threatening – not that it's always easy, Mel has learned, to tell who is nice and who is downright nasty from first appearances.

The fresh chill of a spring morning sneaks in as Mel pulls the door open and she can't help shivering, even though the sun is bright and casting dappled shards of light through the trees and onto the gravel driveway to their house. It's hard to know if the shivers are down to the cool air, or her nerves.

The woman in front of her, whom she'd put at in her late sixties or early seventies, is standing with a tight, nervous smile on her face and a well-worn biscuit tin in her hands. It's the same type Mel used to take to school on Home Economics days for cooking lessons. Seeing it conjures a memory of scones like rocks and banana bread that was so horrible not even the dog would eat it – not that her baking has improved much in the intervening years.

The older woman is wearing a pair of knee-high green welly boots that are muddy in a way only very well-loved and much-worn wellies can be. A long green padded coat, peppered with the occasional mud splatters near the hem, and a red beanie hat hide most of her distinguishing features. A few wisps of ash blonde – or it could be grey? – hair escape from under the hat and frame her ruddy cheeks. She has the look of someone very much outdoorsy – her skin weathered by the sun but her wrinkles minimised thanks to the plumpness of her features.

'Sheila,' she says in an authoritative voice. 'Sheila Quigg. From up the road.' She gestures with a quick nod of her head behind her, which is so commanding that Mel finds herself looking to see if there's a house noticeably close by that she just hasn't noticed before.

'You won't see it from here,' Sheila says, moving her head to try and peek into the hall. Mel moves slightly to block her view. 'It's just over a mile back there,' Sheila continues, unfazed and without missing a beat. 'Up to the left, past the shuck. Not a bad walk on a day like today, all the same,' she adds before her gaze comes to rest on Mel's swollen stomach. She gives a small, curt nod of acknowledgement.

Sheila stares expectantly at Mel, waiting for her to speak, but Mel suddenly feels as if she has lost the ability to make polite conversation. She's controlling her nerves but only just. No amount of rationalising can change the fact she does not know this woman and has no idea what her intentions are. A voice in her head tells her she should introduce herself like a normal human being would, while another screams that she should still be careful not to give away too much information.

'I'm your nearest neighbour,' Sheila says, breaking the now

awkward silence. 'I've seen all the comings and goings, and decided I'd come down and introduce myself. It's always good to know whom you're living alongside. It can get lonely enough out here.'

'I'm Mel,' Mel says, her voice a little strained. 'I'm here with my husband and my wee girl.'

'And another on the way, I see,' Sheila says, her gaze falling once again to Mel's stomach. 'You'll have your hands full,' she says. 'Are you from around here? Your accent doesn't sound like it?'

'I'm from Northern Ireland, yes,' Mel says, still guarded. 'But we're new to this area. We loved the house so…'

'And you'll be living here yourselves? You're not just some fly-by-nights making it into a glamping spot or something? Because the last thing we want is more people flying along these roads in their cars, driving like they're Lewis Hamilton or the like. You'll understand that, with your wee girl and everything.' Her voice is light but it's clear that she is very serious.

'No plans outside of making it our forever home,' Mel says with a tight smile, thinking this woman should be working for the police, wheedling information out of people. 'I'm sure you'll have seen the builders' vans and the like, if you've been watching all the comings and goings.'

'Builders. Yes. I've seen some vans. So it's more than a lick of paint and new curtains you'll be going for then?' She takes a step back and surveys the exterior of the house as if she's bidding for the contract herself.

'Yes,' Mel says. 'It is. But we're going to try and make the most of the original features and make it in keeping, on the exterior at least, with how it looked in its heyday. We'll be putting a small extension in too, to the rear and…' She stops herself because she doesn't want to let Sheila – or anyone – in. She doesn't want to find herself in a place where she feels compelled to share her story. She hasn't moved here to make friends – not now that her trust in people has been irrevocably damaged. No, she just wants to live a quiet life with her little family and keep to herself as much as possible.

'I'm sure it will be lovely when it's done,' Sheila says, and she thrusts the tin in Mel's direction. 'Shortbread. Home-made this morning. Probably still warm if you get to them quickly. Perfect with a cup of tea.'

Mel knows she should probably invite Sheila in for tea. The woman has traipsed over a mile to bring her new neighbours fresh baked goods so it would probably be mannerly, but she really doesn't want anyone in the house who doesn't absolutely have to be there. When she remembers that she is out of milk, she sags with relief. She has a proper excuse for not welcoming guests.

'I'd invite you in, but to be honest, the place is completely upside down and we've not a drop of milk. I was actually just about to get ready to head out to the shop.'

Sheila lets out a loud 'humph' of disapproval then tries to cover it with a cough. 'Sorry, excuse me. These damp mornings.' She thrusts her biscuit tin at Mel again, a final hint to take it from her. 'But yes, of course, I remember what it's like when you move house and everything is at sixes and sevens. But there's never any excuse to run out of milk. Not when you have a wee one in the house!'

Mel colours at the implied judgement. Her skin prickles. Does Sheila think she's a bad mother because she's out of milk? She's about to launch into a long-winded explanation about the broken fridge when she remembers her therapist also telling her she is not obliged to spill her life story to every person who looks in her direction. She takes a deep breath. 'It would be lovely to have you over when we have the place sorted out a bit.' She knows it will be months before the build and renovation will be complete.

'I'll look forward to it,' Sheila replies with a tight smile. 'And remember, we're just up the road. That's me and my husband, Barney. Just the two of us now the wains have grown and gone their own way. Not a one of them interested in farming. But sure, what can ye do? So remember – about a mile up the road, past the shuck. That's us, if you need anything. And if the dog starts barking at you, just tell her to quiet down. Her name's Doris.' She turns to leave.

'Hang on,' Mel calls. 'Let me give your tin back at least.' It's not so much a kindness as a case of not wanting to give her a reason to come back.

'Ach, away o' that,' Sheila says. 'It's only an old tin. I've plenty of them.'

She gives a courteous smile, nods and turns away again to start down the gravelled drive towards the gate, with the gait of a woman well used to walking country roads, and fields, in all weathers.

A wave of guilt washes over Mel.

'Sheila?' she calls. 'Would you like a lift back? I figure it's the least I can do.'

'Not at all,' Sheila says, with a stoic smile. 'Sure the walk will do me good. That fresh country air works wonders, you know. And sure you've enough to do getting to the shop and getting milk in.'

With that, Sheila is gone and Mel is left, biscuit tin in hand, her back nipping just a little, and worried that she might just have made an enemy.

Another one.

3

Even though Sheila has left and the house is quiet again, Mel still feels unsettled. She tries to tell herself that's perfectly understandable given everything she has been through and that it will, in time, pass. She just has to have faith in herself, she thinks, as she has a quick scout around the kitchen to see if there is anything else she should get at the shop. More tea bags, for one. The builders go through them at a rate of knots. And a few more packets of biscuits. As usual she'll just set everything out in the kitchen and they can help themselves to tea and coffee whenever they want. There's no way she has the energy to be making tea for them all day – not at almost thirty-four weeks pregnant.

The sound of footsteps – unmistakably Ed's – on the stairs is a relief. She feels at ease when he is around. He smiles at her as he walks into the kitchen, dressed in a T-shirt and joggers, his hair still messy. 'Morning, love,' he says. 'Who was at the door? I heard you talking to someone.' He walks to the fridge and opens it, his brow wrinkling when he can't see any milk.

'There's no milk,' Mel tells him. 'The fridge is on the blink and the milk was definitely smelling a bit ripe this morning. I'm going to nip out to the shop.'

'I'd a feeling the fridge was in its death throes last night, but I was really hoping we'd get another few weeks out of it,' he says with a grimace. 'Let me get my trainers on and I'll go. Save you the effort.'

Mel smiles, grateful for the offer. She's at the stage of her pregnancy where fitting behind a steering wheel has become a bit of a challenge. 'Thanks,' she says. 'Is herself still asleep up there?' Mel nods towards the ceiling.

'By some miracle, yes.' Ed grins. 'I figure let her sleep as long as she wants. There's enough chaos down here as it is. So, who was at the door?' he asks again, before spotting the biscuit tin on the table. He wastes no time in opening it and the smell of freshly baked shortbread permeates the air. 'Is this something to do with our mystery visitor?'

'It is. We had a visit from a neighbour. I think she was a recon mission to find out as much about us as possible.'

'I didn't think we had any neighbours,' Ed says, lifting one of the perfectly golden biscuits out and taking a large, crumbly bite. 'Hmmmmmm,' he says. 'These are amazing. Maybe we should make friends with her so she'll share the recipe.'

'She said she's our nearest neighbour – lives about a mile away, past the shuck – whatever a shuck is. Her name's Sheila. I can't remember what she said her husband was called. Harry... or Barry... or something. She definitely seemed like the kind of woman who enjoys a bit of gossip.'

'What's a shuck, Daddy?' a little voice, still croaky with sleep, asks and both Ed and Mel turn to see their daughter walk into the room, dressed in her pyjamas and with her slippers on the wrong feet.

'Well, I think it's like a tiny wee stream that runs between fields,' Ed replies, while Mel guides her daughter to a chair and changes her slippers over to the correct feet without saying a word.

'Can you catch fish in a shuck?' Tilly asks.

'I wouldn't think so,' Ed tells her. 'They're usually very small.'

Tilly seems pleased with this answer and turns her attention to asking for her breakfast instead.

'Daddy is going to the shop to get milk and you can have your cereal then,' Mel tells her. 'Or I can make you some toast now?'

'With Nutella?' Tilly asks, immediately brightening.

It's not something Mel would normally offer for breakfast unless it was a special day like a birthday or Christmas, but she figures it can't hurt to break her own rule occasionally.

'As a treat,' Mel tells her. 'Just this once. And I'll pour you some juice.'

Meanwhile Ed has sat down and is slipping his feet into the trainers he abandoned in the kitchen yesterday. 'I suppose we have to expect the odd nosy neighbour. Country folk like to know who are around them, and I don't think it's a bad thing to get to know the people living closest to us. There will be times you'll be here on your own with the babies...'

Mel stiffens, her anxiety breaking through the surface again. She doesn't want to think about being alone without him close by, even though she knows that with the nature of his job, he can be anywhere in the country working on a build.

'I'm not a baby!' Tilly interrupts, indignant. Mel can understand. They've been preparing her for months that there is a new tiny baby on the way and she will be the 'best big girl in the world'.

'Of course not. Sorry, pet,' Ed soothes, before returning his attention to his wife. 'There might be times you will be grateful to have someone on hand if you need them.'

Mel's not convinced.

'She doesn't have to be your best friend,' he continues, and Mel feels herself tense up more. Even after everything that has happened, she still finds herself missing the last woman she'd considered a best friend. 'If this is going to be our forever home then we need to focus on the positive.' He stands up and slides a hand around his wife's waist and pulls her into a gentle sideways hug. 'Isn't that what we've been saying? Things will be good from now on. We have this house. It's going to be the best home for us. This is our new start. That and our new baby. And before you say it, yes, I know that's scary too, but everything is going to be okay. *We're* going to be okay. We're safe. Our baby is safe.'

Mel nods, aware that Ed doesn't like it when she starts to spiral. She worries that, as wonderful as he is, he is losing patience with her and still smarting from her refusal to emigrate. In return, she feels she has to keep her end of the bargain and work on her anxiety and believing that things are on the up.

She takes a deep breath, trying to inhale some of that fresh country air wafting in from the open back door. 'You're right,' she says with a smile she doesn't quite feel.

'Can I have a biscuit, Mummy?' Tilly asks, standing up on her tiptoes, her eyes fixed on Sheila's biscuit tin. 'They smell dee-lish-us,' she says, emphasising each of the three syllables.

Immediately Mel wants to say no. They don't know Sheila Quigg. They've never so much as set eyes on her before today. There could be anything in those cookies. Anything at all. And they don't even know for certain she actually is their neighbour... No, she chides herself. She's being ridiculous – but still she doesn't want Tilly to eat something prepared by a stranger who has just landed at their front door.

'Of course you can,' Ed tells his daughter just as Mel opens her mouth to speak. He glances towards her and she can read the look on his face: *It's only a biscuit. You have to stop worrying.* She wants to scream at him that it's impossible not to worry – hasn't the last year proven to them how fragile life is, and how brutal people can be, but she hears his voice in her head again. *You will drive yourself, and the rest of us, mad if you don't start to move on and stop worrying about every little thing and every person we meet.* She hears that voice and she can picture his expression – tired, exasperated, and close to breaking point. This move isn't just a new start, it's a Hail Mary for a marriage battered by the losses of the last year.

Mel bites her tongue and holds her breath as Tilly reaches into the tin and extracts one of the sugar-dusted treats. She holds back the tears that threaten to fall, hears her therapist's voice in her head reminding her to think logically.

It's a cookie. It's just a cookie. Ed took a bite, she tells herself. He took a bite and he is fine. Sheila Quigg is not the wicked witch come down from some castle with a baked goods equivalent of a shiny red apple to feed Mel and her child in a bid to send them into a dreamless sleep.

Pulling a chair out, Mel sits down, afraid that her wobbling legs will give out altogether if she doesn't. She hates what her life has become, even with this new house in this beautiful part of the world, and she can't seem to steer herself back to shore, no matter how hard she tries. Her therapist tells her to 'give herself some grace' – an expression that has started to set her teeth on edge. She doesn't want to give herself any grace. She wants the whole world to leave her alone.

She was not responsible for that beautiful baby's death. She'd just done what she always did – tried to help to the very best of her ability. That had been all she had ever wanted to do.

4

Looking back, there was nothing much to differentiate Alice Munroe from any of the other woman who had approached Mel to hire her as a doula.

A first-time mother, Alice wanted to keep things as 'natural as possible' when it came to giving birth. That in itself was nothing unusual. The very nature of Mel's business meant that the vast majority of mothers-to-be who contacted her were keen to have medication-free births and were looking for alternative methods to support them during labour and delivery.

Some were just looking to find out more about the hypno-birthing classes she offered and were eager to learn how they could work with their bodies to have a positive birth experience.

Mel encountered more than one or two cynics along the way, of course. Her own mother had fitted into the category neatly – at least at first.

'Mel, are you really trying to make me believe that if a woman just tells herself it doesn't hurt, then it doesn't hurt? That sounds insane,' she had said when her daughter had sat down across the kitchen table from her and attempted to justify the massive career change she was about to embark on.

Shaking her head in frustration, Mel had tried to explain to her mother once again how the practice of hypnobirthing could help reduce stress and anxiety levels, leading to a calmer and more empowering birthing experience for all concerned.

'In my day we just got on with it,' her mother had told her, but Mel didn't want to 'just get on with it' ever again. That's how it had been when she had given birth to Tilly, and Mel had never felt so vulnerable in her life. With the emotional scars still raw, she had decided that she was never going to put herself in that position again, and she would do all she could to support other women so that they didn't end up traumatised by their birth experiences. She hadn't expected to find herself loving it all so much that she'd decide to walk away from her career as a primary school teacher to concentrate on supporting women full-time.

Women like Alice, who was already incredibly nervous about what lay ahead. Mel could see that when she first arrived at the Munroe house.

'My mother thinks I'm making a fuss,' Alice said as she handed Mel a cup of tea. 'That I should count myself lucky to have the NHS on hand to help me, but...' Alice pulled her phone from her pocket, took a seat and started scrolling down her screen.

'I've been reading all these articles, you know. And talking to women on birthing forums, and there are some really horrible stories out there. Awful stuff. Staff shortages. Women not getting pain relief. Babies being put at risk.'

'I'm sure that's only in a small number of cases,' Mel told her, desperate to offer what reassurance she could.

'But what if it's my case?' Alice asked, her hands wrapped

tightly around her coffee cup. 'And another thing I can't get past is, you know, this pandemic and all the restrictions that have been placed on women going in for antenatal care, or to give birth. Partners not always being allowed in, or being shooed out as soon as the baby was born with no time to bond, and no time to support their partner. Thomas – that's my husband – he'd hate that. I'd hate it too. I don't want to do it alone. I know they've relaxed a lot of the restrictions but it's not enough. What if we hit another lockdown?'

Alice's eyes brimmed with tears and her bottom lip trembled, and Mel couldn't help but feel sorry for her. 'It has been tough,' Mel said. 'Really tough. I have my own daughter and she was born just before the restrictions came in. I remember thinking it must be so stressful for any new mummies going through it all – but I'd like to think that's all behind us now.'

Alice shook her head, put her cup down and shuffled back on the sofa – her hands now cupping the hint of a swollen stomach. 'I don't want to take any chances. I'm thirty-eight. I've waited so long to have this baby and I know that time is against me now. I don't want to do anything at all that will risk harming my baby. I'm not a stupid woman or someone who just follows each new trend that emerges. I've done my research and that's why I've contacted you.'

Mel gave her a soft smile. 'And I appreciate that you've come to me. I totally understand you wanting the very best for your baby. That's as natural as breathing. And I understand that birth can be scary – especially with how medicalised it has become. That's why I do what I do. But I want to reassure you that the people caring for you will all want the very best outcome for your baby. I can guarantee you that.'

Mel sipped her tea and took in the room around her. This was a beautiful home – decorated to perfection. Fresh flowers scented the air. Alice herself was an elegant, attractive woman, dressed in cool cream linen trousers and a matching sleeveless tunic top. Her arms were tanned, her hair glossy and straight. A pair of diamond studs and a beautiful but understated wedding ring were the only items of jewellery she wore. Everything in her life looked curated, and expensive. She'd told Mel she was a solicitor – and had 'waited until her career was exactly where she wanted it to be' before she and her husband Thomas – also a solicitor – decided to start their family.

'It wasn't as easy as we thought it would be,' she'd told Mel on the phone two days before when they first spoke. Mel knew this baby was clearly precious to Alice, but it was only during this conversation that she started to realise exactly how precious he or she was.

Alice was not willing to take any chances. 'Don't you think the system is broken?' she asked. 'Our hospitals are struggling to get staff. There's a national midwife shortage. Midwives are leaving the profession because they think it has become unsafe.'

It was clear to Mel that the woman across the coffee table from her knew what she was talking about and was not just some 'hysterical conspiracy theorist' or 'hippy dippy crunchy mum'. She was able to back up her concerns with statistics and case studies, and Mel could see she was talking to a woman who felt as passionately about maternity care as she herself did.

'I think it's obvious there are problems in the system,' Mel agreed. 'That extends into every part of the NHS, unfortunately. I fear we're on the road to stealth privatisation, but I can assure you I've met many midwives who feel as passionately as we do and who work themselves to the bone to provide the very best and safest level of care they can.' But Mel didn't want to get caught up in a debate on the politics of healthcare provision. She wanted to get a proper idea of what Alice needed.

'Let me ask you this,' she said, putting her cup down on the coffee table and leaning forward. 'What do you want your birth to look like? What do you want from the experience – apart from a healthy baby, of course.'

Mel smiled and Alice smiled back, her demeanour shifting. She was more than happy to share her hopes and wishes.

'Well, it's probably no surprise to you that I want to look at natural methods of pain relief instead of medication. That's why I wanted to find out more about hypnobirthing,' Alice said. 'And then when I looked you up, I saw you also offer doula services. It just sounds like exactly what I'm looking for.'

Mel nodded. 'I'm happy to hear that. Hypnobirthing can be so effective at using our inner power and strength to birth our babies. It's a very positive, affirming practice that steers away from negative language. So we don't talk about contractions, we talk about surges. We don't refer to pain, we focus on the individual sensations – be they pressure or tightening. What words we use colours how our body responds. We work with breathing and visualisation to help you feel connected to your body and to the experience, instead of scared of it. Does that sound like something you could get on board with?'

'Absolutely!' Alice replied, her blue eyes flashing with delight that she'd clearly found her kindred spirit.

'And your partner?'

'Husband,' Alice corrected. 'He's a little nervous but he trusts my judgement. Says it's my body so it's important we do what feels best to me. He was impressed by what he read on your website of course, especially the client testimonials. It was he who suggested that we find out more about your doula service, and not just hypnobirthing. He thinks your experience and knowledge will be invaluable. I happen to agree.'

Mel felt a warm glow deep in the pit of her stomach. She

always enjoyed being called 'invaluable'. She found that a lot of people were unsure of the role of a doula, or didn't even know they existed in the first place. If she got a pound for every time she'd had to explain that the word 'doula' came from the Greek for 'woman's servant', and that her role was simply to support a woman during birth, and after if required, she was pretty sure she'd be able to buy herself a very nice designer handbag.

'Is that not the job of a midwife?' her mother had asked when she'd first told her.

'No, Mum. The midwife helps deliver the baby. I won't do that. I'm there simply to encourage the mother-to-be, and to advocate for her. In the way I wish I'd been able to advocate for myself when I was having Tilly.'

Her mum tsked and shook her head. 'I don't understand this new generation,' she'd muttered, 'with all your new trends and notions.'

'It's not new, Mum. Women have been doing it for centuries.'

'Well, I've never heard of it before,' her mother had said, before she launched into a lengthy lament that her daughter would be leaving the teaching profession. Mel had to switch off and simply find her own peace with her mum's lack of enthusiasm. Her mother would never understand that while she enjoyed teaching her class of seven- and eight-year-olds, she loved helping women in labour. Plus, it had the added benefit of allowing her to spend a significant amount of time with Tilly. It was a work-life balance that Mel could only ever have dreamed of before.

As she sat across from Alice, she felt once again reassured that she was on the right career path.

'I can't promise you everything will go exactly as you'd want it to,' she told Alice. 'I'm sure you are well aware that any birth can be a little unpredictable. But I can promise you that if I'm by your side, I will offer you non-judgemental support at a level you are comfortable with. You will always have a strong voice in the room and you will be listened to.'

Alice shifted in her seat. 'That's very reassuring. You've no idea.' There was a pause before she spoke again. 'So, you're happy to help with a home birth?'

Mel noticed Alice's expression had changed. She looked more serious. If Mel wasn't mistaken, she looked worried.

'Absolutely,' Mel replied, keen to reassure Alice as quickly as possible. 'I've been practising as a doula for fourteen months now. I've attended seven births in that time and five of those have been home births.'

Alice raised an eyebrow.

'Mostly they were first-time mothers who all had their own reasons for wanting to have their babies at home,' Mel continued. 'Some, like you, were very nervous of hospital births given the pressure the NHS is under. Although, I have to say, the two hospital births I've attended as a doula have been incredibly lovely and positive experiences for everyone. But yes, I am more than happy to support you while you have your baby at home.'

Alice smiled broadly. 'Oh, that's fantastic news!' she said. 'Because I very much want to have this baby here, at home. I want it to be peaceful and relaxing, you know. Well – as relaxing as giving birth can be.' Alice gave a little laugh and Mel smiled.

'It really can be a peaceful and empowering experience. And it will certainly be our aim to keep you as relaxed as possible so your body releases all those happy hormones that help your labour to progress. Our bodies are absolutely incredible at doing this – we just need to trust them,' she said.

Mel wished, of course, she had her own experience of a natural and empowering birth to draw on. Things had been so different when Tilly was born. Induction. Frequent examinations. Slow progress and an eventual emergency C-section had left her feeling broken. But this job was definitely helping her heal.

'If we agree to work together, I will not take on any other clients with a delivery date less than four weeks before or after yours, so my caseload is fairly limited. Given that, I'd need a commitment from you sooner rather than later as I've had a few enquiries,' Mel said, having sensed that now was the time to seal this deal.

'I'm in. Sign me up,' Alice said with a smile that was so broad Mel couldn't help but return it.

'Brilliant! I'm delighted!' she said.

'I do have one more question,' Alice asked, her face clouded over again with the same worried expression as before.

'What is it?'

'How do you feel about unattended births? You know, free-birthing?'

Mel told her she had never done it before but was open to the idea. The truth being that when she thought of supporting a woman through a completely independent birth – free of support from midwives or other medical professionals – she felt a frisson of excitement.

'Great,' Alice beamed. 'I'm so glad. Because that's what I'm going to do. And Thomas is completely on board with it, but we really would love someone else in the room. As a support for us both. Are you happy to do that?'

There was no way Mel could have known that in offering an enthusiastic 'yes' in response, she was making the worst decision of her life. She could never have predicted the nightmare that would follow.

5

MARCH 2024

34 weeks + 1 day

The soft mewling of a newborn baby wakes Mel from her nap, and immediately she is sure she must be hearing things. There is no baby here. She knows that. The builders have gone to collect yet more materials to add to the ever-growing stash in the yard, while Tilly and Ed have gone into town to get some groceries.

Mel wasted no time in grabbing the window of peace and quiet to rest. The chances for blissful solitude come few and far between these days – especially in the cramped confines of their mobile home. It's a nice caravan – much nicer than the ones she remembers from her childhood holidays, but no matter what she does, it's hard to not feel as if they are all living on top of one another.

It didn't take her long to slip into a deep sleep, one she's now struggling to pull herself out of. She feels herself slide back under its spell, only to be woken again by the mewling getting louder. It must be a lamb in the nearby field, she thinks. Or a kitten wandering around the yard. But it sounds human – so much so that she knows it can't be anything other than the enraged hello of a baby freshly evicted from the dark, warm and comfortable home that is its mother's womb.

But Mel can't understand why a baby would be here – and so close that she can hear it crying. Using all her effort, she prises her eyes open and takes a deep breath in the hope that a lungful of fresh air will pull her brain out of its sleepy fugue. She knows the baby is close – if anything it seems to be getting closer – and she can't leave it to cry.

Her hand moves to her swollen belly. Her maternal instinct to react to a crying child is strong.

Immediately she notices something is wrong. Something is off. Her belly is not swollen as she expects it to be. It's sagging, gelatinous, empty. Mel struggles to comprehend what on earth is happening, her heart rate rising to match the urgency of her need to know what is going on. This can't be, she tells herself. She has been preparing for this baby for almost eight months. She knows with every fibre of her being that he is real. She has felt him move inside her – has seen his grainy depiction on the screen of an ultrasound machine. The chubby little curve of his nose. Legs that look impossibly long, kicking and wriggling. She has felt him hiccup, watching as her stomach jumped along with him. She doesn't understand why he is not still with her. How is her stomach now flat? It doesn't make sense. Forcing her eyes open, Mel pulls herself up to sitting, even though her body feels heavy and her eyes still want to close. Maybe, she thinks, her eyes want to stay closed because they know what's coming. She can feel dread come to rest on her shoulders with a weight too heavy for any person to carry. The baby's cries get louder still and she wants to clamp her hands over her ears just so she can have the peace to think. She desperately wants to make sense of this strange world. Pressing her hand hard and firm into her stomach, sure that if she just presses hard enough she will feel the now familiar outline of her baby, she feels desperation take root. No matter how hard she presses all she can feel is the spongy, empty feeling of a post-partum body.

A warm wetness trickles between her legs. Reaching down, afraid to look, her hand finds itself swamped in the sticky flow of blood. A smell – the unmistakable metallic tang of blood – assaults her nostrils and she knows she has to look. She has no choice. Even though none of this makes sense. Surely, she thinks, this can't be her baby crying. That's impossible. There is no way she has given birth without realising it.

Dizzy and terrified, her chest constricts as she feels the trickle between her legs turn into a tide. Her eyes start to droop again but she knows she has to fight it. There is a baby and it is crying, and it might be her baby... She needs to fight for this poor child. She needs to fight for herself, and for Tilly and Ed. She cannot give in to the darkness and fear. So she does it. She looks. She forces herself to see the horror she has been dreading.

Life draining from her in a sea of red, she sees the baby who is still crying. She knows though, as soon as she sets eyes on him, that something is wrong. He is pale. There is no pinkish tinge of a healthy newborn. His cries quieten and he is deathly still. When Mel reaches for him, her hands are shaking. She recoils in horror when she touches him only to find him cold.

She gasps when he twitches, and he opens his mouth wide, letting out the shrillest scream she has ever heard. Her scream joins his – so loud that it wakes her from the nightmare she thought she'd left behind in Carrickfergus.

The room is still and quiet, save for the thumping of her heart. Mel tries to slow her breathing and centre herself in the here and now. She tells herself she is in her bedroom and what has just passed was an awful nightmare, but it was not real.

With her heart still in her mouth, she reaches for her stomach just to be sure, scared she will feel yielding softness, and not a solid, round and full bump, as it should be. Sitting up, she feels around the bed for traces of warm, sticky blood and for a birthed but silent baby. But all is as it was when she lay down exhausted an hour before. A reassuring kick tells her that her baby is fine, and she can't stop a sob of relief escaping from her throat, drowning out the echoes of the phantom cries in her nightmare.

Defeated and drained, she slumps back against her pillows. All she wants is to be able to leave behind what happened on that awful, awful day but, she thinks, maybe that's too much to ask of the universe. After all, Alice will never be able to leave it behind, and why should Mel be able to carry on with life as normal? She has asked herself this a thousand times and never come up with a satisfying answer.

She tells herself again and again that she did not do anything wrong. She was not at fault. But she can't shake the nagging feeling that maybe she is still responsible anyway. The 'if onlys' weigh heavy on her heart every single day – more so since she discovered she was pregnant. Unexpectedly. Just months after Jacob died.

Pressing the heels of her hands into her eyes to try and stop fresh tears falling, she is relieved to hear the familiar purr of Ed's car engine followed by the rattle of the tyres on the gravel outside.

Although the bedroom window is closed, the structure of the caravan does little to block out the sound of 'How Far I'll Go' from *Moana* blasting in the car stereo.

Mel remembers a time when Ed only ever listened to podcasts or classic rock in the car, and when he vowed that no baby would change that habit. 'The baby has to fit into our lives,' he'd said, as they'd discussed the impending birth of their first-born. 'They won't be ruling the roost! I refuse to be one of those kinds of parents!'

Mel's tears turn to a smile as she thinks of how Tilly now has full DJ duties in her daddy's car. Ed has even been known to listen to his daughter's music at times when she isn't with him – although he swears this is accidental.

Mel switches on the camera app in her phone to act as a makeshift mirror so she can assess just how haggard she looks before greeting her family. She doesn't want them to know she has been crying. Taking in her pallor and the dark circles under her eyes, she wonders if she might be on the anaemic side. There's no doubt she has been neglecting her diet of late.

The car doors slam closed outside and Mel hears the chatter of Ed and Tilly as they walk towards the caravan. She is over-whelmed by the need to see them, and to be close to them. Being in their company is the best distraction from her dark thoughts. Coming out of her bedroom, she hears them chat conspiratori-ally about chocolate buttons that they absolutely 'must keep a secret from Mummy'.

Smiling, she shouts 'Gotcha!' as she pops her head through the door and into the living area. They both startle.

'What were you two talking about?' Mel asks, her voice exag-gerated and one eyebrow raised.

'Oh, nothing,' Ed says back playfully. 'We were just talking about all the healthy, tasty and nutritious broccoli we bought at the shops. Isn't that right, Tilly?'

Never one to miss a beat, Tilly nods solemnly. 'Yes, Daddy. All the broccoli, and the cauliflower too, don't forget?'

'So you weren't talking about *chocolate buttons* then?' Mel teases, and they both shake their heads in a move so perfectly synchronised and symmetrical that no one could ever doubt they are father and daughter.

'So what would this be, then?' Mel asks, reaching for the familiar purple packaging she has spotted on the kitchen counter. Tilly erupts into laughter with Ed following suit.

'I think we might be able to share these,' Mel smiles, basking in the warmth of this simple interaction.

'Maybe we can share these too?' Ed says, handing her a bundle of flyers and envelopes. 'Mostly bills, I imagine.' He grimaces before giving her a reassuring wink. They are well prepared for the feeling their bank accounts are haemorrhaging.

Mel flicks through the post, discarding the junk mail and setting the bills in their own little stack. She's surprised when she comes across a handwritten envelope which, given the shape of it, she is pretty sure must contain a card. Its presence comes as a surprise to her. So few people know their new address. She and Ed had agreed they could keep that information on a strictly need-to-know basis because there were people whom she never wanted to know where she was.

But maybe, she thinks, she should've driven that message home harder to her mother – a woman famed for her lack of ability to 'hold her own water' as the saying goes. Not to mention the fact her mother thought selling up and moving on was a bit of a 'drastic overreaction' to everything that had been happening, being of the firm belief that everything would die down given enough time.

If she didn't know better, Mel would swear her mother was perfectly okay with her only daughter losing her business. It wasn't something she had ever fully understood in the first place – this newfangled way of approaching birth.

Her mother saw it all so differently to how Mel saw it, and felt it, so it would come as little surprise to find out that the entire population of Carrickfergus had been given chapter and verse on the big move. Her mum will have revelled in pitching the renovation of the old farmhouse as some sort of *Grand Designs* adventure.

'Is that a card?' Ed asks as Mel walks back into the kitchen. 'Our first New Home card maybe?' He smiles. 'Who's it from?'

As Mel slips a fingernail under the edge of the envelope seal, Ed turns back to the fridge and starts putting away the milk, eggs and cheese he has just purchased.

'I bet it's just from the estate agent or something,' Mel says. 'It will be one of those standard-form cards they send out to all their clients when all is done and dusted and they've made their money.'

'Can I see it, Mummy?' Tilly asks, her hand already reaching out. 'Sometimes when I get cards they have some money inside for toys. Is there money for toys?'

Mel smiles, gesturing towards her daughter with the envelope. 'You can see it, sweetheart, but don't get your hopes up about money for toys. It's not a birthday card, honey.'

Clearly disgusted at the revelation there will be no trip to the toy shop in her near future, Tilly shakes her head and turns her attention back to leafing through the CBeebies magazine her daddy bought her when they were out.

Mel pulls the card from the envelope herself, seeing the words 'Happy New Home' written across it in beautiful pastel colours. Perhaps it is because she is still shaken from her bad dream, but she can't help but feel a sense of foreboding as she turns the card over in her hands. She's not sure what she's expecting. It's not like monsters can jump out of it, or that it is likely to cause her any physical harm. Once again she finds herself trying to rationalise her fears. There is no reason for her to expect this to be anything other than the standard card sent from their estate agent or conveyancing solicitor to wish them all the best in their new home.

Still, Mel has to steady herself before she opens the card to read what is written inside. And her heart plummets. 'It must be lovely to be able to start all over again,' she reads, and sees the signature. A single letter 'A' written with the exact same flourish Alice uses.

This can't be happening, she thinks, bile rising. How on earth does Alice know their new address? Even with her loose lips, her mother would not have given Mel's address to Alice of all people. Not in a million years. The voice in her own head – the one that likes to gaslight her into believing she's just being paranoid – whispers that the way a person writes a capital letter A isn't enough to confirm the narrative currently forming in her head – that Alice knows where they are and that she is not about to let things go.

Mel watches her family – her daughter peeling stickers from the insert that came with her magazine and meticulously placing them exactly where they are meant to go on the page. Ed is chatting with her as he puts the shopping away. He looks surprisingly relaxed and worry-free – more so than she has seen him in months. She does not want to rain on his parade with her doubts and fears. Not now. Nor does she want him to revert back to his 'should have moved out to Australia' stance.

'Who's it from, Mummy?' Tilly asks, jolting Mel from her thoughts. 'What does it say?'

'Ah, it says, "Welcome to your new home" and I was right, it's from the man who helped us buy this house,' Mel lies, simply grateful she doesn't sound as shaken as she feels.

'We should put it up somewhere,' Ed says.

Mel feels the colour drain from her face. She doesn't want him to see it. She doesn't want him to notice it isn't signed and to start asking questions. She has to find some way out of this and some way to fix it. Just under three weeks – that's all it has taken for Alice to find them. Maybe Ed was right. She should've listened to him and got them as far away from Alice as possible.

Think. Think! She tells herself. 'Sure, this place isn't our new home,' she says. 'This is just a stopgap. I think I'll keep the card safe for when the work is done and we're in the finished house.' She's impressed by how easily the lie trips off her tongue.

Her plan, of course, is to tear it into tiny pieces before burying it in the bottom of the bin. Or maybe she will just hide it away somewhere.

Just in case she needs it in the future, as evidence.

6

It's next to impossible to get any meaningful level of privacy in a mobile home. Mel just wants an hour or so alone to scan the Internet but she has to do it surreptitiously. Ed does not approve of her 'torturing herself' as he puts it.

'If you look long enough you'll always find something upsetting about you,' he has said on numerous occasions. She doesn't want to correct him and tell him she doesn't need to look 'long enough'. In fact, the barrage of hateful comments and judgemental takes are remarkably easy to find. All she has to do is search her name, or click into any parenting forum. Even the forum she had used religiously while carrying Tilly and in her daughter's early years has become a no-go zone. She has been frozen out, subjected to the worst name-calling by these people she used to consider friends.

But she has no choice now. The card sits heavy on her mind. What if Alice shows up at the new house? What if she calls to Tilly as she plays in the yard, and this time there is no fence to stop her from grabbing her daughter and running? There's nothing stopping Alice from waiting until she knows Mel and

Tilly are alone without the protection of Ed, or a gang of burly builders, or even a neighbour or two nearby. Isolation isn't always a good thing. She'd been foolish to think moving would be an end to it all. Foolish to think Alice would just let her disappear and start rebuilding her life elsewhere.

The anniversary of that awful day was approaching and Mel should've expected that it would add new fuel to this particular bin fire of emotions.

She had learned over the course of the past year that Alice's rage, like her grief, comes in waves – calm at times, and with reckless force at others. Something deep inside Mel screams that this time, it will come like a tsunami. The card is only a warning shot. A reminder that she is still out there – and she knows where Mel is.

Sitting cross-legged in her small bedroom, she switches on her laptop, desperate to judge just what level of anger she is dealing with. Alice has, of course, blocked her on all social media. She has blocked Mel's phone number and her email. But she has not blocked her from the forums she frequents – most likely because Mel has long since abandoned any account Alice would've been familiar with. She uses ghost accounts now, secret ways to log in and read without being recognised. It doesn't help much, but it does help her when it comes to knowing her enemy.

It breaks her that it's come to that. She'd thought she'd found a friend for life in Alice. Their bond had been immediate and strong – but not strong enough to survive tragedy.

Alice doesn't post as much as she used to, at least not openly. As Mel scrolls through the familiar forum groups, searching her own name, she knows that despite Alice's quieter approach, she will still find threads in which every detail of her life will be picked over.

It doesn't take long to uncover them. Mel suspects she isn't the only person with a variety of ghost accounts to access the forum. She's relatively sure Alice has a selection of usernames and fabricated identities to keep the conversation going. It's too much of a coincidence that the members who shout loudest about how 'dangerous' Mel is are all newly registered, without profile pictures or identifying details.

They don't care if what they say is the truth. Some of the things Mel has read about herself over the past year have been pure fiction – assertions that Mel has always been reckless, that she didn't so much as leave teaching but was pushed. That she should never have been around children at all. That someone should take her beautiful little girl from her and keep her safe...

The most recent thread Mel finds is from a user by the name of Big Bad Wolf – with the title 'She can run, but she can't hide'.

Well, well, well – it seems the demon birthing coach has run for the hills. I wonder if she would like me to tell everyone exactly which hill she has run to. Would it be wrong to dox her? After all, we have to make sure she doesn't get up to her old tricks in a new setting?

#KeepOurBabiesSafe #KeepOurBabiesAlive

Alice, she thinks, is never going to let this go. Pressing the heels of her hands into her eyes, Mel fights the urge to cry. It's all just too unfair. Staring at the screen, she tries to form some sort of plan on how she can handle this – not that she has been able to think of anything effective over the course of the last year.

She can't just let it lie though. What if Alice *does* dox her? She's not expecting to be completely anonymous here. Northern Ireland is a small place where people revel in knowing every detail of one another's lives. But she had hoped that it could be quieter. That she could go about her day-to-day business without worrying quite so much about wicked whispers. All this effort, all this money, all the tension with Ed to relocate here as opposed to his dream destination – and now she worries it could still all go tits up.

Fuck it, she thinks, maybe it's time to speak up after all. Or at least try to. She clicks on Alice's profile page and on the envelope icon on the top right-hand side of the screen. If she can't call her, or message her through normal means, she will message her here and hope that she reads it.

The low hum of the television in the main living space reassures her that Ed is still distracted by the documentary he was watching. Tilly is asleep. This is her time to do it, even though she knows there is a chance it could just stir things up even more. She has to at least try, but she knows she also has to be careful. Never put anything in writing that you wouldn't be happy sharing with the entire world – isn't that the rule? She knows she can't write anything that Alice might share, and she knows that is exactly the kind of thing she could – and might – do.

Alice,
      It's Mel. I got your card. Can we talk? Don't you think it's about time?
      M.

She hits send just as the door to the room opens and Ed walks in. Without thinking, she slams the lid of the laptop shut and his eyes widen a little. 'Hiding something from me?' he asks, the hint of a smile playing across his lips. She knows if she just keeps her cool, she will be able to get away with this without him finding out.

'Okay,' she says, 'you caught me. I was looking at more baby clothes.'

He shakes his head and rolls his eyes. 'We have bags of baby clothes already. We really don't need any more.'

'Yeah, but a lot of those are for baby girls. And this is a baby boy. Doesn't he deserve his own things?'

'And you've bought enough of those already!' Ed says, but his tone is light and the teasing is loving.

'It's only a couple of tops,' she lies.

'I suppose I'll let you away with it this time.' Ed sits down on the bed beside her and places one hand on her stomach. 'This boy deserves the best of everything, as does his mum.'

When he kisses her on the cheek, his stubble scratching her skin in just the right way – the way she loves when she's not heavily pregnant and *sans* libido – she breathes him in and reminds herself that what they have is what really matters.

'I love you,' she tells him, feeling overwhelmed with love for him and the need to make their problems go away. And one problem in particular.

7

34 WEEKS + 2 DAYS

'Mel Davison?' A tall, thin woman, probably in her early forties, stands in the doorway to the waiting room, looking around as she speaks.

The woman has a friendly look about her – her face is scrubbed clean of make-up, revealing flawless skin, and her glossy, chestnut, curly hair is pulled back into a loose ponytail. Mel immediately feels self-conscious about the hormonal zit that is currently blooming on her chin, and the frizzy, untameable nature of her hair.

With a smile, the vision in scrubs calls her name again followed by 'Don't be shy, ladies,' and the women in the room, each cradling a different-sized bump, smile and giggle. It's a busy morning in the midwifery clinic at the health centre and Mel's grateful that it's finally her turn.

'Just coming,' Mel says, easing herself to standing. She winces, aching from the increasing weight of her unborn baby, but more so right now from the discomfort of the cramped bed in the caravan. Last night had made for an awful night of half-sleep as she wondered if Alice had seen her message. Or replied.

She dared not risk getting up and checking and possibly waking Ed. She'd checked this morning though – and no, there was no reply.

'Hi, I'm Lindsey and I'm one of the midwives,' the woman says as she leads the way into the small side room and directs Mel to take a seat beside her desk.

Everything about this room screams 'clinical setting', Mel thinks. From the blood collection tubes, with their myriad of different-coloured tops, to the poster on the wall featuring a cross section of the female form, complete with a baby *in utero*, head down and ready for delivery.

Another poster illustrates what each extra centimetre of cervical dilation looks like, while still another of a smiling, happy mother, vernix-clad baby to breast, not so subtly reinforces the message that good mothers breastfeed.

Mel feels a trickle of sweat bead at the back of her neck, and she rubs her clammy hands on her dress. She's annoyed at herself for being nervous. She who knows intimately about the process of birthing a baby. She built a career on it. Or at least tried to.

'So I see you're newly registered here, and you've just moved to the area. I've had a quick look at your notes. Thankfully your old midwifery team sent them through quite quickly and I didn't have to go chasing them. They were very helpful,' Lindsey says. Her voice is soft and her demeanour gentle but still, Mel feels flooded with nerves.

A small green strand of yarn comes loose on the cuff of her cardigan and she tries with shaky, sweaty fingers to thread it back through the tight-knit loops in the wool. She can distract herself easily by focusing on the fact she doesn't want to cause irreparable damage to one of the few remaining items of clothing that still fit her. This baby will be her last. Ed has already offered to get the snip later this year so there will be no more pregnancies in her future – and no need to ever buy new maternity wear again.

After a beat, while Mel works at the cardigan cuff, Lindsey speaks again. 'I can't imagine it's easy making a move across the country this far into a pregnancy. That will be a challenge for you all. And for your daughter too – big changes all round?'

It's a question, not a statement, and Mel is pretty sure she senses judgement in the other woman's tone. She's been met with this judgement before. People thinking she is making a rod for her own back by introducing so much change to her young daughter all at the same time.

'It's not ideal,' she agrees, shifting in her seat, trying to move the bony elbow or knee that is digging into her ribs. 'But Tilly's a resilient little girl and very happy to be here. We found our dream home – one that will be the very best place for two children to grow up in – and it was too good a deal to pass up on. You'd pay twice as much in the east for it. We were ready for a change, especially with the baby on the way, so... you know...'

Lindsey nods but she doesn't speak. The silence sits between them until its awkwardness forces Mel to say more. She never has been a fan of an awkward silence.

'We were going to move here in the late summer, after the birth,' she tells Lindsey. 'We wanted to move before Tilly is due to start school, obviously. But then we thought maybe it would be harder on her if we waited and moved with a newborn so close to such a big transition as school. So we decided we'd get it over and done with now, and give her some time to adjust and get to know the baby.'

'Ah,' Lindsey says with a smile that seems sincere, although Mel would concede the last year has proven she is not as good a judge of character as she once thought.

'Well hopefully, it's not *too* upsetting,' Lindsey says. 'And you all settle in well.'

As Lindsey chats, she takes a blood pressure cuff and slides it around Mel's arm before pressing the button on the monitor to start it inflating mechanically. Soon it is painfully tight and Mel fights the urge to wince. She doesn't want to make a fuss. She'll be happy to stay under the radar as much as possible.

'Do you know what you're having?' Lindsey asks, even though Mel is sure that her baby's gender is already written in her notes.

She is hit with a now familiar, weird and painful combination of excitement and overwhelming guilt as she nods. 'We're having a wee boy.'

In any other circumstance, she wouldn't be able to hold in her joy at having a son. One of each has always been her dream and while she adores raising Tilly, and would have welcomed any new addition to their family, she can't wait to find out what it's like to be a mother to a son. But of course, she dreads it too. It feels wrong. Unfair. Cruel even, she thinks on her darkest days. Alice never got to raise her son but, all being well, Mel will get to enjoy that experience. She knows that every person who knows of Alice and Jacob will feel a pang to hear her news, so she must be mindful not to sound too happy.

The beep of the monitor distracts Lindsey from making any comment and they both glance at the reading of 140/90 now displayed. Mel knows immediately what that means.

'Hmmm.' Lindsey frowns. 'It's edging towards high.'

Mel blinks back tears. She knows this reading isn't edging towards anything. It's high already. It might be on the lower end of the high scale but with over a month to go, maybe even closer to two months, that is not a number she wants to see.

She strokes her stomach, willing her son to be okay, and

loses the battle to hold in her tears. Embarrassment washes over her. She did not want to cry, but here she is with high blood pressure and the worry that all this will be too much for Tilly to manage, and Ed's comments about Australia. And the awful, inescapable knowledge that a baby died on her watch.

'Do you think it's possible you're feeling a wee bit stressed this morning?' Lindsey asks as she subtly shifts a box of tissues across her desk. Mel gratefully takes one, immediately twisting it in her hands nervously.

'You know stress can elevate your blood pressure,' Lindsey continues. 'With everything you're trying to manage at the moment – moving house, caring for your wee girl... and everything – it'd be no surprise if you were feeling a bit overwhelmed. Have you help at home?'

Mel shrugs. 'Well, my husband is at home, and a great help, obviously. And the builders will be doing the vast majority of the heavy work. I'll just be doing a bit of painting, and maybe hanging curtains, but I doubt we'll even be ready for that before the baby comes.'

Lindsey's brow furrows with what looks like concern. 'Heavy work? Builders?' she asks, her gaze dropping to her patient's swollen stomach.

'We're restoring the house,' Mel says. 'It has great bones but has seen better days. And we're building an extension too.'

'And where will you be living while all this is happening? With a newborn?' Lindsey asks, incredulity – and possibly judgement – written across her face again. 'Lord, you don't believe in doing things by halves, do you?' she adds with a little laugh.

Feeling defensive, Mel says, 'Originally, we thought we'd be able to do it bit by bit around us, but once we were in and realised just how big and messy a job it was going to be, we moved into a mobile home on the site during the build instead.

So we'll have somewhere relatively dust- and mud-free. And we'll get some of the bigger work done before the baby arrives.' She shifts in her seat, realising she has just done one of the things she used to tell her clients not to do – when she still had clients. She'd over-explained her reasons instead of telling herself that no one is owed an explanation for every choice you make in life.

'You're a brave woman,' Lindsey tells her, with an expression that makes Mel think she wanted to say 'stupid' instead of 'brave'. She scribbles something in Mel's antenatal notes. 'I'm not sure how I'd manage in a caravan with a newborn,' she continues, her head bent. 'But I suppose they are fancier these days than they were in the past. Some of them are nicer than my house.' She gives a little laugh but Mel is still tense. She's desperate to know what her midwife has just written in her notes. Is it perhaps some judgemental comment on their living conditions? Mel fears that she is under more intense scrutiny than other mums-to-be because of Jacob's death. She fears that every single decision she makes will be held up and used against her.

'Okay, how about you get up on the bed and we'll have a little look at your tummy!' Lindsey puts her pen down on the desk and claps her hands together.

Mel immediately does as she's told in an attempt to prove she's a 'good girl' and not the loose cannon some people have labelled her.

She lies down on the narrow examination couch and pulls up her jumper, exposing a collage of old and new stretch marks snaking their way up and down her abdomen – a vivid reminder that this is not her first rodeo.

Lindsey washes her hands, then rubs them together to warm

them before she starts palpating Mel's stomach – feeling for the baby's position.

'And you're feeling plenty of movement?' Lindsey asks, as she presses down dangerously close to Mel's already sensitive bladder.

'Oh God, yes. He never stops.'

'That's a good thing,' Lindsey says before standing straight again. 'Of course, you'd already know that.' She pauses. 'Given your line of work.'

Mel freezes, unsure if this is just a referral to this being her second pregnancy or something much more pointed. She knows there are plenty of midwives who were cynical about her work as a doula and a hypnobirthing coach. She'd encountered a few who resisted her presence in the labour ward – and that was of course before Jacob and Alice.

'Yes,' she mutters in response. 'I do.'

'Good. So, you know, any concerns at all, you call here, or the foetal assessment unit at the hospital. Don't hesitate. Although I guess you've already learned that lesson the hard way.'

Mel wants to scream that she did everything she was supposed to do. Everything that Alice wanted her to do. That it wasn't her fault. But experience has also taught her that there are a lot of people who don't care about the truth – Alice herself, who was still stirring the pot from across the country, being chief among them.

8

THEN

Alice's due date had come and gone. She was now just over forty-two weeks pregnant and still intent on continuing with her plan to freebirth her baby. A plan that had seen her refuse all prenatal care – convinced most of it was unnecessary and even invasive. Mel would've found it more reassuring if she'd been checked along the way, but at the end of the day she was only there to be a support and a witness to Alice's delivery. It was not her place to interfere with the plans Alice and Thomas had put in place for their baby's arrival.

Mel had made sure to visit her every day after her due date, unable to escape the uneasy feeling that nipped at her with each one that passed.

Alice frequently greeted Mel with a 'I'm trusting my own body, so please, don't say anything. My baby will come when they are good and ready! They are moving. All is fine. It must just be extra comfy in there.'

On the seventeenth of April, two weeks and two days past Alice's due date, Mel's phone had rung while she was on her way to Alice's house. As soon as her friend's name popped up on her dashboard display, she knew instinctively that things were finally underway. A wave of relief washed over her as she answered the call.

'Good morning, Alice,' she said.

'It's happening,' Thomas said while Mel could hear Alice groaning in the background. 'Are you on your way?' There was a shake in his voice and Mel could imagine all the emotions he was going through. He was about to become a father to a much wanted, much loved baby, and yet that great endorphin rush conflicted with the fear of seeing his wife in discomfort. No matter how much Mel had worked with both Alice and Thomas to prepare them for what was to come and to learn it was nothing to be feared, she knew there would still be moments when it would feel overwhelming. The realisation that your life is about to change forever is a big one.

'I'll be with you in about five minutes,' Mel told him. 'It's all going to be okay. Try and centre yourself. Take a moment to just breathe and then get that birthing pool filled!'

'It's already filling,' he said. 'And I've the oil burner lit, and the curtains pulled.'

'And how's Alice?'

Mel heard a laugh – small and nervous – and unmistakably Alice. 'You're on speaker phone and I'm good. Didn't I know it would be okay? Didn't I say this baby would come in their own time and I just had to be patient?' She sounded euphoric and Mel felt a rush of love for the woman who had already become one of her most trusted friends. Ed had started to joke that Alice was becoming his wife's mistress due to how close they had become, but Mel knew her husband had a great fondness for Alice too. And for Thomas. They had shared many dinner parties together already and Thomas had proven to be a worthy golfing opponent for Ed.

'You did,' Mel told her friend, unable to stop smiling. 'I'm just turning into your street. Hang on. I'll be right in!'

* * *

Everything progressed beautifully – until it didn't any more. In a matter of minutes, Alice went from feeling very much in control to very much overwhelmed.

Her surges became more frequent, longer-lasting, and she had little to no respite between them, and while Mel knew this usually indicated that the mum-to-be was in the transition phase – and almost ready to have her baby – there was something about this that just felt all wrong.

It wasn't long before that gut instinct became a nightmare. When Mel thinks of it even now, she can't quite remember how it all happened – instead she is assaulted with snapshots of the following hours. Noises. Sights. Smells. The expressions on the faces of Alice and Thomas, and the paramedics... and the doctor and nurses.

Baby Jacob Munroe entered this world silently at 10.14 p.m., while his mother was under general anaesthetic and his father and Mel sat staring at the greying white walls of a hospital waiting room, completely shell-shocked by what had just happened. His grandmother didn't sit down. She paced the corridors, shaking her head, occasionally bellowing at a broken Thomas, 'How could you let her do this?'

The woman didn't even acknowledge Mel's existence. Mel had the strongest feeling that if she did, the resulting outburst would be catastrophic for everyone.

Their clothes were still wet from helping Alice from the birthing pool. Their eyes were red. Thomas clung to a small stuffed elephant which he had insisted on bringing with him because every baby deserved their own cuddly toy.

Mel couldn't think. She could barely breathe. She just kept asking herself over and over again how it could have gone so very wrong. His heartbeat had been fine an hour before. Alice had felt him moving.

But he was gone. A blur in scrubs with a disembodied voice told them that. 'He'. Alice had been right. Her baby was a boy.

'Jacob,' Thomas said as he nodded to acknowledge that he had in fact heard the awful news. Mel couldn't speak. She couldn't move.

The doctor had his theories, of course, about what exactly had happened. Theories they would explore in a post-mortem. Theories that would give them answers but which would never give Alice and Thomas back what it was that had been so cruelly taken from them, before they'd had so much as the chance to see him open his eyes.

Mel left the hospital when Thomas went in to see his wife and to hold their baby for the first time. She couldn't bring herself to be a part of a grief that raw any more. She doubted she was welcome anyway. This was a time for family, and she knew it was also a time for blame and anger.

As the taxi drove her back to Alice's house to retrieve her car, the thought kept popping into her head that she had known something was wrong, hadn't she? She'd felt it in her bones that something wasn't right an hour or two before it all went wrong. Running it through her mind time and time again, she tried to pinpoint what it was that made her feel uneasy. Asked herself if things would have been different even if she had spoken up? It's not like she had anything solid to go on. It could've just been that the baby was so far overdue and there was no medical help on hand and... All the 'coulds' didn't matter one bit. She tried to hold on to everything that happened but her memories were already becoming muddled. Her mind fuzzy with exhaustion and trauma.

She knew she'd have to reach out to Alice sooner rather than later – not only as her doula but as her friend. Her very dear friend. Alice had joked many times she'd need Mel more after the baby was born. They'd planned to continue with their weekly coffee mornings, and their daily phone calls. This was only the start of their friendship, they'd told each other, and Mel knew she needed to say something. She just wasn't sure where to start. After staring at her phone for the entirety of the taxi ride, she typed the only words that really seemed appropriate – 'I'm sorry'.

She let herself into the house with the key Alice had given her a few weeks before and immediately was confronted with the sights, smells and mess of a birth gone wrong. What had looked like a cosy nest just hours before now looked like a bomb site. The birthing pool with its soiled water; stained, sopping towels on the floor. Discarded latex gloves, the candles now burnt down to stubs, the smell of incense now stale in the air. Mel couldn't leave the room like that. She couldn't have Alice and Thomas come home to this. Not after everything.

Even though she was exhausted and had not slept in almost twenty-four hours, Mel set about cleaning and tidying. It was the very least she could do, she told herself. So she emptied the birthing pool before dragging it out to the patio to hose it down. She picked up the towels and Alice's discarded clothes and put them on to wash.

She gathered any waste and disposed of it, washed up the dirty mugs and glasses that had been sitting around the room. She wiped everything down, mopped, and tidied the cushions on the sofa. She even went so far as to go out to the shop and stock up on milk, freshly baked bread and scones, even though Thomas and Alice already had a well-stocked fridge. She did everything she could think of to make sure that when they did come home, they wouldn't have to worry about anything other than trying to start to come to terms with what they had just been through.

When Mel finally left, their house was in some sort of order, but her mind was not. She was so tired and so broken she could barely see straight. She just wanted to get home, hold Tilly to her as tightly as she could, and cry herself to sleep. Before she set off on the drive home, she looked at her phone one more time. It was silent. There were no messages from Thomas or Alice – not that Mel really expected them to respond. She just hoped they knew that her heart was breaking right along with theirs.

9

MARCH 2024

Mel knows she is being extra snappy with Ed, and with Tilly for that matter. She feels guilty that she swore when Tilly knocked her juice over and soaked the carpet in the caravan. Tilly had looked at her, eyes wide, instantly aware that her mother was not in her usual gentle parenting mode. There was no admonishment that 'Mummy said a bad word' – in fact Mel had seen tears forming in her daughter's eyes and immediately felt awful for raising her voice.

'I'm not cross with you, Tilly,' she soothed, even though at that moment she *was* cross that juice had been spilled on the floor. She'd told Tilly to be careful when she'd handed her the drink just seconds before. But now she was going to have to get down on her hands and knees and mop up the spill – not an easy feat at almost eight months pregnant.

Ed is in the bedroom on a Zoom call with a client which is less than ideal to say the least, but his options for makeshift office space are limited given their confined quarters. In time, he'd clear out the third bedroom in the caravan and set up on a desk and chair, but for now he could either be found at the kitchen table or in their bedroom, giving her one fewer space to be able to truly relax. Or check her phone or laptop. Every time she so much as reaches for either of them, Tilly seems to appear like a device-seeking missile asking for just 'a wee five minutes' on YouTube or watching *Bluey* on the Disney + app.

At least, she thinks, Tilly can't read yet. It might be frustrating to have her daughter clamber on top of her begging for a look at her phone, but it would be worse if she were able to pick out words from the screen and start asking awkward questions.

As she mops up the juice, she feels a second wave of guilt wash over her. Between the move and her being heavily pregnant, she has been relying on YouTube and *Bluey* to act the role of de facto babysitters. She is certainly not playing the part of the ideal mother at the moment. Poor Tilly doesn't get the interaction she used to at nursery, but nor does she get her mother's attention to sit and work through an afternoon of arts and crafts, or take a walk through the park. Mel has not been the mother she wants to be and none of it has been helped by the stress of the situation with Alice.

She feels her bottom lip wobble, a mirror image of the sorrowful look on Tilly's face. She has to fix this, once and for all. Of course she has immense sympathy for what Alice has been through, but her loss can't be used as a reason to keep damaging Mel's life. And she can't allow it to continue damaging her relationship with her daughter, never mind the baby who has still to be born.

Later, when Ed has finished his work and is curled up on the sofa with a now perfectly placated Tilly, Mel disappears back into the bedroom and logs in to see if Alice has replied to her message.

She hasn't, although Mel can see from the two blue ticks on the screen that she has read it. Frustration burns inside her. She knows Alice is grieving. Mel knows she is hurt, but surely she realises that it was a tragedy and not down to anything Mel did or didn't do.

She searches her own name again, already feeling the familiar uncomfortable, sickly feeling that she gets anytime she goes online these days. She has become much too used to seeing her name followed by a barrage of slurs and lies. People are only too willing to sit in judgement of something they really know nothing about.

Big Bad Wolf has been online again.

I've made it my mission to make sure every community group who offer any kind of support to expectant mothers or parents of young children in and around Mel Davison's new home know just exactly who she is. I cobbled together a selection of the newspaper articles about her, and screen-shots from social media, to give them the full picture. She won't be able to peddle her wares anywhere else again.

Mel's blood runs cold as she imagines emails and letters being disseminated around offices as people who have no idea what really happened make their mind up about her. She's bad news. No community service provider is going to take a chance on someone with a reputation like hers – not that she thinks she could ever comfortably step back into her former profession. That particular dream has long since morphed into a nightmare.

But still she wants – no, needs – to stop this poison about her being circulated. Anger flares in her that Alice continues to make her life so difficult. As tears slide down her cheeks, she decides that enough is enough. If Alice doesn't have the manners to reply to her message, then she'll give her no choice but to do so. As Mel sees it, she can do this in one of two ways – she can go the legal route. Report her for harassment. Send a solicitor's letter. All things that Alice in all her guises could spin to make it look like Mel had it in for a grieving mother.

Or she could do what she should've done in the first place. She can go and see her face to face – and this time she's not going to wait for Alice to respond to her message, or post yet more hateful lies online. She knows where Alice lives and even though she hasn't set foot inside that house since the day Jacob died, and even though the very thought of stepping over that threshold again makes her feel sick to her stomach, she has to make it stop. Tomorrow, she thinks. She'll do it then. She'll tell Ed she wants to go and see her parents. She'll pop Tilly in the car and she'll drive back across the Glenshane Pass and up past Belfast and... and well, then, maybe she shouldn't bring Tilly. Her daughter doesn't need to be caught up in this. No, she'll just tell Ed that she needs a day or two away from the site and the noise. Tell him that her blood pressure is high. It's not a lie. Or make up some admin that she just forgot to do before they moved and now needs to get finished before the baby arrives. Whatever, she'll think of a reason and she'll go back to Carrick-fergus and to Alice's house, and she will do whatever it takes to put an end to all this stress.

The following morning, she steels herself to have the conversation with Ed, hoping that he will be okay with her going for a day or two and leaving him with Tilly and the building site, as well as his own work to manage.

She makes him scrambled eggs on sourdough toast before mashing up a boiled egg into a cup with some salt and butter and giving that to Tilly for her breakfast. It's one of Mel's own comfort foods – egg in a cup. It was her mother's go-to whenever Mel was sick, or sad, or just needed a little extra spoiling as a child. Thankfully, Tilly is as fond of it as her mother was at that age.

'We're going all out with breakfast this morning.' Ed smiles as he pops a capsule into the coffee machine and switches it on. The caravan is filled with the aroma of coffee, eggs and toast. The windows are lined with condensation and while rain is lashing the outside of the van, Mel allows herself a moment to appreciate how cosy it is. She has – she realises once again – so much to fight for. Her family – this little army within these four walls – are what really matters.

'It's only eggs on toast,' she tells him, but she knows it's unusual. Normally it's a bowl of porridge or a slice of toast, maybe with some chopped banana or a sprinkle of berries.

'It's yummy eggs and toast,' Tilly says, as she loads her spoon with another mouthful of food. 'I think it might be my favourite.'

Ed laughs. 'I think you change your mind about your favourite things every single day, Tills. Yesterday you said Cheerios were your very favourite thing ever.'

Tilly tilts her head to one side, as if she is mulling over the benefits of eggs versus Cheerios. 'They are both my favourites. Just like you say me and the new baby will be your favourites.'

Mel smiles as she watches her husband gently ruffle their daughter's hair. 'You're my favourite girl, and the new baby will be my favourite boy,' he tells his daughter with a warm smile. In these moments it's hard to remember that all is not perfect in their world.

'And you're my favourite daddy and Mummy is my favourite mummy,' Tilly replies decisively.

Sitting down at the table with them, Mel knows that it is a case of now or never and she really, really needs it to be now.

'Ed,' she says as she reaches for her coffee cup, 'I was thinking I might go and visit my parents. I've a few things still to clear up, just some paperwork they want me to help them with, and I figure now would probably be the best time to go.'

Ed smiles, laughs a gentle, mocking laugh. 'I'll give you your dues, Mel, I didn't think it would take this long, so I'm impressed in a way.'

'What do you mean?' she asks, her brow crinkled. She thinks he's just teasing but she's not 100 per cent sure.

'I knew it wouldn't be long before you wanted to go back up the road to see your parents.'

'It's been almost three weeks. I was used to seeing them almost every day,' she protests, realising, as she does, just how much she misses them.

'They say cold turkey's the best way to beat homesickness,' he says. 'That's what Emma did when she went to Australia. She didn't contact a single one of us for a month – apart from a once-a-week text message to confirm she was still alive, that none of us were allowed to reply to. She swears it made her get used to her new, detached way of life much quicker.'

Mel wants to reply with a sarcastic 'good for her' but she doesn't. 'I don't want my life to be detached,' she says, feeling her grip on her coffee mug tighten. 'They're my parents and of course I miss them. I was just thinking, you know, in a week or two I'm going to want to stay close to home until after the baby is born. I've no desire to give birth on the 212 bus to Belfast.' She forces herself to smile, to keep this all light.

'No,' Ed says and laughs. 'I can't imagine that would be much fun. And imagine if you had to name the baby after whatever part of Northern Ireland it was born in?'

'Castledawson Roundabout has a certain ring to it,' she says with a smile. 'But, honestly, I was just thinking it would be good to go and maybe stay up a night or two and get a good rest. You know I've not been sleeping well. I could help them with this paperwork and that would ease my guilt at moving away from them too.' She wonders when she became such a proficient liar.

'And is Miss Tilly here going with you?' Ed asks.

Before Mel can answer, Tilly speaks. 'I want to stay here with you, Daddy. And help you make the new house all builded.'

'You *are* my best helper,' Ed says. 'And your mummy could do with lots of rest before your baby brother comes along so you can stay if you want, as long as Mummy doesn't mind – and you know sometimes you have to be super quiet while I'm working.'

Tilly puts one finger to her lips just to prove she can be as quiet as her daddy wants. Mel should be completely relieved but there's a part of her that feels a little rejected. Not that she can blame her daughter. She has become the neurotic, hormonal, always-tired one, while Daddy has blossomed into his fun-parent era. If she were a four-year-old, she'd choose to stay with Ed too.

'If you want to go, then go,' Ed says. 'I know this has all been stressful. Tilly and I will have great fun just the two of us. We promise we won't make too big a mess.'

Mel hopes she doesn't make too big a mess either.

10

MARCH 2024

34 weeks + 4 days

'Why don't you just put your feet up, pet, and I'll make you a wee cup of tea?'

Mel's mum has been in full-on smother mode from the moment she arrived yesterday. You would think it had been a year, and not just a few weeks since they had last seen each other.

'You have to take it easy. High blood pressure is no laughing matter. You've come here to relax and that's exactly what you're going to do. Although I'll be honest, Mel, both your father and I are a little disappointed that Tilly isn't with you,' she'd said.

Mel had forced a smile on her face and explained how, as much as she loved her daughter, there was little to no chance of getting a rest with Tilly Davison around. 'I've always known you love my daughter more than you love me,' Mel had joked.

'We love you the same,' her mother had said as she had given her a warm hug. 'Sure, isn't she just an extension of you? She's your wee mini-me.'

A mini-me, Mel thought, who preferred to be with her daddy. Even though Mel knew why it was more sensible for her daughter to have stayed in Derry, and even why her daughter found spending time with Ed more enjoyable, but she didn't say that to her mother. Mel didn't want to give her anything else to worry about – not on top of Mel's high blood pressure and the crash-and-burn of her career. So instead, she'd smiled and agreed, and changed the topic to talk about the weather and the new road up from Derry to Belfast. Safe, mundane conversation.

She's let her mum look after her in the way only a mum can, and it has felt so nice. Even though she has so much running through her mind, having someone else cook and clean, and hold her hand while telling her everything will be okay has been soothing.

Or it had been. Today, when she wants to go out to see if she can get Alice to talk to her, it feels a little claustrophobic.

She turns down her mum's offer of a cup of tea – the third of the morning – ignoring the wounded look in her eyes at the refusal. 'I think I'm in danger of turning into a cup of tea,' she explains. 'And I need to watch my caffeine intake. Especially with my blood pressure.'

'Oh God, yes. I didn't think. You're right, of course. You never really think about tea having caffeine in it. I know I only really think about coffee. Well, can I get you a glass of juice? Or water? Or maybe milk to help with your heartburn?' she asks, busying herself in the kitchen as if it's not already perfectly clean and tidy. The woman just can't ever seem to sit still.

'Actually, Mum, I think I'm going to go for a walk. Get some fresh air in my lungs,' Mel says.

'There's no need for that. If you want to go anywhere, I can take you. Or your dad can. He likes to be kept busy, you know. I'll ask him.' Her mother makes to leave the room, no doubt to shout from the bottom of the stairs for her husband to come down from his small study to be at their beck and call.

'No! Mum, honestly. I need to get a bit of exercise. The walk will do me the power of good and it's a nice day for once. There's been so much rain lately.'

'Do you want me to come with you?' her mum asks, and Mel knows it's not going to be easy to get her to drop it and let her go out on her own.

'There's no need. I'm fine. Honest. I'm thirty-six, Mum. I think I'll be grand taking a walk on my own.'

'But what if you take a funny turn?' she asks, and Mel wonders if what she really means is, *What if you run into that woman who is trying to ruin your life?* She can only imagine what her mother's reaction would be if she told her she was going to hunt down *that woman*, and that's why she wants to go out on her own.

'I'll have my phone with me so I will call you if I start to feel anything out of sorts. I promise. I'm actually feeling good today, Mum, and I just want to make the most of it. I fancy a nice walk to give my head a wee bit of quiet to think through everything.'

Mel hopes that will suffice as a polite way of saying she is doing this on her own.

Her mother sighs. 'Well, if you're sure? And if you promise you'll call me if you need me?'

'I promise. And thanks, Mum,' It strikes her how much she means it. Her mother may have dismissed her hypnobirthing as 'airy-fairy nonsense'. She may have told her that she was overreacting to move away from home, but Mel knows that behind those words, her mother cares for her deeply. And she always, always has her back. Her concern comes from a genuine place. One that Mel only really understands now that she is a mother herself. That feeling of needing to do whatever it takes to protect her children. There is no drive like it.

She tried countless times last night to phone Alice, but the calls just went straight to voicemail – a sure sign if ever she needed one that Alice still has her number blocked. It's not a huge surprise but it does mean there's only one thing for it.

Mel knows the only way to get to speak to Alice now is to go to her house and stand her ground. As soon as she'd made that decision last night, she had wanted to get it over and done with but had held off until this morning.

Nervous energy has been pulsing through her body since she woke up and she knows she has to do this now before she combusts.

* * *

Alice lives about a fifteen-minute walk from Mel's parents' house. As Mel turns onto her street, it strikes her that she's not been in her house since the night Jacob died – when she went back to clean up and collect her belongings.

Or to 'dispose of the evidence' as Thomas put it when he had called her the following day, his voice shaking with rage and grief. She shivers when she thinks of those words, and of how cold he was to her. How scared she had been of the possible repercussions and how much she had questioned whether or not it was – in some way she couldn't think of – her fault after all.

For all her bravado, she can feel the nerves kick in as she walks farther into the leafy cul-de-sac where the Munroes have made their home. Alice had told her they'd bought the house because of its location and how they believed it would be a safe place for their children to play.

So many of us take for granted that there will be children, Mel thinks. Alice was pregnant when she'd shared that story – she'd had no reason to suspect that she would one day be walking into her home with an empty belly and empty arms. There would be no child to worry about letting out to play. It was cruel.

Mel wraps her coat tighter – it's not that she finds it particularly cold, it's actually quite lovely; it's more that she wants to wrap her arms around her tummy and around her boy. This will be painful for Alice, Mel knows that, but that doesn't mean it doesn't have to be done. Even with everything that has been lost, they still both deserve to move on.

The exterior of the house looks much the same as it did a year ago. The garden is well tended and on its way back to life after a cold and particularly rainy winter. Mel's heart startles when she spots Alice's car in the driveway. She's home and this is the last chance Mel has to turn on her heel and walk away. She contemplates it for a moment. She could go back to her mum's, and then back to Ed and Tilly, and she could agree to move to Australia like Ed wants and all this would go away. Then again, she thought that moving to Derry would help fix things and it hadn't.

No, she reminds herself. She has to go into this with a positive attitude. She doesn't deserve what she is being put through and nor does her family.

Taking a few deep breaths to try and centre herself, Mel reminds herself she is doing the right thing. Even though she can feel her whole body shake as she exhales, she knows she has to push through. So that is what she does. She raises her hand and knocks on the stained-glass panel of Alice's front door. And then she waits.

There is no answer. There is no sign of a shadow moving behind the coloured glass. There is no sound of footsteps coming down Alice's beautifully tiled hall, the one that leads

from the room where she laboured just over a year ago. So Mel
knocks again, before crouching to peek in through the letter box.
There is still no obvious sign of Alice, or anyone else for that
matter, but she can see a Yankee Candle burning on the hall
table, and a TV or radio appears to be emitting a low sound from
somewhere at the rear of the house.

'Alice!' Mel calls through the door. 'It's Mel. Look, I know you
might not want to, but I really do want to talk with you. I think
we need it. *I* need it. Please.'

There is no response.

Frustration blooms in Mel. Now that she has decided she
wants to talk, and has gone to the effort of coming back up to
Carrickfergus and putting her nerves aside, she really hoped to
make it happen. She stands for a moment and contemplates her
next move. Spotting the side gate, she remembers how Alice used
to leave it unlocked, along with her back door so that friends – the
kind of friends she and Mel had become – could let themselves
in. Mel used it herself many times in the past. But today when she
gives it a good rattle, she finds it's locked. There's no other option
but to go back and try again out front. A flicker of movement
behind the glass catches her eye as she turns the corner, and for a
second she wonders if Alice is about to open the door and invite
her in. But it stays firmly closed and all that follows is a loud slam
somewhere in the bowels of the house. Knowing that means there
is, at least, someone home, Mel knocks twice more, fighting the
urge to batter at the wood. But Alice doesn't appear.

'Please,' Mel pleads through the letter box, unwilling to
admit defeat. 'Alice, we both need this. Haven't we all been hurt
enough? Don't we both deserve to move on? Don't we both need
to talk about what happened? If we don't, how can we ever come
to peace with it?'

The hall stays empty.

Dejected, Mel hauls herself back up to standing, her back protesting at being bent over with the weight of a wriggling baby pulling at it. Tears, fuelled by frustration, prick at her eyes. Maybe Alice doesn't feel the need to move on with it? Maybe she's enjoying this game of cat and mouse too much.

Not wanting to come across as a total lunatic, Mel decides the best course of action is probably just to give up and head for home. She can try again tomorrow. And the next day if necessary. Perhaps if Alice sees how determined she is, she will eventually give in.

Her phone buzzes in her pocket as she is walking out of Alice's driveway. It'll be Ed, she thinks. He's probably sending another picture of him and Tilly having the 'best time ever'. She hates that she feels jealous about that.

She takes her phone out of her pocket and looks at the screen to see that it's not Ed. It's not her mother checking in on her either. Alice's name is illuminated. Mel turns immediately to look back at the house but only catches the shifting of a curtain, as if someone has been peeking out but doesn't want to be seen. She looks back at the screen, taps it and reads the message from the woman who has made it her mission to destroy her over the last year.

Meet me at Creed in an hour. We can talk then.

* * *

Creed is a coffee shop they used to go to together. Mel thinks that is probably a good sign. The fact Alice is willing to meet her at all is a good sign. And it's somewhere public, so she's less likely to make a scene. Or at least Mel hopes she is less likely to make a scene.

Mel taps in a quick reply confirming that she will be there and, as she sends it, she feels Teddy kick and wriggle inside her, as if to reassure her everything will be okay.

'I know, wee man,' she whispers to her tummy as she walks away from Alice's house. 'We're going to make sure this is an end to it all.'

11

THEN

The days following Jacob's birth were the most surreal of Mel's life. She kept replaying everything that had happened that evening over and over again to try and figure out just when it went wrong and why.

She felt broken into so many pieces she wasn't sure she would ever be able to put them back together. But as tough as that was, she knew it was nothing compared to what Alice and Thomas were going through. That must've been pain on an unimaginable level and there was no doubt in Mel's mind it was the kind of wound that would never heal.

She desperately wanted to visit Alice in the hospital. Maybe if they talked this through together it would help all of them. But Alice wasn't answering her messages, and she dared not call. She knew from driving past their house that they were not at home, so Mel called the hospital only to be told that Alice was not taking calls. Or visitors.

Mel could understand that. Alice was not only recovering from the physical trauma of her birth, but she was spending time with Jacob. The hospital had a cooling crib which allowed bereaved parents to spend extra time with their babies before they had to say goodbye.

Mel felt sick to her stomach every time she imagined their pain but she knew this this wasn't about her. She was at the bottom of a long line of people more entitled to grieve for Jacob than she could ever be, but his passing filtered into every moment of every day of her life. Even when she looked at her own, beautiful, precious daughter she felt the cruelty of what had been lost like a blow to her solar plexus. Her body ached with exhaustion, grief and shock as she struggled to eat, to get dressed, to brush her teeth. The experience weighted her to her bed even though a voice was screaming inside her to get up, parent her child and get on with things.

Three days after Jacob's birth, Mel's phone rang and her stomach immediately dropped when she saw Thomas's name on the screen.

She wanted to talk to him, of course. And to Alice. But she was also terrified – unsure of what she could say. There were no words that could make any of this better. Nothing that could make any of this less horrific. All she'd be able to do was offer to help in other, practical, ways. She could come and sit with Alice. Cook up some food for the freezer. Help plan the funeral.

She took her phone into the kitchen, away from where Ed and Tilly were playing together on the floor, and answered with a voice as shaky as her hands.

'Thomas...' she said.

'Why did you do it?' he asked, his voice thick with emotion.

Mel froze. 'I... what do you mean?'

'Coming back here, cleaning everything up...' he said.

'I thought it would help. I didn't think you'd want to come home to face all that. I wanted to make it less awful,' Mel stuttered.

'Or were you disposing of the evidence?' he asked, and his words hit Mel like a thump to the stomach.

'Evidence?' she gasped.

'Of what went wrong,' he said, his voice breaking. 'I... I don't understand what happened. Alice trusted you. I trusted you.'

The room around Mel started to spin. Was he actually implying that she was to blame for all this? 'I... I didn't do anything wrong,' she said, even though she had already asked herself the same question a thousand times. It always came back to the same answer though – and it was the one she had to give Thomas. 'I was there as a doula. To provide support and encouragement. I'm not a midwife or a doctor. You both knew that. It was very, very clear.' She hated that she sounded so defensive to a man who was going through a parent's worst nightmare, but she couldn't believe the anger towards her in his voice.

'But you have experience. You've been to so many births. How did you not know when something was going wrong? We trusted you to know.' The sound of Thomas's sobs was heartwrenching and Mel felt nausea rise. She didn't know how to deal with this man in his grief, but she knew she had made her role very clear from the start. And she got how hard it must be for him, and for Alice, to come to terms with what had happened. Of course they would want to blame someone who wasn't them. They'd feel a desperate need for it all to make sense.

'The police want to talk to you,' Thomas managed to say. 'They've spoken to us and we've told them everything. Now they want to talk to you.'

'The police?' she stuttered back.

'Due to the circumstances of Jacob's birth and death, they are investigating. One of them asked if we were trying to hide something by having the house cleaned up so quickly. They've asked a lot of questions about you.'

Jesus Christ, she thought. This is a police matter? Could she
be arrested for some imagined crime? Could she be hauled away
from her family? She could barely breathe as she slid to the
floor, the phone still in her hand. She knew she hadn't stepped
outside of her remit as a doula. She didn't pretend to be anything
other than a birth coach. She didn't make up medical experience
or perform any procedures. Even with it being an unattended
birth, she had not stepped outside the confines of the law. Alice
and Thomas hadn't either. It's not illegal to refuse antenatal care.

'Surely they don't think we caused this?' she blurted, even
though she felt mired in guilt all the same.

'Didn't we?' Thomas said, his voice cold.

'We didn't,' she said, not quite managing to keep her voice
steady. 'Look, why don't I come round and we can talk about it.'

'There's nothing to talk about,' Thomas said. 'And please,
don't come round. We don't want to see you, Mel. Just stay away.
From us, from the house, from—'

'—the funeral?' Mel asked. Surely they weren't going to shut
her out. Alice was her friend.

'You're not welcome,' Thomas said. 'You should've known.
You should've helped him.'

The phone call was ended before she had a chance to say
anything back and she found herself in shock, wondering what
the hell had just happened. She had not expected it to be like
this.

She'd anticipated that she might help them plan Jacob's
funeral and that she would absolutely be there on the day to
support her new friends. But instead they seemed to be blaming
her for things going so wrong. Suggesting she'd – what, hidden
evidence? Even the word 'evidence'. And the police were going to
speak to her. How would she break that news to Ed? Would they
come to the house? What the fuck was going to happen?

12

_____

MARCH 2024

Having found a seat in the corner of the coffee shop, Mel is sitting with a decaf latte in front of her that she can't bring herself to even taste. Anxiety has started to take hold and she jumps every time the door to the cafe opens. Any bravado she felt earlier, any confidence that she can face this woman and ask her outright to please just her get on with her life, is melting away.

She's all too aware that Alice's actions have not always been rational. She's taking a chance that Alice could just turn on her. While she'd felt better about meeting in a public place at first, thinking it would offer her a level of protection, she's starting to worry. Alice could use this as just another chance to humiliate and hurt her. The cafe is busy – packed with chattering shoppers who have called in for a coffee and cake, and mothers with their children getting a little break and a treat. It would provide a perfect audience for Alice and her anger.

Mel can feel a headache starting to build. She massages her temples, hoping that will be enough to lift it. 'Could I get a glass of water, please?' she asks a passing waitress who smiles and says 'of course'. Maybe this was a bad idea. Her mouth has gone dry. The smell of coffee hangs thick in the air and even though it's an aroma she usually loves, now it is making her feel sick.

She glances at the clock on her phone. She still has time to leave. To just message Alice back, now that she has been unblocked, and say she has changed her mind.

Two minutes after the hour is up, the door to the cafe opens and Alice is there, silhouetted against the sun now brightly shining outside. Mel knows there is no turning back – no running away.

What she doesn't know is how to react. Should she get up and greet her? Should she stay seated? She's not sure what's appropriate and all these thoughts jumble through her mind. There was a time, of course, when she would've jumped up and hugged her friend close. A part of her – the part that had come to view Alice as a soul sister of sorts – still wants to hug her, even now. She wants to grieve alongside her. In no way could she have felt Alice's loss as keenly as Alice has, but she has felt it all the same. She felt a connection with Alice's baby before he came into this world and she had looked forward to watching him grow. She'd wanted to cuddle him. To rock him back and forth. She thought she'd sit with Alice while they watched him crawl on the rug at their feet. She wanted to see her friend light up inside at being called 'Mama'. More than any other of her clients' babies, she had felt that this little one was going to be in her life for a long time. Even with everything that has happened, she still feels his loss like a searing pain in her chest. As she watches her former friend step inside and close the door behind her, she hurts for the woman who lost the most important thing in her life.

Alice is dressed casually but looks as well put together as she always did. She's dressed in designer leggings and an oversized hoodie, with her feet clad in pristine white trainers. Her is hair swept back into a flawless ponytail. Her face tells a different story, Mel thinks. It's thinner than she remembers. So much thinner that it can't just be due to no longer being heavily pregnant.

Frozen to the spot for a moment, Mel watches as Alice glances around the coffee shop, trying to find her. Mel takes a deep breath and raises her hand to give a little wave to indicate her presence. She has never been so conscious before of her gestures, or her facial expression, of how she looks, of how swollen her stomach is. There is no manual on how to act in a situation such as this.

Alice nods in response before making her way to the counter to order her own drink. Maybe, Mel thinks, she should have ordered a coffee for Alice while she was waiting, but then again this is not a friendly coffee and cake date and, she realises, she had half-expected to be stood up.

The waitress returns and places the glass of water on a paper coaster on the table in front of Mel, startling her out of her thoughts. Still, Mel manages to say thank you and sound relatively normal despite her mouth now being drier than the Sahara Desert. After she takes a long drink, she begins to feel a little better. Still, she places her wrists against the glass, hoping the icy cold water inside will help cool her pulse points.

When Alice approaches, she has a takeaway coffee cup in hand. It would seem, Mel thinks, that she is not planning on staying.

Mel's chest constricts as a vision of the lid being torn from the cup and the steaming hot liquid being thrown in her face flashes through her mind. Instinctively, she turns her head away, just in case. She wills herself to get it together, and keep it together.

Breathe in and breathe out, she tells herself as she tries to slow her pounding heart. She should be able to do this – to find her centre and keep calm. She taught this after all. But even with her best efforts, she finds it's not easy. Just as not breaking down into tears is not easy.

The chair opposite makes a jarring, scraping sound on the floor as Alice pulls it back from the table and sits down. An immediate shift in energy sends a chill right through Mel. Teddy kicks and moves inside her at the very second she looks directly into Alice's eyes, but she doesn't allow herself to react. She doesn't want to appear insensitive. Or unnerved. She's not stupid. She knows this will be hard for Alice to see her here with an unmistakably round and heavily pregnant stomach. She's aware that's a cruelty in itself. She's also aware that if Alice is waging a revenge campaign against her, flaunting her pregnancy might just push the woman over the edge.

'I thought you'd moved away,' Alice says, her voice unexpectantly hesitant and unsure. Mel is surprised. She certainly wasn't expecting Alice to be nervous too.

'I did,' she tells her. 'I mean, I have. We have. I've just come back to visit my parents for a couple of days.' She doesn't challenge Alice about the card. Not yet.

Her eyes move to Mel's stomach. 'Keeping well?'

'Mostly. Yes.'

'Good,' Alice says, bringing her coffee cup to her lips and taking a sip, her gaze never leaving Mel's.

There's a beat of silence. A moment in which Mel questions yet again what the hell she's doing, and just what might be running through Alice's mind. She notices, for the first time, that Alice's hands are shaking, her pale pink nail polish is chipped. *I'm not the only one who is a nervous wreck*, she thinks.

'Look, first of all, thanks for coming to talk with me,' Mel says, thinking her voice sounds strange – strained and needy – as she speaks. 'I appreciate it. I know things aren't easy.'

'They're not,' Alice immediately replies. 'It's a nightmare, to be honest. My mind keeps going back to everything that happened, especially now that his anniversary is approaching. I *hate* that I have to call it his anniversary and not his birthday. Every child deserves a birthday.'

Mel can't find the right words to say. She just nods in agreement.

'It's hard not to live each day now thinking about everything on a this-time-last-year basis,' Alice replies, a slight wobble in her voice. Yet Mel is impressed at just how composed she sounds, even with the tremor.

'I can understand that. It all runs through my mind all the time too. I can't imagine how tough this is for you and Thomas.' Mel is trying her best to keep the emotion from her voice because she knows that *whatever* has happened, she is not the real victim in all of this. She hasn't lost a child.

Alice gives a sad nod. 'It's been worse than anything else I have experienced in my life. Every day. Every *single* day I wake up and remember again. And it hurts again and I get *angry* again. It shouldn't have happened. It's not fair.'

Mel is surprised that while Alice is talking of her anger, she doesn't *sound* angry. She sounds sad. Broken even. And even though she is wearing her designer leggings, and her hair and make-up are flawless, Mel can see just how diminished by her experience Alice has become. She can see the bags under her eyes – dark circles that concealer can only do so much to cover. Her previously larger-than-life personality – the part of her who felt so deeply and passionately about the things she believed in – has shrunken into non-existence.

For the first time, Mel starts to doubt that this woman in

front of her could be physically or emotionally capable of carrying out any meaningful act of revenge. Has Mel just mistaken raw grief for malicious intent?

'It *isn't* fair,' Mel says. 'None of it was ever fair. You *should* be planning a birthday party now for Jacob. You should be watching him take his first steps. And I'm so sorry that you can't do that.' She takes a deep breath before continuing. 'But when I say I'm sorry, I mean that I am sad for you, and Thomas, and Jacob. You have to understand, Alice, I didn't cause what happened. It was one of those awful, awful things that are impossible to wrap your head around, but it wasn't my fault and I don't deserve what has happened since – just like you didn't deserve to lose Jacob.'

'Did you think it could go so wrong?' Alice asks, her face solemn. 'All those times we talked through the birth plan.'

'I think we both knew on some level that, in theory at least, it *could*,' Mel says as gently as she can, reminding herself she has to be careful with every single word she says. 'We just didn't believe it *would*. Or at least not like this. I've asked myself if I should have urged you to seek help or advice the more and more overdue you became, but we were so far into it all – so close to the end – by then, and you'd made your wishes so very clear.'

Alice stiffens and Mel knows she's said the wrong thing.

'I'm not blaming you,' she says quickly. 'Please don't think I'm blaming you. I'm just trying to explain honestly. You'd hired me to support you, but we'd moved on from just a business relationship, hadn't we? I very much considered you my friend. You *were* my friend.' Mel's voice cracks, her grief at losing their special bond in this awful mess pushing its way to the top.

Alice blinks and a tear rolls down her cheek, followed by another, but she doesn't speak.

'I've gone over it all many times. Asked myself if things

would've been different if I had walked away or tried to force you to listen. Maybe you'd have had second thoughts about the free birth,' Mel says.

'"Maybe" is a brilliant word, isn't it?' Alice replies, rubbing at her cheeks with the cuff of her hoodie which she has pulled up over the heel of her hand. 'Fucking useless word, mind. But a good one all the same.' She gives the briefest of smiles – one that screams of trying to hold in the most unimaginable pain – before her face crumples again. Quickly, she takes a deep breath and settles herself.

'The thing is,' Mel says, knowing that she has to keep going now that she has started, 'even with all the thinking and all the maybes, I know I didn't do anything intentionally wrong. And I know that you know it too. Whether you want to admit it to yourself or not.'

'So, you *are* saying it was my fault,' Alice says, but her tone is not accusatory. It's one of acceptance and for some reason, that's harder for Mel to deal with. Tears flood her eyes and it's her turn to try and wipe them away, using a paper napkin which she had already partially shredded to pieces while she was waiting for Alice to arrive.

'Does it have to be anyone's fault?' Mel asks. 'Is it not just bad enough that it happened? I get that you have a need to blame someone because what happened was brutal and it was unfair and you didn't deserve it. But I don't deserve it either. And neither do my family. It has to stop, Alice. It has to stop now and if you can't do that for me, then do it for Tilly. Do it for this baby who deserves a normal childhood.' Her voice is a little louder now. A few of their fellow customers have turned their heads for a nosey at what is unfolding in front of them. Mel takes a deep breath while Alice stares at her for a beat before speaking.

'Mel, I don't know what you're talking about. Your family?

What do you mean? And as for you – yes, I know I treated you awfully. I know I've damaged your business beyond repair, but I was completely lost in my grief back then. I couldn't think straight. But I don't know why you're asking me to stop.'

Frustration bubbles up inside Mel. 'I got the card, Alice. You sent a card to our new home and I know it was some sort of message.'

Alice raises her hands as if in surrender. 'Okay, you've got me. I sent you a card. I wanted to wish you well. Felt guilty, perhaps, that you had left. Was that because of me? Because of what happened? I know someone who works in the estate agent's. They gave me your address and I thought... just maybe... it was time to draw a line... Before his anniversary. Look, I know I've been awful – really awful – but I didn't know what I was doing half the time. It was like I was in a daze.'

'Were you in a daze when you went to Tilly's nursery?' Mel blurts. 'The day you called her over? Told her you were going to take her on a trip?'

Alice's face blanches at first before it colours. 'I'm so sorry. I didn't even realise. I was out walking – I had to get out of the house – and I wasn't even thinking about where I was or what I was doing and then I heard the sound of children playing. I looked up and it was Tilly's day care. I knew it immediately. I didn't expect to see her outside but she's such a beautiful little girl that I spotted her straight away. I wasn't even thinking. I called her over but I swear I didn't tell her I was going to take her away. We'd barely said two words to each other before one of the staff came over and hurried her back inside. That was the long and the short of it.'

Feeling completely wrong-footed by all of this, Mel finds herself at a loss for words. She has so many questions and no idea of where to go to get the answers. It suddenly all feels too much.

'Are you okay?' Alice asks. 'You're very pale?'

When Mel looks at Alice, she sees her expression is one of empathy and concern. Shaking her head, she sighs. 'No. No, I'm not okay. There's so much hate out there. You must have seen it – you were a part of it for a long time. People saying vile things online. Twisting everything. Blaming me. It's still happening. And in real life too. Why do you think we moved? I couldn't go anywhere without being harassed. We had eggs thrown at the house. Threats. Someone sent us excrement in the post! I've had threatening phone calls. And it's not stopping, Alice. When I went to see the midwife, she made it clear she knew exactly who I was. There have been posts online in the last few days... just so much...'

Mel feels a soft hand on her arm as Alice reaches across the table. 'I'm so, so sorry,' Alice says, her voice now thick with tears.

Mel wasn't prepared for this. For contrition. The adrenaline coursing through her veins tells her that every part of her body was ready for a confrontation. She wasn't expecting Alice to apologise. To look genuinely sorry for her. It unnerves her a little and she's not sure if she can trust it.

'How can I help put this right?' Alice says as she tries to brush away her tears before starting to fumble in her pockets. 'Do you want me to put some sort of statement out on social media? Say I was in a place of deep grief when I spoke to the press last year? Tell them what a good friend you were to me... before?' She extracts a tissue from her pocket and dabs at her eyes. 'If I ask people to leave you alone, maybe they will? I could tell them you're pregnant and you don't need the stress.'

Mel notices Alice's gaze fall again to her stomach. It must be so incredibly painful to be around pregnant women.

'I'm not a monster,' Alice says as she makes eye contact again. 'Or at least I don't think so. I did lose my mind though – for a while at least. If I could go back and change it all, I would. I'd change so much.' There's a beat in which Mel just knows that Alice is talking about so much more than her reaction after Jacob's death. Mel allows her own mind to travel to that place too – a place where different decisions were made and Jacob was safe and well and gurgling in a high chair beside them right now.

But they both know the past can't be changed. Only what happens next.

'I know I should never have let it go this far,' Alice says.

'You've been grieving,' Mel replies, relief making her a little giddy that all this unpleasantness could be coming to an end. That their move to Derry really can mark a fresh new start for them all. They could transform the house into the home of her dreams. They wouldn't have to move to Australia and away from her parents after all. She was sure that once the house was in order, and Ed could see his children enjoying the rural surroundings of their new home, he would settle. They had been happy at the prospect of staying in Northern Ireland before. They could be normal again.

'I'll always be grieving,' Alice replies. 'I don't think that's ever going to go away. But I can tell you this – being angry, it doesn't make it any less painful. It doesn't help. So let me see what I can do.'

The smile on Alice's face is small, tempered by the tears still welling in her eyes. There may be room for a fresh start here, but things will never be like they used to be. Mel knows that. They won't be the friends to each other that they once were. It will always be too painful to exist in the same space together. But to think they could at least stop being enemies, that would be enough.

'I'd really appreciate that, Alice,' Mel says as her throat tightens. So many emotions exist in this space right now.

'There's one more thing,' Alice says, her voice dropping to little more than a whisper. Mel freezes, her nerve endings immediately on red alert, fear swooping back in.

'Don't look so worried. I promise you this is nothing to worry about!' Alice says quickly.

'What is it?'

'Well, you remember when I was carrying Jacob, we used to say it would lovely to see our children grow up together and play together?'

Mel gives a nervous nod, her mind racing.

'Well...' Alice says as she sits back, and smooths her hoodie over a neat – but definitely very much there – baby bump. Mel can hardly believe she didn't notice it before, but then again Alice's hoodie is so big and shapeless, and she had been standing in the shadows when she walked in, and Mel just never thought...

'You're... you're pregnant?' Mel asks, even though the answer is blatantly obvious.

'I am,' Alice says, her voice shaky. 'Eighteen weeks yesterday,' she adds. 'And I'm absolutely terrified.'

'I can understand that,' Mel tells her, instinctively reaching across the table, taking Alice's hand. 'It's good, though. It's good news. Yes?'

Alice nods, laughs and smiles as the tears continue to fall. 'The best. More than I could've hoped for. I'm taking no chances this time, Mel. None. And we're trying to keep it quiet – we don't want the added pressure of everyone sticking their noses in and judging every little thing I do. I know it's probably as much as I deserve – I was so public after Jacob dying – but I want to protect this little one. More than anything. I don't want him or her to become a headline before they are even born.'

'I understand that.' Mel feels the exact same away about the baby she is carrying. How she doesn't want him caught up in all the tension that has gone on before. 'I'm just so very, very happy for you. I'm sure everything will be well. Have faith.'

Alice nods. Smiles and cradles her stomach. 'I'm trying my very best. I think I'll feel better after the anomaly scan. We might even ask the sex of the baby – although a part of me is a bit worried about how I'll react to either answer.'

'Again, that's very understandable.'

'And do you know what you're having?' Alice raises an eyebrow and takes another sip from her coffee.

'We do.' She can't help feeling a little nervous to share the news. 'We're having a little boy.'

Alice swallows and puts her cup back on the table, her eyes brimming with tears. 'That's just the very best news,' she says. 'You are so blessed.'

'I know,' Mel says. 'It was a little shock to the system at first, but now we can't wait to meet him.'

'It can't be too long to go?' Alice asks.

'About five and a half weeks. All being well.' As soon as Mel says those words she wonders if she has made a mistake. They feel so loaded now. She cannot take 'all being well' for granted.

'Well, for my part, I'll do what I can to make it as easy for you as possible. I'll let people know that I was acting out of grief, and that I in no way blame you for what happened. Then hopefully that will be enough for them to stop,' Alice says, and smiles.

13

Back at her mother's house, Mel decides to change into her comfy tracksuit bottoms and baggy T-shirt. Catching a glimpse of herself in the mirror, she marvels at the freshly reignited flames of stretch marks crawling up her tummy. There are few new marks but those which accompanied Tilly's journey into the world have turned a livid red again.

Mel's mind turns to Alice and her neat little bump. Her stretch marks from carrying Jacob – not that she had that many – will barely have faded before being tested again now. Mel hopes that it's a comfort to her; that she feels her son is still with her in some way. Cheering her and his baby brother or sister on.

Kicking off her trainers and slipping her feet into the fluffiest pair of socks she owns, she notices they feel tighter than normal. Her ankles are puffy and moving quickly towards the cankles stage. She tells herself it's probably just a result of walking in and out of town today, but she also knows this could be a sign that her blood pressure is increased. It would hardly be surprising, given the day she has had. She makes a promise to herself she will spend the remainder of the day with her feet elevated, and as stress-free as possible. Her body will thank her for resting too – her back is also protesting after her physical activity.

Kneeling on the soft thick-piled carpet of her mother's spare room, she rests her elbows on her bed and rocks back, allowing the full weight of her stomach to hang freely. Just taking the pressure and weight off her back feels incredible and she lets out a small moan of relief.

Now comfortable, she decides to call Ed and tell him where she has been and what has happened. She hopes he will share in her relief. Hearing his voice on the other end of the line, she can't help but smile. It's comforting to her that he doesn't sound stressed. In fact, he sounds as if he has just been laughing at something.

'Hang on a moment so I can step outside,' he says and in the background, Mel can hear Tilly chatting and laughing too. A wave of love for her girl washes over her. Even though Mel has only been gone since yesterday, she already misses her daughter so much. She always feels like a part of her is missing when they aren't together.

'Who's there with you?' Mel asks. 'Who is Miss Tilly talking the legs off?' She expects him to tell her it's one of the lads from the site. Or even that Tilly is having a full-on conversation with her dolls, or her imaginary friends. She doesn't expect him to tell her it's their neighbour from the top of the hill.

'It's Sheila,' he says brightly. 'And I think they've been talking the legs off each other. That's why I came outside. I can barely hear myself think between the two of them rabbiting on in my ear. Tilly seems to have really taken to her.'

'Sheila? What did she call down for?' Mel asks, feeling a pang of irrational jealousy. She can't put her finger on it, but something about Sheila feels a little off.

'Maybe she's come down here to get herself a younger man?'

Ed teases. 'I might be tempted, you know. While the cat's away and all that...' He laughs and Mel forces a laugh back that she absolutely doesn't feel.

'Seriously though, Ed?' she asks. 'What brings her back down from t'big house?' She adopts her very best Yorkshire servant voice in a bid to make her question sound as light as possible.

'She came down earlier to drop in a fruit loaf. Said she'd baked too much and thought that maybe the builders would like some with their tea. Tilly told her you were away for a few days. Next thing I know she's back again an hour later with a shopping bag full of food and she's telling me she's going to cook us dinner. That woman just doesn't take no for an answer, and she was a dab hand at getting Tilly on board. It worked out quite well though. She cooked the most delicious dinner of bacon and cabbage with mashed potatoes. I swear, I've never tasted the like of it. We've just finished and I'm about to serve up some ice cream for afters.'

'But you don't even like cabbage!' Mel protests as she pictures Sheila moving around the kitchen in the caravan as if it's her own. Does she not have Barney – or whatever his name is – to cook for? Mel wonders. And what's this about her arriving with a bag of shopping? Mel bristles – does Sheila not think she is capable of looking after her own family?

'Maybe no one has ever cooked it right for me before,' he says and deep inside she knows he is teasing her, the way they always interact with each other. They normally thrive on teasing and banter but today, irrationally, it makes her feel odd, as if he is criticising her.

'At this rate, you'll not be wanting me and my substandard cooking back at all,' she says, as she rolls her hips and stretches her back further. She lets out a groan.

'Are you okay?' Ed asks, his voice immediately serious and full of concern.

'Achy back,' she tells him. 'I went for a walk.'

'Are you not supposed to be resting?' There's no mistaking the sternness in his voice this time.

Now, she realises, is not the time to tell him about going to see Alice – despite how positive the interaction had been. She can imagine how he will respond and it's not great. As a couple, Mel and Ed rarely fall out. They have mostly rubbed along quite nicely over the eight years of their relationship – resolving most disputes quickly and without residual resentment. Mel knows she's lucky. She has always known that about Ed. Lucky that he crossed the bar in Belfast to chat to her while she was on a night out with her teaching friends. Lucky that he asked for her number and actually did get in touch, and not just ghost her instead. Lucky that he is a man passionate about work, and family, and her. A man who is fiercely protective and who does not like conflict. But even with all her good luck, she senses that admitting she had intentionally sought out Alice would lead to the mother and father of all arguments.

It won't matter to him that she got so much from the meeting. Not initially anyway. His first reaction won't be relief that she has made some form of peace with Alice. He won't be able to see past the risk she took.

He'll say that if she was really concerned Alice was waging some sort of campaign against their family, she was at best naive and at worst, stupid, to walk straight into the lion's den.

On one level she can understand why he would feel that way. But it had paid off. Hadn't it?

'I *am* relaxing and I have *been* relaxing,' she tells him. 'Right now I'm in my comfiest joggers and that super-baggy oversized

T-shirt of mine you love so much. And I'm in my room, stretching out my back, and let me tell you, it feels great.'

'Good,' he says, seemingly mollified a little. 'You know I love you very much, Mel.'

'I love you too. And Tilly of course. Give her the biggest hug and kiss from me, please.'

'Should I give Sheila a big hug too?' he asks. 'Test the theory that she might be after a younger man after all?'

'I double dare you!' she laughs.

Mel's mother stays quiet over dinner. She doesn't give her usual run-down of all the gossip from the neighbourhood WhatsApp group, or of the latest news from the women of the church choir she's a member of. She doesn't talk much at all outside of the niceties of asking for Mel to pass the salt and pepper. The tension is palpable, the scraping of knives and forks on the plates taking on a particularly jarring quality.

None of them are eating very much – there is, however, a lot of just moving food around the plate. Mel can't help but notice that her mother looks pale and tired, not at all like the vibrant and ever-busy woman she normally is.

'I needed to talk to her,' Mel says. 'I'd stayed quiet for too long.'

Her mother swallows the minuscule piece of pork chop she has been chewing for an impossibly long time and places her knife and fork on the edge of her plate. She doesn't speak, though. She lifts her glass and takes a long drink of water before finally meeting her daughter's gaze.

'I don't know what to say to you, Melissa,' she says. 'So,

maybe we just eat our dinner and leave it at that.' She doesn't lift her knife and fork though. She just looks at her plate for the longest time and occasionally shakes her head.

'She'd sent a card. To the new house. And people were starting to post again online,' Mel starts to explain, but her mother raises one hand to signal to her to stop.

'Melissa, it's been a long day. Let's not do this now.'

'But can't you see that I needed to do it? Before the baby comes. I don't want his early days and weeks to be filled with stress and worry.'

'So what? You put yourself directly in harm's way? The woman who came to Tilly's nursery and said she would take her away? The woman responsible for the calls, and the letters and the abuse? You willingly chose to be in the same space as her. Running over there trying to make *friends* – like none of this happened! When there's a doctor who has already warned you about your blood pressure? Because it's not like we've enough to worry about, or we've not been under more than enough pressure this past year.' Her mother pushes her plate away from her. 'Actually, you know what? I feel a little under the weather. I think maybe I'll just go upstairs for a wee lie-down.'

She pushes back in her chair, it making a loud screeching sound, and stands up.

'Mum!' Mel calls, feeling the weight of her mother's disapproval heavy on her shoulders. 'I wasn't trying to make friends. I was just trying to fix it. Can't you see that? It's exactly because of the stress we've all been under that I *needed* to see her in the first place! I don't get why you're so annoyed about it. Surely you wanted all this to be fixed?'

She glances over to her father, hoping to find some support, but he has his head bowed, clearly unwilling to get involved in what is unfolding.

'Melissa, I thought you were a smart girl,' her mother says. 'You really don't understand why I'm so annoyed by this? You didn't even have the wit to tell me or your father where you were going. We didn't know where you were – just that you'd gone out for a walk. You were gone for hours and when we tried calling your phone, you didn't answer. We didn't know if you were okay, or collapsed somewhere, and that's without even bringing *that* woman into the equation.'

'I'm a grown woman!' Mel protests, her defences now well and truly up and any appetite she had now well and truly gone. 'I'm not some silly wee girl of Tilly's age. I'm well able to go out for a walk by myself.'

'But it wasn't just a walk, was it? It wasn't just stretching your legs like you said it was. You went out to meet Alice fucking Munroe!'

Mel's mother never swears and the curse sounds alien coming from her mouth. Mel stiffens, can't think what to say or how to react.

'You moved across the country because you felt you weren't safe here because of her!' her mother continues. 'You took our only granddaughter away from us because you were tired of *her* casting a shadow over your life, and then what do you do? Come back here five minutes later and actively seek her out? Go to see her without telling anyone where you are or when to expect you back? Can I remind you that this is the woman you were convinced had it in for you. The woman *you* called "unhinged".'

'And you told me I was more than likely getting myself stressed out over nothing and being paranoid!' Mel protests. 'For God's sake, make up your mind!'

'We played it down because we were trying to help you get through it. The worry was making you sick! It was making us all sick! But today, you just wander back in here all smiles as if the last twelve months of a living nightmare hasn't happened and announce everything's all okay now, and we're just supposed to forget what she has put you through?'

Mel doesn't think she's ever seen her mother shake with rage before now, but here she is and her jaw is taut, her fists clenched as she rests them on the table. Tension vibrates in the very air around them. Her mother's speech is tight, staccato. Mel looks to her father once again in the hope of some form of support.

But not only is he not providing his usual voice of reason, he is reaching out for his wife's hand – his focus purely on comforting her.

'I was *fine*, Mum. I am fine. I don't know how many times I have to explain that I had to face her because enough is enough.'

'Could enough have not been enough *before* you moved away?' Her voice cracks. 'Before you turned your whole life upside down and ripped our family apart? And do you really believe that suddenly she's changed and is the kind of person you want in your life again? Around your children?'

'I didn't say that! I didn't say we were going to be friends again. I'm not doing this to make friends. I'm doing this to heal a horrific situation. But it's different now anyway. If you'd just let me tell you. She's pregnant too. Almost halfway there. She wants to move on just as much as I do.'

Exasperated, her mother sighs and shakes her head.

'Melissa, love,' her father chips in, resting a hand on her arm. 'I know the girl was grieving and that's awful. No mammy in the world deserves to lose her baby, and certainly not how she lost her wee man. But I'm with your mum on this. You've been hurt enough. Fair enough if she stood up and said sorry, and even better if she's going to try and stop all these lies that have been spread. And of course, we're very happy if she's going to have a baby now. I hope it all goes well for her, but no we don't think

you should have let her back into your life, love. Not in any big
or small way. She's bad news and she'll always be bad news.'

Mel blinks back tears.

'I'm sorry if what we're saying upsets you, love,' her mother
says, her voice a little softer as she sits back down. 'But I can't
stay quiet on it. And God alone only knows what Ed will say
when you tell him. People like her don't change, Melissa. If they
have hurt you so badly once before, they will think nothing of
hurting you again. Who do you think will be left picking up the
pieces then? When you're hurt and you've a wee baby to look
after along with Tilly, and a house falling down around your
ears? I'm sorry, but I can't watch you invite someone back into
your life who is just going to destroy you again.'

'I'm not inviting her back into my life,' Mel says, even though
she knows that's not entirely true. 'I just wanted to resolve
things. I wanted to make things right. Before the baby comes. I
don't get why that's so hard for everyone to understand.' She
stands up. 'Mum, Dad, I love you both with every part of me and
I love that you care and that you worry, but... it's complicated.'

She looks around her, feeling almost as if the room is spinning as much as the thoughts in her head. 'I think I'm going to
get an early night. I'm not hungry.'

'Melissa!' Her father calls after her as she turns to leave the
room, but she doesn't stop, and she doesn't look back. She
doesn't dare try and speak to them again because she knows her
words will come out a garbled sobbing mess. She feels like the
stroppy teenager she once was getting scolded by her parents for
not tidying her room. Embarrassment blazes across her face.

As she closes her bedroom door, she feels a twinge in her
back. She has stomped up the stairs far too vigorously for a
woman this far into pregnancy who has already walked the

length of the town and back today. *How pathetic am I*, she thinks as she slumps onto her bed, tears coursing down her cheeks.

Here she is in her childhood bedroom, with an aching back and swollen ankles. She's scared to tell her husband the truth of why she is here. Her parents are disappointed in her. Her daughter doesn't seem to miss her at all as long as she has Sheila from up the road spoiling her. It's not that she wants Tilly to be miserable, but some sign she's missed would be lovely.

Her house is nowhere near ready to live in, and she knows Ed would sell it in a heartbeat and move to Australia. She has no job. No career. Will she find herself back in the classroom? Losing the freedom of being her own boss and being able to be there for her children?

And on top of all that, meeting Alice – which she thought had been a positive development – has only served to upset her parents even more.

This isn't how this stage of her life was supposed to be.

Her phone vibrates in her pocket and she fishes it out, half expecting it to be Ed ready to drop another clanger to round the day off nicely.

But it's not Ed. It's Alice.

I've posted something online now. Look at my Insta.

15

Mel contemplates just how much she really trusts Alice as she opens the Instagram app on her phone. It would be especially cruel for her to have made promises she had no intention of keeping.

But Alice had perfected 'especially cruel' over the last year. Mel's argument with her parents has kicked up a lot of painful memories. Not least the police arriving at her door on the day of Jacob's funeral. 'Just some questions,' they'd said before they had proceeded to grill her on the nature of her agreement with the Munroes.

Had she suggested or encouraged the unattended delivery?

No.

Had she told them she was experienced enough to deal with any 'minor hiccups'?

No. She made it clear she was not a medical professional. She could show them copies of her agreement with the Munroes. She'd had it specially altered to apply to an unassisted delivery.

Had she offered alternative antenatal care?

No. Apart from antenatal classes in hypnobirthing and relaxation. But that wasn't 'care' in the medical sense.

She'd watched as the officers had exchanged looks – looks which screamed that they thought she was clearly off her head and into 'mumbo jumbo' as one of them had put it.

They'd asked her what exactly had happened in the days leading up to Jacob's birth, and about the night in question. Why did she go and tidy up the Munroes' home? Did she take anything away from the premises? Why did she send a text message apologising?

'Apologising?' she had asked, exhausted with shock and grief.

'Mrs Munroe received a text message some hours after the birth of her son. It said, "I'm so sorry". Was this an apology or admission of culpability?'

She could hardly believe what she heard. 'Culpability? No,' she'd said. 'No. It was a message of condolence. I was – I am – so very sorry for their loss. Why would they take it to mean anything else but that?'

How could Alice ever have sincerely thought she was to blame? Grief made her cruel and Mel only hopes that the healing that comes with a new pregnancy, a new life, has quieted the cruel streak.

Her hand is shaking as she tries to type Alice's name into the search bar. Pausing, she takes a deep breath. With a slow exhalation, she tells herself it will be okay. Alice is happy now. She is expecting another baby and wants to move on while always, *always*, remembering Jacob. Mel reminds herself that the Alice who sat opposite her today was calm and composed and had seemed entirely genuine.

Right, she tells herself, there's no point in putting this off any longer. She picks her phone up again and opens the screen to continue tapping Alice's name in.

The account pops up almost immediately. Alice Munroe. Her bio is short. 'Married. Mum to one *angel emoji* baby – 17/04/23'. Seeing the date of both Jacob's birth and death is stark and Mel pauses for a moment to take it in. Alice's profile picture is a black and white shot of her face in profile – it's simple yet beautiful, and perhaps perfect for her four thousand and some followers.

At the top of her Insta grid, Alice has pinned an image of white writing on a black background – the headline reading 'An Apology'. Breath catches in Mel's throat as she clicks on the image to open it.

Family, Friends and Followers,

This statement is an apology and an explanation. I sincerely hope you will take the time to read it with grace.

As you will be aware, in April last year Thomas and I suffered the most devastating loss when our beautiful boy, Jacob Thomas Munroe, was born sleeping after a prolonged labour at home.

A number of factors contributed to Jacob's death – some of which I have addressed publicly before. I don't intend to address them again now and I won't be commenting on free-birthing in this post.

What I will be focusing on is issuing an apology to the one person who has been unfairly harmed by my words and actions over the last year. And I want to apologise to you all for quite unintentionally painting a picture of what went wrong that is not accurate, or fair.

My only excuse is that I was mad with grief. Any parent who

has ever lost a child will understand exactly what I mean by that. There is no loss like it and I would not wish this pain on anyone. Not even my worst enemy. In my pain I needed to blame someone, and I was not strong enough at that time to blame myself.

So I directed my pain at Mel Davison – my birthing coach, doula, and a woman I had very much considered my friend. I told the world that Mel had misled us and had offered services better suited to a midwife. I blamed Mel for not spotting the signs that something was going catastrophically wrong and getting the proper help.

THIS SIMPLY WAS NOT TRUE.

At the time I made the statement I was so completely mired in my pain that I convinced myself it was. I needed to point the finger at someone and I could not face blaming myself. I was a coward, but I was broken at the time. As broken as a person can be.

As I worked through my grief, I shared my story with as many people as I could. I did not consider the consequences for Mel and her family when I did this. If I am being honest, I did not care if they faced any consequences. I was hurting and I think I wanted everyone else to hurt just as much as I was.

I have caused significant pain to Mel, who was gracious enough not to make life even more painful for me than it already was. There was so much she could've said but she did not. She lost her business, her reputation and so much more, but still she kept hold of a dignity I could only dream of. She did not react with the anger I deserved.

Mel was a consummate professional throughout our time working together but more than that, Mel was my friend. She was in no way responsible for Jacob's death and should never have been forced to carry even one ounce of blame or guilt for the tragedy that occurred.

This is my unequivocal apology to you, Mel. And to my friends and family – I am sorry for misleading you.

I can only hope you find it in your hearts to forgive me for my actions.

Alice x

16

34 WEEKS + 5 DAYS

Mel has barely slept. She has instead read Alice's statement over and over again and tried to take it all on board. She can hardly believe that it's true and yet, there it is, and it has been flooded with replies all through the night.

Each time Mel has refreshed there has been something new: someone telling Alice she has been brave to come clean and how no one should underestimate what trauma can do to a person; a couple of posters determined to continue to blame Mel – people who say she was a birthing coach, she should have been more than aware of when things were going badly, or telling Alice she was completely reasonable to expect Mel to be a safe pair of hands in the room.

Mel has had to sit on her hand to stop herself from launching into a response in her own defence. She has no desire to get into an argument with people she doesn't know over something they clearly know nothing about. It's hard though, now that Alice has come clean, not to share the statement far and wide and send it to everyone who has been openly rude towards her. It's hard to resist a great big 'I told you so' moment to the haters and the people who hadn't had her back.

She will though – for now anyway. She has a few more hurdles to get over before she addresses the whole issue publicly herself. There are people she needs to talk to. Calmly. People who will have to admit she has been right all along.

Of course, she wants to show it to her parents – prove to them that she had not been wrong to meet Alice yesterday.

But, most of all, she has to talk to Ed about it. Tell him that she met with Alice and they had come to an understanding of sorts. She could lie to him of course. It would be just another lie of omission, she thinks. She runs throughs the pros and cons of withholding the truth while she showers. Does she really think he will believe that Alice has spoken up now without any prompting? Just as she happens to be back in Carrickfergus?

As soapsuds cascade over her pregnant belly, she realises it might help Ed feel more relaxed to know that Alice is pregnant too. Now that she has something so positive to motivate her to stay out of trouble, she won't dare try to target Mel. No doubt, though, he will focus on the risk she took in meeting Alice in the first place, and not the outcome.

Mel rinses off and gets dressed, deciding she won't rush into this. She wants to think about exactly what she's going to say to Ed before she speaks to him. Brushing her hair, she allows herself to feel really positive for the first time. Yes, she has to handle this carefully, but surely they will all have to agree that it has worked out well. The apology is out there for everyone to see. She can start repairing her reputation now. She can hold her head high in every new appointment, and in the postnatal ward and baby clinics. She is no longer a villain.

Her stomach rumbles, reminding her that not only has she

not had any breakfast yet, but that she also barely touched her dinner last night before she lost her appetite.

She's so hungry she's verging on nauseous so, with a final spritz of perfume, she leaves her room and makes her way down to the kitchen.

Both her father and mother are sitting at the table, mugs of tea in front of them and heads bent together deep in conversation.

'Morning,' Mel says sheepishly as she walks into the room. By the way they jump apart she's quite sure that she was the subject of their very serious-looking conversation. At least she'll be able to ease their worries by showing them the post.

'Morning, love,' her dad says. 'Would you like some tea and toast? Or maybe coffee?' He's already on his feet and heading for the pantry cupboard, his back turned to her.

'That would be lovely, Daddy.'

Her mother sits, stiff and pale, at the table, looking as though she hasn't slept a wink. Mel suddenly feels selfish for not showing her the post last night and lifting the worry from her shoulders earlier.

'Mum, look, I'm sorry about last night. It's just—'

'It's grand, love,' her mum tells her.

'But it's not, Mum. I know you and Daddy are just trying to watch out for me and I hadn't really realised how much of an impact this had on you.' Mel takes her phone from her pocket and gets ready to show them what Alice has said online. She'll just wait for her dad to come back into the room.

'Love, sit down, would you? There's a couple of things I need to talk to you about.' Her mother's tone of voice is one Mel knows all too well. It tends to precede bad news. She does as she's told, immediately flooded with unease despite being in such a positive frame of mind just seconds before.

'What is it, Mum?' she asks.

Her mother shifts in her seat, rubs her hands together and looks up with eyes that definitely have been crying. Immediately, Mel jumps to the worst possible conclusion. 'Are you unwell? Or is it Ed? Is it Tilly? Has something happened? Are they okay?' She feels the air leave her lungs – in fact it feels as if it has left the room entirely. Surely nothing bad can have happened – not when she has just been so sure everything is going right for the first time in a long time. Even though she can hardly bear to hear whatever it is her mother will say next, she can't stop herself from examining every line and wrinkle on her mother's face for clues as to what has happened and just how catastrophic it might be.

'Love, God, no. They're fine. Your mother is fine. No one is ill or hurt. It's not them,' her father says, as he comes back into the room with a mug of tea which he places in front of Mel. She feels the reassuring squeeze of his hand on her shoulder. 'Marie, maybe Mel should have something to eat and drink first. This toast will be ready in a minute.'

Mel doesn't know whether to laugh or cry. Fear has her on edge but her father's simple belief that she can put her emotions aside while she eats a slice of toast is laughable. A bite of toast would choke her now.

'I'm not hungry,' she tells him. 'I know something is wrong and I need to know what it is.'

'I don't want you getting upset,' her mother says with a small voice. 'But I didn't realise that Ed didn't know you'd met with Alice. I assumed you'd told him, and I didn't even think when I mentioned it to him.'

'You spoke with Ed?' Mel's heart plummets. He will not be happy to have heard this from her mother. He will not be happy that she didn't tell him. He will be absolutely enraged that she went to meet Alice at all.

'Why... Why did you speak with him?' she asks – so many possibilities running through her mind. Had he phoned to speak with her? Surely, he would have called her directly. Had they called him to float their theory that she has lost the run of herself in going to meet with Alice? Were they hoping her husband would come and talk some sense into her? Were they all ganging up on her?

Mel's mother looks from her to her father, and it's obvious see she is struggling to figure out what to say.

Mel's father sits down beside his daughter, clearly all thoughts of toast on hold for now. 'We were concerned for you. We thought it—'

'— best to run to my husband instead of talking to me?' Hurt tightens her chest.

'No, love. It wasn't like that. Not at all.'

'Well, what was it like, then?' She can feel tears welling in her eyes. 'Tell me.'

'Something arrived this morning.' Her mother's voice is barely more than a whisper.

'What? Something arrived?' Mel can't get her head around this. 'What are you talking about?'

'I've put them outside.' Her father looks absolutely stricken.

'Them what?' Confusion mixes with her annoyance.

'Flowers,' her mother says. 'A floral arrangement. We didn't know what to do, so we called Ed.'

Mel struggles to process what they are saying.

'We... we've had to call the police,' her father tells her.

'What? Why?' she stutters, feeling dizzy now, unable to figure out what is happening and why.

'They are a very specific kind of arrangement,' he says, his face pale. 'The kind you might send to... to a funeral.'

Nausea rising up in her, she pushes her seat back and gets up to go outside and see exactly what has been left, but the firm grip of her father's hand on her arm stills her.

'You don't need to see them, love. You'll only upset yourself.'

'And they were for me? These flowers? Someone sent flowers for my funeral? Who would do that?'

Her mother shakes her head and sniffs before her face crumples, leaving her husband to speak.

'No. They're the kind of flowers you'd send to a child's funeral. And there was a baby loss sympathy card with the most awful message.'

Mel's stomach lurches and her hand flies to her mouth. She can't understand this. It makes no sense. Today of all days. It makes no sense. She shakes off her father's hand. 'Are they in the back garden?'

'Mel!' her father says as she walks to the back door. 'We've called the police. They'll deal with it. Come and sit down, pet.'

But Mel has a masochistic need to see them. She needs to see exactly what they are talking about. This is a fucking funeral arrangement sent to her parents' home. This is inarguably fucked up.

With trembling hands, she opens the door and steps out onto the paved patio. There, a floral tribute made of ivory roses in the shape of a teddy bear is resting against the wall, pale blue ribbon tied in a bow around its neck.

Mel has seen this very display before. It's exactly the same as the one she sent to baby Jacob's funeral. The crisp, white envelope of the card stands out against the soft ivory of the rose petals. She reaches for it even though she really, really doesn't want to. She doesn't want it to be real. It makes it feel like a hex.

A curse. A wish that her baby will never take his first breath either.

Slipping the card out of the envelope, she looks at the image of a sleeping baby, complete with angel wings. She turns it over and sees, in handwritten scrawl, 'You do not deserve to be a mother. Your babies would be better off dead.'

17

Mel can't stop shaking. Her father has guided her inside and added some sugar to the cup of tea she still can't bring herself to drink. She is finding it impossible to get the image of the flowers out of her head, or the memory of the words scrawled on that hateful card. There's no other possible explanation for this. This is a threat. It is cruel. It is terrifying.

'We didn't want you seeing it,' her father says. 'We knew it would upset you and you need to mind yourself.' Her mother wraps a cardigan around her shoulders, but still she shakes. Her heart is thumping so hard that she can feel it in her throat, just as she feels bile rising.

'Try to take a few deep breaths,' her mother says. 'It's okay, love. It's going to be okay. The police are going to come out and look at it and they'll sort it out once and for all.'

'But who would do it?' Mel asks, unable to wrap her head around why anyone would wilfully cause so much distress to a pregnant woman. It has to be someone who knows she's back in town. Maybe one of the posters on Alice's Instagram who still thinks Mel is responsible for Jacob's death. Maybe they were annoyed by the apology. But why would they be? It has to be someone who's truly sick in the head. 'Does the card say which florist it was from? Would they know? We can ask them,' she says, words falling on top of words as her speech races, as if trying to keep up with the thudding pace of her heart.

'Sweetheart,' her mother says and takes a hold of Mel's hands, 'there's no florist's name but I think it's pretty obvious who's behind this. I know you won't want to believe it after your cosy little meet-up yesterday, but you've said it before yourself in the past, that woman is unhinged. This is exactly the kind of thing she would do.'

'No,' Mel says, 'No. She posted an apology online last night. Here, I'll show you.' She reaches for her phone but can't help but notice the look on her mother's face, one which screams of pity. Silly little Mel being taken in by this fake apology, only to be hurt even more with these disgusting flowers.

'Why would she post this apology – openly – and share it with everyone she knows if she were still trying to hurt me? It makes no sense. And you don't know her. You didn't sit opposite her yesterday and see the look on her face and hear her talk.' Mel thinks of how Alice was. How she talked. How she seemed so bloody genuine and so like the woman Mel had known before.

Finding the Instagram post, she turns her phone towards her mother who reluctantly takes it from her hands and starts to read, shaking her head the whole time.

'See!' Mel says, her head spinning from how quickly her earlier euphoria has been vaporised. 'It can't be her. I don't believe it!'

'Pet, when we spoke to Ed—'

Mel drops her head in her hands. She'd forgotten they'd spoken to Ed as the image of those flowers – those awful flowers

– imprinted itself in her brain. He's going to be so angry. So worried. And so sure that Alice is behind this. Who else would know what flowers Mel had sent to Jacob's funeral?

It's a question she has to ask herself. 'Those are the same flowers I sent when Jacob...' Her voice trails off as her world continues to fall apart. She thought she had fixed it. She believed she had. In many ways she still believes she has because she cannot imagine for a second that a woman who knows the pain of losing a child would wish the same on someone else.

'Just breathe,' her father tells her as he takes her hand. The feeling of his strong, warm hands – the hands that have kept her safe her entire life – are usually enough to ground her, but today Mel's skin prickles and suddenly she doesn't want anyone to touch her, or look at her, or breathe in her direction. In fact, she's fighting the urge to run for cover to somewhere she is safe and alone, and able to hide from all of this.

Her mother, meanwhile, is still talking. She's telling Mel how Ed is on his way to support her and how she had said no good would come of yesterday's meeting.

Or how she can't believe Mel would keep her meeting with Alice from Ed. How selfish she had been to put herself and her baby at risk. 'Just why would you do this, Mel?' her mother asks, utterly exasperated. 'It was bad enough. Why did you have to go and make it worse?'

Her mother doesn't mean to do it, but it's there. It has always been there. There has always been something in her expression since the day Mel announced her career change that has screamed disappointment. She has never quite understood her daughter's desire to leave a steady and reliable teaching career to become a doula. She didn't really hold any court with hypno-birthing. Mel had listened to enough well-meaning 'in my day we just got on with it' stories to leave her under no illusions about that. And when Mel had eventually told her that Alice was opting for an intervention-free birth, she had been unable to hide her shock. Her mother's judgement only grew day by day as Alice went past her due date. It didn't matter how many times Mel explained she was just there as a support and to follow Alice's wishes, her mother still told her 'what that wee girl should be doing'. Mel knows in her heart that ever since that awful day, her mother has been battling not to say 'I told you so', knowing that if she did, it could fracture their relationship forever.

And it seemed today might just be that day.

How can her mother not understand that Mel had just been trying to fix a mess of her own making. That she knows she should never have agreed to work on an unassisted delivery – especially once Alice had withdrawn from antenatal care. She knows her actions had turned her family's life on its head and she wanted to fix it. She wanted to stop it.

She thought she had.

Something inside her still believes she has. She cannot see this being Alice. She feels this deep in her gut, but can she turn to her mother, who is ashen-faced and distraught at what has happened and tell her she's wrong? Mel's wise enough to know her mother isn't open to hearing that.

'I was trying to make it better,' Mel tries to explain. 'I wanted to make it all stop.'

Her mother just shakes her head sadly. 'Well, that hasn't quite worked out for you, has it?' she says, wiping away her tears. 'Those flowers this morning? My God, Mel. It's sick and twisted. That's what it is.'

There's nothing Mel can say to challenge that. It *is* sick and it *is* twisted.

'I'm going to call her,' Mel announces reaching in her pocket for her phone. 'I'm going to ask her outright.'

'No!' her mother exclaims.

'I'm not sure that's a good idea,' her father says, a look of alarm on his face. 'I think we should leave it to the police from this point.'

But no, Mel thinks. Putting this in the hands of the police, setting them on Alice, will just make things so much worse. It will fracture all the progress they made yesterday – set everything on fire all over again.

'Daddy. I need to call her. I really don't think that Alice could be behind this. Not the Alice I spoke with yesterday. You should've seen her, Dad. Heard her. You saw her apology – how can you think that's anything but genuine?'

'For goodness' sake, Mel,' her mother snaps. 'Who else could it be? Who else is so angry with you they'd want to do something as sick as this? Who else have you hurt so badly they'd put you, and us, through this? Who knows you're staying here? You can continue being blind to what's obvious to everyone else if you want, but I raised you to be smarter than that!'

Her mother's words hit just as hard as she'd intended – each of them landing like a slap to the face.

She's freshly determined to prove her mother wrong, because the alternative – finding out that Alice had intentionally been lying yesterday – makes her feel sick to her very soul.

Ignoring her parents' protestations, she leaves the room, scrolling for Alice's number as she goes.

Alice answers after two rings and Mel holds her breath as she tries to judge the tone of her voice.

'Morning, Mel,' she says, her voice soft and warm. 'So you saw the post? You've seen the responses? It's had so many shares, too. My phone hasn't stopped ringing... if this is a taste of what you've had to go through, I'm so very sorry. I've deleted some of the shitty comments. I know you'll have seen them. I was going to call you today anyway. There's still so much I'd like to talk to you about. My... my memory of that night is hazy. PTSD, my counsellor said. It plays havoc with your memories. I know this is a big ask but—'

'Alice,' Mel interrupts. 'Before anything else, I really need to ask you something.'

'Sorry. You know what I'm like. I start talking and end up blurting my whole life out for whoever is listening. The truth is, I'm shitting myself. I'm kind of expecting you to hate me even more now you've read other people's takes on it all—'

'Alice,' Mel interrupts again.

'God, sorry. Sorry. What was it? What did you want to ask?'

Mel's heart is thudding hard in her chest. She doesn't know how best to word this. If there even is a positive way to ask a question like this. She takes a deep breath.

'Alice, something was delivered here, to my parents' house – something upsetting.' She doesn't quite know how to tell her just what the item is, conscious that it will invoke memories of Jacob and his funeral, of the flowers Mel had sent. Flowers that were turned away at the door and returned to the florist.

'What is it?'

Mel takes a deep breath. 'It's awful,' she says, a crack in her voice. 'It... it's a floral arrangement. Exactly the same, in fact, as the one I sent for Jacob's funeral. And there's a card. Telling me my children would be better off dead.'

There's a sharp intake of breath on the other end of the line. 'Oh God. Mel, I'm so, so sorry. I can't...' Alice says before releasing a loud sob – as if her grief is only ever a heartbeat away. 'Funeral flowers?' she croaks.

'My parents... they are just in pieces, and I need to ask...'

'...if it was me?' Alice's voice is shaky. 'I can assure you it was not. I would never. Do you know what florist they came from? Could you check with them? Oh God... is this my fault? What I told people before? I didn't think...'

'There's no florist's name. But whoever sent them knows me. And they clearly know I'm here with my parents too,' Mel adds, the reality of just how scary this is hitting her hard.

'So, it could be someone who saw you in town yesterday?'

'I don't know,' Mel replies, assessing every word, every little intonation to try to find any sign of a lie – any reason she should not believe what Alice is telling her. She finds none.

'What can I do to help?' Alice asks. 'Can I do anything to make it better? Should I say something else? Make it extra clear? We can't have people upsetting your parents. We can't have people upsetting you! Not when you're pregnant.'

Something in Mel's gut tells her that getting Alice to say more online would be the wrong thing to do. She can't put her finger on it – it's just a strong feeling.

'No, please don't say anything else. You don't want to pull attention back your way again. You're pregnant too. You have to take care of yourself. My parents have called the police. They can look into it.'

'The police?' Alice's voice is laced with fear.

'Yes. My parents are very distressed by it. They did it before talking to me.'

'They think it's me, then?' Alice sounds panicked. 'I understand why they wouldn't trust me and think I'm the bitch from hell, but I promise you that it's nothing to do with me. I don't know how to prove that, and maybe it's rich of me to ask you to take my word for it but...'

The sound of a car pulling into the driveway catches Mel's attention. Ed has arrived. 'Shit!' she swears. 'Look, I have to go.

My parents called Ed and he's here. I need to talk to him. He doesn't know I met with you.'

'Shit!' Alice sobs. 'Oh Mel, I'm so sorry. I have made this all worse for you.'

'No. No. It's not you who has made it worse,' Mel says, hating that Alice sounds so distressed too. The last thing she wanted to do is upset her, especially now she's pregnant again. She has enough to worry about.

'The only person to blame is whoever sent those flowers. And it's me for not telling Ed before now. Please, don't beat yourself up. You need to look after yourself. Is Thomas there to look after you?'

There's a pause, as Alice tries to steady her breathing. 'Not right now. But I'll call him.'

'Good. I'll call you later. Please take care. I'll make sure to tell the police you've nothing to do with this.'

Alice says a rather muted goodbye as Mel watches her daughter climb out of the back of the car and run headlong towards her grandparents, grinning widely. Ed, on the other hand, is not smiling at all. Not one little bit.

18

Tilly bundles into the room and straight towards her mother, immediately showering her stomach with kisses. 'I missed you so much, baby brother,' she says dramatically in a style that is unmistakably her own. She wraps her arms around Mel's middle and hugs tightly.

'Did you not miss your mummy too?' Mel's mother asks as she follows Tilly into the room. It's obvious she is trying to be bright and cheery for her granddaughter, but there is no mistaking the tension that hangs heavy in the air.

'A little,' Tilly says. 'But I was having fun too with my friend Sheila. She has ducklings. That's what you call baby ducks, Granny. She said I can come see them sometime.' Tilly's face is so solemn as she shares her newly gleaned knowledge as if she had uncovered the Dead Sea scrolls.

'Is that so?' her granny asks, as she scoops her up into a hug.

'Ducklings?' Mel asks Ed as he walks into the room, using the non-controversial question as a way to gauge the full extent of his mood.

'Yes. As Tilly says, that's what you call baby ducks.' He's

smiling but the passive aggression is obvious in his voice. 'Tilly and Sheila were talking about them last night. Sheila said she knows just where to go to feed some ducks. She offered to take Tilly some day.'

'I wanted to get one to bring home and live in our caravan, but Sheila says it's too messy in our garden for ducklings, but maybe when the house is all done and I'm back in my big bedroom. Or maybe we could get chickens in the garden.' Tilly looks up at her mother, eyes wide and a pleading expression on her face.

'Maybe,' Mel tells her, wishing she could prolong this exchange with her daughter because she's all too aware that Ed is wound up. But at the same time as dreading talking to him, she knows she *needs* to talk to him. There's no point in trying to put this off.

'Tilly, why don't you go into the kitchen with Granny and Grandad and get a nice cup of milk? I happen to know there are some yummy cookies in the cupboard too. I'm sure Granny will let you have one,' Mel says and watches her daughter's eyes brighten at the promise of sugary treats and the kind of spoiling that only comes at a grandparents' house.

As Tilly and her granny leave the room, Ed and Mel just look at each other, a hundred things being said in the silence between them, until they are alone.

'First of all, are you okay?' he asks. Mel shrugs. She's not sure she is okay, but perhaps, she thinks, he's referring to her blood pressure. Ed tends to have a more logical and practical approach to any crises they face.

'Physically, I'm okay,' she says. 'Emotionally is a completely different story.'

'Well, I'm not sure what you expected. If – and it's a big if – you think Alice is truly capable of all the things you've been telling me she is capable of, why would you go and face her? Jesus Christ, Mel!' His voice is raised but stops just short of shouting. She imagines he doesn't want either Tilly or her parents to hear him.

'But it wasn't her. I asked her outright and she was so open with me,' Mel says to her husband before relaying to him all that had been said the day before. She is aware that while she speaks, he is at times shaking his head or rubbing his temples. What she does not see is the look of relief she's been hoping for on his face. He doesn't even look relieved when she shows him the Instagram post and lets him read through all the replies. He just shakes his head even more.

'Mel, who is it then? Who would send funeral flowers, for God's sake? And wish harm to our babies?' His voice cracks and Mel sees for the first time just how close to breaking point her husband really is.

Mel reaches out to Ed, desperate to comfort him, but also desperately wanting some comfort herself. He pulls away, his face tight with anger and worry.

'I don't know who it is,' she says. 'But the apology seems heartfelt. Here, read it.' She hands him her phone and watches as he scans the post, his face giving nothing away.

'If you'd sat across the table from her yesterday like I did, you'd fully understand where I'm coming from. She was so genuine, Ed. Like she used to be. Back when we both considered her a friend. And you have to admit things had gone a little quieter recently, at least from her end.'

Mel knows she's asking a lot to get him on board with this take. They both believed that Alice had been behind fake accounts, and had continued to spread poison even after she'd stopped posting so much under her own name.

'People don't just change. They don't stop, Mel,' he said. 'This isn't something that could be explained away as an innocent mistake. This was sending *funeral flowers* to your parents' house. You can't dress that up as a coincidence or a misunderstanding. That the flowers were sent here, when you just happen to be here, despite moving to the other side of the country? You don't seriously believe that's not suspicious. Who else knew you were back? Me? Your parents? She's the only person you've spoken to since you've been home.'

'Someone might have seen me in the street,' Mel offers, knowing she is clutching at straws, but it's all she's got. The look on Ed's face screams of frustration and disappointment. It's the look she fears he has been hiding for the last few months since she knocked back his suggestion that now was the perfect time to emigrate.

'She's pregnant,' Mel blurts out. 'Almost halfway there. She doesn't want any attention from people, especially not the press, so she's kept it quiet. She doesn't want any bad feeling any more – not now when she's trying to look to the future and focus on getting their baby here safely. She doesn't have the energy or motivation to send something so vile now. If you maybe sat down and spoke with her, you'd—'

'I will not be sitting down and speaking with her! The only people who should be sitting down and talking to her are the police. And I don't care how sincere her apology seemed to you. Or that she's pregnant. The only pregnancy I care about right now is yours. Ours. The only children who matter are our children,' Ed says. 'I will not allow *anyone* to put them at risk.' His voice is so stern Mel has no doubt at all that he means every single word.

19

The atmosphere in Mel's parents' house is still icy cold even after the police have taken statements and left. To both her parents' and Ed's disgust, the police said there isn't actually all that much they can do about the flowers and the note – there being no clear and defined threat against Mel or her children.

'They are *funeral* flowers!' Ed had protested. 'And they say our children would be better off dead!'

'This is definitely unpleasant, and we can certainly go and speak with any individual you think may have sent them and, of course, we will keep a record of it,' the uniformed PSNI officer said as he reached for another one of the biscuits set out by Mel's mother. 'Our advice in situations like these is to keep a diary of any interactions and/or strange experiences, and perhaps look at getting a restraining order if they persist, but...'

'So you're telling me that someone has to directly threaten or physically harm my daughter or her family before you will take this seriously?' her mother had asked, enraged.

'Regretfully, that is the case. We can't arrest someone for a crime they haven't committed,' the officer said.

'But surely this shows intent!' her mother had said, exasperated as Mel had watched, torn between feeling utterly horrified by the flowers but also firmly convinced there was no way Alice would've sent them. Even in her most unhinged days, she would not have been that cruel. It would be easier, of course, if she were to blame. The mystery would be solved. Mel would know who exactly to look over her shoulder for. Her mother and Ed might be terrified that Alice could've sent the flowers, but Mel was more terrified that she hadn't. It meant this whole situation was out of control. Someone was out for blood.

The conversation with the police had gone around in circles for another half-hour before they said their goodbyes, leaving them in this awkward, tension-filled silence. Mel's head hurts from trying to make sense of it all. She hates seeing her mother so upset. She hates that Ed is cross with her. She hates that in trying to sort this all out, she's just managed to make it a whole lot worse.

Her mother gets up to make more tea. Ed walks out to the garden to take a phone call, and her father leaves to take the floral tribute to the dump, announcing that he can't settle with it near him.

Mel, meanwhile, is just trying to make the most of the silence. A sleepy Tilly is cuddled up beside her, lip petted, after having had a big cry that she is no longer able to fit on her mummy's lap due to her expanding baby bump. It had taken a lot of soothing and reassurance to get past that particular issue, and Mel had to draw from the deepest reserves of her soul to find some. Poor Tilly, she thinks. Caught up in all this but much too young to understand any of it. Not why her mother is on edge, or her granny is upset. Or why Daddy seems cross. It breaks Mel's heart, and she hopes that Tilly realises just how much she is loved. Mel is soothed by the warmth of her daughter's body beside her own and by the simple action of stroking her daughter's hair.

Tilly yawns and looks up at her mummy, her soulful blue eyes – the same as her father's – pleading. 'Mummy,' she says, 'are you coming home with us?'

Mel's not sure how to answer. Maybe she should stay, to help her parents over this upset. They are clearly very shaken. A selfish part of her thinks it will give her a little more space to maybe have another chance to talk with Alice. Make sure she is okay if the police come to visit her. Ask her if she has any idea who might be behind the flowers. Could it be the mysterious 'Big Bad Wolf' from the parenting forum? They seem to know a lot about Mel after all. Shit... maybe she should've mentioned them to the police when they were here. Maybe if she stayed, she could call down to the police station and do just that.

'I'm not sure, baby,' Mel says. 'I might stay and help Granny and Grandad a little. And sure you're having so much fun with Daddy and Sheila anyway.'

Tilly blinks and her beautiful blue eyes fill with tears again. Her bottom lip juts out, and while she doesn't start to wail, it's clear she's having to use all her energy to hold it in. Her grip on Mel's arm gets a little tighter and she cuddles in closer, burying her face into Mel's side as her little body starts to shake. Mel feels her heart crack. How could she possibly think of not going home with her precious little girl?

'Tills, would you like me to go home with you and Daddy?'

Tilly doesn't speak but Mel feels her head nodding up and down against her arm.

'Okay, baby,' Mel tells her. 'I'll go home with you and Daddy.'

Tilly's little arms wrap even tighter around Mel, letting her know she has done the right thing.

An hour later they drive away from her parents – her mother

having hugged her extra tight and told her to take care and be sensible. Mel found it impossible to ignore the tremor in her mother's voice as she did so. Hugging her back, she had done her best to match the tightness of her mother's embrace.

Ed remains unusually quiet, but Tilly is more than making up for his silence, telling Mel how Sheila has promised to teach her to make 'nanana bread' and how she had beaten her daddy at Connect 4 – which Mel knows will only have been because he let her win. Normally, Ed would be joining in with his daughter's chatter – the two of them making a brilliant double act – but today his eyes remain firmly on the road ahead.

As they get closer to Derry and start driving through the beautiful scenery of the Glenshane Pass, Tilly starts to flag. It's impressive she's kept chatting for this long, Mel thinks, given that they are more than an hour into the journey already, but there's no mistaking that her chatter is getting slower and quieter, little by little.

Soon she stills, and the car goes quiet. Mel glances behind her and sees that yes, Tilly's eyes are closed and her head is turned to one side, her beautiful rosebud lips slightly parted as she sleeps.

'That's her out for the count.'

Ed is quiet for a moment, the only noise between them the low hum of the car engine and the rumble of the tyres on the road. Unsure of whether to try and break the awkward silence between them, or just let it hang for another while, Mel shifts in her seat.

'I spoke with Emma,' Ed says eventually. 'Earlier. I called her and told her about everything that's been happening.'

Mel doesn't speak, unsure of where this is going, but feeling a prickle of uneasiness at the back of her neck.

'Look, the last thing I want to do is make things more difficult for you, but I'm not sure how much more of this stress we can deal with. You've seen how clingy Tilly was with you. And your poor parents. We could have a whole new, improved life out there with her, you know. Your parents could come and visit. I'd pay for their flights.'

Mel tenses, hating that they are back to this conversation again, but she says nothing. She's not sure what she wants to say anyway. Her head is much too messy right now.

'She's been having a little look around at job opportunities. She said I'd have no problem getting something. They're crying out for construction industry workers over there, and my experience project managing the build of large-scale developments would stand me in really good stead. She said you could easily find a teaching position – if you wanted to, that is. I don't mind if you want to be at home with the kids for a little bit. Just imagine it, days in the sun, afternoons by the pool and a summery Christmas.'

He sounds so enthusiastic, so excited about the possibility of something they decided not to pursue a long time ago.

'You know Emma's my only sibling. And with Mum and Dad both gone, it's just the two of us. I miss her, you know. A lot. Yes, the house here will be great and the countryside is beautiful, but imagine the life the kids would have in the sun? Tilly and the new baby would have their cousins on hand to play with. Emma is sending over some property listings...'

'Ed,' Mel says, stopping him before she becomes much too overwhelmed. 'I love that you've put thought into this and it all sounds idyllic, but our life is here. My parents need me – even if I have just caused them a whole heap of stress. Not to mention we're balls-deep in debt investing in the new house. We wouldn't make anywhere near a good return if we tried to sell up now. The place is even more of a shell than it was.'

She looks across at her husband, sees the tension in his jaw and the tighter grip of his hands on the steering wheel.

'We'd cope,' he says. 'Emma is on board to help out. I even had a chat with Fergus before – just to suss out if he knew of any developers who might be willing to buy the project. Given that the work has started, that the materials are there and that planning permission is all in order, I think we'd have a solid chance.'

'You spoke to the builder about selling the house?' Mel asks, incredulous. 'When was this exactly? After my mother called? You just dropped it casually into conversation before you jumped in the car?' She does her best to keep her voice just a little above a whisper, keen to make sure she doesn't wake Tilly.

Glancing at Ed, she sees his face colour just a little.

'No. I spoke with him yesterday.'

'Yesterday?' She's taken aback. Why on earth would he have spoken to Fergus, the site foreman, yesterday? Things were still 'normal' yesterday.

'I was just asking. It was curiosity more than anything. Trying to suss out the market. I wasn't committing us to anything. Just thinking...' He turns the car onto the road that leads to their new home. The home he just so happened to be asking about selling.

A thought arrives, unbidden, in her head. A thought that is at first so preposterous that her immediate reaction is to push it to the farthest recesses of her mind; but even there, it niggles.

It niggles as she carries Tilly back into the caravan, and as she sits watching TV in sullen silence with Ed later that evening.

It even niggles as she tries to sleep, forcing her to get up out of bed and go through to the living room where she makes a cup of caffeine-free tea. She can't stop thinking that it is all just a little too coincidental. Ed has been asking about selling the house. He has been talking to Emma and she just happens to know, with no time to go off and investigate, that there are job opportunities for him? And all this at the same time those flowers – that only Alice, she and Ed knew about – arrive at her parents' house? A thought – cold and brutal – flashes into her mind. Could Ed have sent the flowers, knowing how easily she got spooked at the moment?

No, she thinks. Not Ed. Not her Ed. The man who would walk over hot coals for his family without so much as a second thought.

The same man, she thinks, who has always wanted to move to Australia and who thought he might finally have a chance last year when everything went south.

But still, he wouldn't be so cruel. Actually, it's beyond cruel. It's evil, and she cannot believe that her Ed would behave that way. Those flowers were awful. Her poor mother and father had been distraught. If he was the kind of man who would do that, then he really wasn't the man she was sure she had known all these years.

That thought chills her to the bone.

20

34 WEEKS + 6 DAYS

Mel wakes with a jolt, for a moment unsure of where she is. All she knows is that her back hurts, there's a cramp in her leg and she's perilously close to falling off the edge of whatever it is she's sleeping on.

The caravan, she remembers. And the sofa. The sofa she'd escaped to when her thoughts had kept her awake into the small hours. Somehow she had managed to drift off and sleep until it was light. And until someone started knocking, loudly and persistently, on the caravan door.

'Shit!' she hears Ed exclaim, almost stumbling into the room as he tries to pull on his tracksuit bottoms and make himself decent. 'I wondered where you were,' he says when he spots Mel trying to haul herself, with as much grace as she can muster, into a sitting position.

'I couldn't sleep... and then I did,' she tells him, but she can see he's not really listening. His hoodie is halfway on, pulled down over his head and ears as he tries to finish getting dressed.

'One minute!' he shouts at the door. 'I'm coming.' He turns his attention briefly back to Mel. 'Are you decent?'

'As I'll ever be,' she says, stretching her back to try and release the tension in her muscles.

'Mummeeeee! Daddddeeee!' Tilly shouts from her room, her calls echoing around the caravan.

'I'll get her,' Mel tells Ed, who is just reaching out his hand to open the door and see who is banging on it in such a heavy-handed way. As Mel passes him to go and fetch Tilly, she hears Fergus's gruff, low voice. She glances at the clock and sees that it has already gone eight. She'd normally be up and dressed by now – something Fergus isn't long in reminding her.

'Ah now, I thought you'd be up and ready!' Fergus's booming voice fills the caravan. 'It's almost the middle of the afternoon!'

'Sure we're up now,' Ed says, 'apologies. Why not come in and get a cup of tea while I get myself sorted?'

'You don't need to ask me twice if I want a cuppa,' Fergus answers, as Mel comes back into the kitchen, Tilly in tow. She tries not to wince at the sight of the muddy footprints Fergus has left behind him.

Standing at six foot something, and as broad as he is tall, Fergus dominates the room. His mud-spattered high-vis vest is straining over a muddy-brown woollen jumper. The muddy brown is, of course, a perfect colour to camouflage the mud and dirt that clings to his work clothes, and what looks like the occasional blob of dried ketchup. It's the ground-in dirt of a man who works with his hands in all weathers.

'Ah, now. This must be the star of the day!' he booms as he spots Tilly. She stares back at him as he opens his arms wide and launches into a raucous and not entirely tuneful rendition of 'Happy Birthday'.

Of course, Tilly looks at Mel, puzzled, who in turn looks to Ed. None of this makes sense to any of them. Fergus, who doesn't seem to pick up on their confusion, just continues singing, inserting 'wee doll' in the place where he would normally sing the name of the birthday boy or girl.

When he finishes, with a particularly loud final note, he looks at Tilly expectantly. Is he waiting for applause? Or thanks? Or tears of joy? Because he'll get none of those, Mel thinks. Because this doesn't make sense.

'Mister, it's not my birthday. My birthday is in Feb-rou-airy,' Tilly says, carefully over-pronouncing February.

It's impossible for Mel to tell whether or not Fergus reddens any further – the ruddiness of his cheeks already providing ample glow of their own. He does have the good grace to look confused.

'Is there another wee one hiding around this place some-where?' he asks, 'because I don't think teddy bears would really be your thing, Ed.'

'Teddy bears?' Ed replies, and Mel feels Tilly's hand grip her own, excitement immediate at the mention of a stuffed toy.

'Aye. Outside, at the gate. Wrapped in plastic, and a big happy birthday balloon... I thought...'

Mel freezes, while Tilly runs from her to look out the window towards the gate.

Ed shakes his head. 'Nothing to do with us. Must be a mistake.'

With a shrug of his shoulders, Fergus shakes his head. 'Didn't look like a mistake. It looks very firmly attached to your gate, probably to keep it off the ground given that it's right and muddy out there today. To be honest, before I saw the "Happy Birthday", I wondered if it was some kind of memorial.' At that he drops his voice to a whisper, and turns his body slightly away from Tilly. 'You know, the kind people leave at the side of a road after an accident?'

'That's probably what it is, then,' Ed says. 'Although I don't like that they've fastened it onto our gate. It's not like it's not completely obvious someone is living here now.'

Fergus and Ed chat back and forth but Mel can't hear what they are saying any more over the buzzing sound in her ears. It may well be a memorial, but not the kind either Ed or Fergus think it to be.

She might still be in her pyjamas and wearing her oldest, least graceful cardigan, but she figures no one is going to see her anyway and even if they did, she wouldn't care. Her trainers are still sitting where she discarded them last night in front of the sofa and she slides her sockless feet into them.

'Mel, what's wrong?' Ed asks. She glances up and sees his eyes dart between Fergus and Tilly before they land back on hers.

'Nothing,' she lies. She doesn't want to make a scene or risk letting Fergus in on their private business by voicing her fears in front of him. 'I just want to have a look at it.'

'Mel, it's muddy out there and slippery. Sit down and I'll go look,' Ed says, but he's still in his bare feet and hardly in a position to head out the door to check. And she wants to check now.

'Can I come and see?' Tilly asks, already running to fetch her wellies from the hallway between the bedrooms.

'No, darling,' Mel calls after her. 'You're still in pyjamas. I'll be right back.' She can't have Tilly come with her. Her instincts are telling her that what is out there might not be pleasant. The flowers yesterday and now this? She can't help but feel the weight of dread land on her shoulders. She wants to keep her daughter as far away from it as she possibly can.

'But you're still in your pyjamas too!' Tilly whines, the full force of her four-year-old petulance starting to build to its soul-crushing crescendo.

'Tilly, I said no!' Mel snaps, sending her daughter straight into full meltdown mode. Fergus raises his hands in a gesture that screams '*I didn't say or do anything wrong*' and Mel dares not even look at her husband's face right now.

She knows she is acting like a madwoman rushing to get a look at a teddy bear and a balloon. But she also knows no one else really understands her fear. No one else believes she is any real danger, but she feels it in her bones. She doesn't think it's just hormones and lack of decent sleep. It's no coincidence, she realises, that the items have been left here on today of all days.

Today is the anniversary of Jacob's due date.

Her feet in her trainers, laces loose, and fighting the ick feeling of her bare skin on the worn insoles, Mel ignores the cacophony of noise and tension inside the van and walks as calmly as her thudding heart allows across the gravel, her feet sliding on patches of bare, muddy ground.

The balloon is bobbing in the air. Bright and colourful. A stark contrast to the dull and muted earthy tones of a wet spring morning. Its message of 'Happy Birthday' is emblazoned in garish metallic script. There are thin ribbons in blue and silver trailing from the knot of the balloon down to where a cuddly toy, a hideous royal blue bear, is wrapped in cellophane and pinned to the wooden gate. The bear's dark, glassy eyes stare back at Mel from behind the rain-dappled plastic. With shaking fingers, she pulls and pokes at it, trying to see if there's a card, or a note, or something that proves her wrong.

Her heart thudding, she feels pressure building inside her head as she pulls back the cellophane, aware that Ed has come out of the caravan and is calling her name as he walks across the crunching gravel towards her.

'Just leave it,' he says, pulling at her arm, as she slides her hand inside the tight ribbon wrapped around the bear's middle.

It takes a moment for her brain to recognise the sensation

she's feeling. It's a release. A slice. A sting. Wet. And then the pain, burning and throbbing at once. She sees the cheap fur of the bear darken with her blood. Panic rising, she tries to pull her hands out from the cellophane that is now spattered with her dark, sticky blood, but her hand is caught – snagged on something sharp.

Mel can't fight the pain any longer, nor the panic. Nor can she block out the shouting from Ed, or the call to Tilly from Fergus the burly builder to stay back and 'not worry about Mummy'.

With a screech, she manages to pull her hand free and is immediately aware that between her fingers there is a loose flap of skin, and a ragged pulsing as blood runs down her hand. Ed is shouting for help as Mel tries – and fails – to keep conscious and not lapse into a faint.

21

'Do you have anyone with you here today?' the doctor asks as a blood pressure cuff starts to tighten around Mel's arm. The emergency department at Altnagelvin Hospital is busy, loud and too warm, and Mel is starting to feel increasingly woozy.

She wishes Ed was with her, but it was Fergus who had brought her to hospital, making awkward conversation the entire time. He clearly wasn't used to having a crying, injured woman in his van. She'd been almost as relieved as he had been when he dropped her at the door to the ER and left to go back to the site. But now, she wishes there were someone there to hold her hand and help calm her down.

'No. My husband is at home with our little girl,' she says, her mouth dry. 'We didn't want to bring her here,' she adds. 'She's only four.'

'Ah, I understand,' the doctor says. 'I'm sure she was delighted to see a teddy bear tied to her gate. You were lucky she didn't try and get her hands on it.'

'Yes,' Mel replies, only too aware of the fact. It's been all she has been able to think about since it happened. If it has caused a nasty injury to Mel, she dreads to think what damage it could've done to a little four-year-old's hand.

The blood pressure cuff continues to tighten and starts to hurt like hell, making her wince. She tries to hide her discomfort, embarrassed by it. She watches the numbers on the screen as if she could will them to behave. She's not stupid though. She'll be shocked if they are anything other than astronomically high with everything that has been happening, both this morning and yesterday at her parents' house. And that's not even taking into consideration the intrusive thoughts she has been having about Ed and his plans.

'Hmmm,' the doctor – who of course falls into the 'looks impossibly young' category – grimaces. 'That's definitely higher than I'd like. Have you been feeling a lot of movement from baby?'

Mel thinks so. Yes, she has been distracted by the pain and perhaps not quite as aware of his movements as she'd normally be, but she's sure he has been moving. Hasn't he? Wouldn't it be perfectly horrific karma if something unthinkable were to happen on today of all days?

'Yes... well, I think so. I'm sorry. I'm not quite with it today,' she says, as if it weren't absolutely obvious to any outside observer.

'I think we'd be best to get someone down from obs and gynae all the same to have a quick look at you. Given that you're here, anyway. So, we'll give you the gold star treatment today, Mrs Davison. We'll get an X-ray to check there is no debris in that wound, just to make sure we're not missing anything before we stitch you back up. I hope you don't have other plans for the day because I imagine you will be here for a while,' he says, frowning performatively. Mel has a feeling that telling people they are in for a long wait is par for the course.

'I can give you some IV paracetamol for the pain,' he says. 'It should make you comfortable at least. I'm afraid that's as strong as we can go because of baby.'

She nods and mutters a quiet thank you. Once upon a time she'd have engaged him in talk about his work, and about 'baby'. She'd have told him she likes to practise alternative methods of pain control. That she's an advocate of hypnobirthing. But she doesn't. She's too tired to get into it. Too much in need of something to dull the pain in her hand and her head.

Not one word is uttered as he slides a needle into her arm to site a cannula. Mel is incredibly grateful that he is not asking her any further questions. He attaches the paracetamol drip and Mel feels relief wash over her as the medication starts to take effect, and the doctor leaves her in peace. The physical longing to be with Ed and Tilly in their own safe space – away from questions and worry – is strong. Left alone, she quickly realises, means giving her enough time to overthink even more. How is she going to handle this?

Her gut screams at her it's not Alice behind the sinister bear and balloon, but is she just being naive? The Mel that existed just two days ago would have had no qualms at all at pointing the finger to her former friend. In a way, she'd understand that Alice was becoming more unhinged in the run-up to the anniversary – but she was not the same person she was two days ago. She had sat, face to face, with the woman who had become her nemesis, who now had waved a white flag and brokered a peace of sorts.

That same woman had been utterly bereft to hear about the flowers being sent to Mel's parents'. If she was lying about her upset, then she had given an Oscar-worthy performance. Besides, Mel knows that even at her most twisted, Alice wouldn't have risked causing physical injury to Tilly.

But then again… Tilly had been so sure that Alice was trying to take her somewhere 'special' on the day she was seen outside the nursery.

It would be easier, she tells herself, if it was Alice. She'd be able to direct the police directly to her house. She'd be able to do something. Surely this would count as the direct threat or injury the police had told her she would need for them to take decisive action?

Not that it mattered. She believed Alice. She believed in her apology. Why would Alice expose herself by posting on social media about her own lies if she didn't mean it?

Which only means it had to be someone else. Someone unknown who is hell-bent on revenge. Or worse again, her own husband trying to scare her into making the big move she has always resisted. If he had risked harm coming to his own daughter just to make his case, then he was not the kind of man she wanted to spend even a minute more with, never mind the rest of her life.

It's too much, she thinks, to wrap her head around. This day last year, everything had been fine and happy in her world. She had been full of hope and excitement for Alice's impending new arrival and now, here she was, not sure who in the world she can trust.

22

She should've predicted that this would end with her being taken up to the antenatal ward to undergo a foetal CTG trace. Once again she has heard the words 'higher than we'd like' – this time from the midwife who had hooked her up to the monitor, wrapping elastic belts around her stomach to hold the transducers in place before telling her not to move about too much.

Outside the room she hears the chatter of nurses in the ward, the beep of infusion pumps, phones ringing and the shuffle of slippered feet as patients walk up and down the corridor.

At least, she thinks, being here gives her the chance to hear her baby's heartbeat and watch the rhythm of it on the monitor. She has more than enough knowledge to know it's a good, steady rate, as it has been for the last two hours. Her blood pressure might still be high, but her son appears to be coping well enough. He is still wriggling and stretching, safely encased in her uterus. Thank God. She doesn't take anything for granted any more.

Hopefully the midwife will return shortly and tell her she's good to go home, and she can get back to Ed and Tilly. Her need to be near them now is almost overpowering – her desire to keep Tilly under her watchful eye all-consuming. She can't help but feel she is at risk of losing it all at any time.

Someone tried to hurt them. *Did* hurt her. The realisation that she has been injured – her skin sliced open – keeps coming at her in waves, as if her brain can't quite process it fully. It pushes it down, until an ache or twinge drags it to the surface and the shock hits all over again. She can't help but shudder as she remembers how easily her skin was split.

The door to her room swings open and the midwife returns, this time with a doctor in tow. His head is already tilted to the side, no doubt in preparation for delivering news that Mel isn't going to want to hear. Mel is more than able to read the signs these days.

'What is it?' she asks. 'The baby's okay, isn't he? I've been keeping an eye on his trace.'

The doctor, a man in his mid-thirties dressed in green scrubs with his hair perfectly coiffed as if he were an episode lead in *Grey's Anatomy*, takes a seat at the end of the bed.

'Your baby is fine *at the moment*,' he says. 'And hopefully, he'll stay fine. We've no reason to worry too much at this stage. But your blood pressure, well – that does present a bit of a concern. So all things considered, I think we'd be happier if we kept you in for a little while just to monitor things.'

Mel's heart sinks. She wonders if he has included her in this mythical happy 'we all' group because while her priority is of course to get her baby here as safely as possible, she very much would be happier not to stay in hospital.

'Are you sure that's necessary? I feel okay,' Mel says, even though she can feel a headache starting to squeeze at her temples and is well aware that's a sign her blood pressure is elevated.

'You may well *feel* okay,' the doctor tells her, 'but the numbers indicate that there is cause for some concern. I think it's better in these circumstances to be safe rather than sorry. I thought you'd understand that more than most.' He glances at the silent nurse who gives him, then Mel, a knowing look – which Mel immediately recognises. It's the same knowing look Lindsey the midwife gave her. The same knowing look she's become painfully used to. *They're keeping an eye on me*, she thinks. *They really think I'd take a chance with my own baby.* She resists the urge to tell them to go to hell.

But then, she remembers, she just said she felt well, even though her head hurt. Even though her readings were high. It was that easy, she realises, to lie to herself.

Maybe they're all right. Maybe she shouldn't be trusted.

There are three other women in the ward Mel is moved to. Two of them are in the early stages of induction, swaying between excitement and nervousness, and are chatting animatedly to each other. A year ago, Mel wouldn't have thought twice about chatting to her room-mates and doing her best to reassure them. She'd maybe even have offered a few pointers for staying calm and in control. But the Mel that exists now just wants to keep her head down and get through this stay, however long it might be, without drawing any attention to herself.

She's about to slip her AirPods in to stream something through her phone when she hears the younger mum-to-be in the bed beside her start to cry. Since arriving in the ward, Mel has been able to ascertain that the young woman has been admitted for fluids and anti-sickness medication to try and help with her hyperemesis gravidarum – a severe form of pregnancy sickness.

Her cries are pitiful and don't seem to get the attention of the two excited ladies in the beds opposite. Mel might just want to keep herself to herself – she might have the urge to pull the curtain around her bed and shut everyone else out – but she can't because her heart aches for the young woman who is clearly having such an awful time.

'Excuse me,' she says. 'Are you okay? Can I get you anything?'

The younger woman shakes her head and sniffs.

'I know it's hard,' Mel tells her. 'But it will be worth it. When you have your baby in your arms. I know that probably seems forever away now, but it will come sooner than you think.'

'I hope so,' the woman replies, her expression pitiful. 'They told me it would get better after twelve weeks but here I am at nineteen weeks and it's getting worse, if anything. I'm so tired. I've another wee one at home. It wasn't like this when I was expecting him. I can't get anything done and I just feel so awful all the time.' She breaks into a fresh bout of tears.

Swinging her feet over the side of her bed, even though she's been warned to stay on bed rest for the remainder of the day, Mel shuffles to the chair beside her room-mate's bed and pushes a box of tissues towards her.

'Thanks,' the younger woman says. 'Sorry for crying. I'm feeling so sorry for myself.'

Mel smiles. 'It's okay to feel sorry for yourself sometimes. Pregnancy can be tough, even when it's all going well. You're better to let the feelings out rather than bottle them all up.'

'My partner says I'm letting them out a little too much. He's getting fed up with my crying and I know that makes him sound like an arsehole, but he's really not. He just feels so useless.'

Mel nods sympathetically. 'You know it's not your job to pretend to be well when you're not, just to make someone else feel a little better.' She hopes she has said this as sensitively as possible. What she really wants is to tell the young woman her partner needs to catch himself on.

The woman smiles. 'Maybe I'll try that.'

'And if you don't mind me saying... I'm a—well, I used to be, a hypnobirthing coach. I'm not saying your hyperemesis isn't very real and very debilitating, but if you looked into some relaxation practices, it might help reduce your anxiety, and that can make your symptoms a little less severe or even just a little more manageable.'

'Really?' the woman says, her face brightening a little.

'I saw it in a few of my clients. It won't make it go away but—' Mel says.

'—if it helps at all, I'll be willing to give it a try!' The young woman cradles her stomach. 'It's stopping me feeling the connection I really want to have with this little one and it's not her fault. Do you offer hypnobirthing here? Is there a class or something? I'm Lucie, by the way. Thanks for coming over to talk to me. I've felt a little out of place here.' She nods towards the chattering women. It must be so hard for Lucie to feel a connection to two women on the brink of having their babies when she is feeling so absolutely wretched and nowhere near her due date.

'I'm Mel. And sorry, I'm not running any classes at the moment.' She feels herself colour, the truth of why her business is no more haunting her. She reminds herself she doesn't owe the world her entire story. She doesn't have to invite judgement, but still, she feels shame nip at her. 'There's bound to be something on offer locally though. I'm not from around here so I'm still finding my feet about what provision is out there. I can have a little look around for you?'

'That would be brilliant.' Lucie smiles and seems to start to visibly relax just a little. 'What has you incarcerated here, anyway?' she asks.

There's no way Lucie hasn't noticed the bandaged hand but

again, Mel doesn't need to get into that. This isn't about her
injury anyway. That has no impact on her pregnancy at all.

'High blood pressure. They want to monitor me for a bit.'

'You can't have too long to go?'

'Five and a half weeks. But I'm definitely ready to get it over
and done with now. Physically at least. We've just moved here
though, so I hope he doesn't come too early. I'd like to get things
in order to some degree before all the chaos kicks in again.'

'Moving when you're heavily pregnant is a flex,' Lucie says,
and Mel notices her eyelids have started to look heavy as if she
could fall asleep any second.

'You look tired. Will I leave you to get a rest?' Mel asks.

'Sorry. Yes. I think the medication has kicked in and I need to
sleep.' Lucie stifles a yawn.

'No need to apologise. You rest and hopefully the sleep will
do you good.' She gives Lucie's arm a squeeze with her unin-
jured hand before getting up and shuffling back to her bed,
grateful for the distraction from her own worries for a bit.
Maybe this is the perfect time for her to get some sleep
herself.

'Thank you,' she hears Lucie mumble. 'Thanks for listening.
It means a lot.'

* * *

When Mel wakes, the lights are dimmed in the ward and the
curtain between her bed and Lucie's is pulled across. Their two
room-mates are not in their beds. Mel suspects they may have
gone on one of their walks up and down the corridor to try and
get their labours moving. Whatever the reason, she's not
complaining. She's grateful for the peace and quiet.

Picking up her phone, she sees there are a few messages

from her mother, and also from Ed. He asks what he should do with the bear and balloon on the gate.

She answers:

MEL

Take them down but don't get rid of them.

A couple of minutes pass before she gets a reply.

ED

Why would we not get rid of them?

Can he really not have thought that these could possibly be connected to Jacob? It was the first thought that came into her head – how could it not have been the first thought that came into Ed's?

MEL

Because after yesterday, I don't think we can rule out that whoever is behind the flowers sent to my mother's might also be behind this. And we need to bring it to the police.

Three dots appear on the screen as if he is tapping in a response and she watches and waits for it to appear. The dots disappear and no message flashes up. A minute later, it starts all over again. Eventually, his words land.

ED

Mel, I'm sure it's more likely to just mark some accident or the like on the road. I don't think we need to be getting hysterical thinking it's related to Jacob. And on the off-chance it is, then I think we know who is responsible. We need to send the police to speak to your 'friend'.

Mel tenses. She can feel venom in the word 'friend'.

MEL

> I don't think Alice is behind this. But I do think it's Jacob-related.

ED

> I think you're very naive to think Alice isn't involved. No matter what she has said, or how she looks. Even if she isn't the person who tied that blasted thing to the gate, she has to bear some responsibility. She's stirred the pot for the last year. She's whipped this all up and it just seems it's only ever going to get worse. What next? Tilly gets hurt? Gets taken? Oh, that's right – your friend already tried that one. The one you don't want to blame, even though she has had no qualms pointing her finger at you. Even though she's created a virtual army of people to do her bidding that we can't seem to get away from.

His words cut as sharp as whatever sliced through her hand earlier. His anger is palpable and her head just won't stop spinning. It's a side of him she is unfamiliar with and she doesn't like it. It makes her feel under attack. And it's making her head spin even more.

She's starting to feel as claustrophobic in this hospital ward as she does in the pokey little bedroom of their caravan.

Nothing in her life feels as if it fits any more. She doesn't know who she is, or what her purpose is. She doesn't know if she can fully trust the man whom she has adored for the last eight years. She's not even sure she can trust her own mind.

She tries to think of how best to respond to him, but he is so angry and she is so confused that she knows any reply will likely just make things worse. She feels vulnerable enough right now, in this hospital with medical staff whispering about her, judging her. A kick in the ribs from her baby boy reminds her that she's not in this alone and she lies on her side so she can cradle her stomach and concentrate on feeling him move beneath her skin.

Ten minutes pass and her phone pings again. She unlocks her phone to read a new message from Ed.

> I love you, Mel. So much. You and our family mean more than the world to me. I know I get wound up but it's because I want to keep you safe. I'm going to put some security cameras up first thing tomorrow around the site. It's not much but it might be a deterrent of sorts. Keep our wee man safe and rest while you have the chance. xxx

Mel lies back on the starchy hospital pillows and closes her eyes and tries to quiet her mind. Just like she told Lucie, she knows getting stressed out is not good for either her or her baby. She tries to follow her own advice and practises some of her breathing and mindfulness techniques. She reminds herself of what really matters. While all this drama is going on, she is creating a miracle in the form of her baby boy. Eventually managing to find a sense of peace, Mel starts to drift off to sleep, only to be hauled back into consciousness by the vibration of her phone. She swears inwardly and looks at the screen. The number is listed as private – probably a spam call or possibly, just possibly, a call from a prospective client. It still happens, occasionally. Someone finds her number in the back of a drawer and calls her, not realising she's not working any more.

Deciding to answer it, she does her best to sound personable despite feeling anything but.

'Is that Mel?' A whisper of a voice, one so low she can barely make it out.

'Yes,' she says, holding the phone against one ear while pushing her finger tight into the other to try and block out the ambient noise of the ward. 'Who's calling? How can I help you?'

There's a muffled reply. Whoever is calling must be in a bad reception area because it's hard to make out what is being said.

'Hello?' she says again, trying to keep her voice low. She's not sure if Lucie is still sleeping and she doesn't want to wake her if she is.

She turns the volume up again and that's when she hears it. A low, muffled cry. Her first instinct is to take the phone from her ear, but she can't. What if someone is in trouble? she thinks. What if it's one of her old clients? One of their babies? Babies she witnessed being birthed into this world.

'Are you okay?' she asks, her voice rising. 'Who is this? Do you need help?'

There's a rustling noise, some heavy breathing, and the crying in the background starts to come to into sharper focus. It's louder now and she can tell it's the unmistakable cry of a baby. Shrill and sharp. She tenses.

'Hello?' she says again 'Are you okay? Is the baby okay?'

The crying intensifies and it sounds as if the baby is right beside the phone now, their cries pleading for help that isn't coming. There is no soothing voice of someone taking care of them. Whoever the caller is, they checked if it was Mel who answered, but they've not spoken since. She can't hear their heavy breathing any more. She can't hear any movement in the background. All she can hear is the baby, who by now is so hysterical that their little voice is growing hoarse. She can't understand how anyone can leave an infant to cry like that. There has to be a good reason. A serious reason.

'Please!' she begs. The shrill cry is almost unbearable. 'Your number was private. I don't know who this is. I want to help but I can't if I don't know who or where you are.'

Mel hasn't realised she has been getting louder and louder herself until the curtain around her bed is pulled back and a nurse with a worried expression is staring directly at her.

The nurse is talking, but the sound of the baby's cries are drowning out everything else and Mel can't hear what she is saying. All she can focus on now is trying to find out what is going on and get to the person on the other end of the line. What's the alternative? Just hang up? She can't bring herself to do that knowing there is a baby in distress and that there might be a hurt parent, unable to help their child. The very thought of it makes her sick to her stomach. If the person calling had the wherewithal to choose her number and to say her name when she answered, she is sure that means they must have some sort of faith that she will actually be able to help them.

'Please,' she says, panic now clear in her voice. 'I need you to help me to help you.'

The nurse, a short, tired-looking woman with cropped brown hair and wrinkled scrubs, walks towards her but Mel just raises her hand, gesturing to the nurse to stay back.

'Mrs Davison,' the nurse says, her voice authoritative and now loud enough to be heard over the phone. 'The other patients are becoming distressed.'

Not half as distressed as I am, Mel thinks, as tears of frustration start to well in her eyes. 'But there's a baby, and it's crying, and I don't know what's wrong,' she says.

'Who is it calling you?' the nurse asks, taking another step forward.

'I don't know,' Mel replies. 'It's a private number.'

'Let me see.' The nurse reaches out to take hold of the phone.

'No,' Mel protests. 'I need it. I need to be there if they speak. We need to get them help. Something is wrong. I know it.' The feeling of being totally useless and unable to help rushes in, reminding her of the night of Jacob's birth. That feeling of desperately wanting everything to be okay but knowing she has no control over the unfolding situation and is unable to help. Desperation claws at her.

The nurse takes the phone anyway, forcing it from Mel's hand. She glances at the screen, before lifting the handset to her ear. Mel watches her, feeling an almost magnetic pull between her and the phone. She wants – no, needs – it back in her hand.

'There's no one there.' The nurse's voice is soft and her eyes full of what looks to Mel like pity. Something plummets deep inside of her. There was, she thinks. There absolutely was someone there and now they're gone, and they've left her terrified she's letting someone else down who might need her help.

She wants to protest. To argue her case, but she can read the changing expression on the nurse's face very clearly. She is well versed in understanding an *I don't believe you* look.

23

---

35 WEEKS

Mel has not slept well, despite feeling utterly exhausted. She couldn't get the sound of the crying baby out of her mind. The nurse had tried to tell her it was probably a 'butt dial' or a wrong number, but she clearly wasn't aware of just how many prank or threatening calls Mel has received over the past year.

They had started about two weeks after Jacob had died. Silent phone calls at first. Then the occasional shout of 'baby killer' down the phone. One caller had told her she was a witch and was going to burn in hell for the 'unholy practice' of promoting hypnobirthing. She'd considered changing her phone number at one stage but then they had become less frequent. In fact it had been a few months, so this one coming now of all times is unlikely to be some sort of random coincidence.

Her mind is on Ed and Tilly waking in the caravan. She has to trust they are okay, but it feels so wrong to be away from them. Maybe she's being naive, but she has an inbuilt belief that there is safety in numbers and that she and her little family are always, always stronger together. They've always said they can get through anything if they have one another. Mel has always believed that to be true. Believed that nothing else really mattered but her family unit. Maybe Ed is right and it is time to consider moving. Yes, they'd had words and he'd been short with her but weren't they all under incredible stress just now? Hadn't she snapped at people recently too? She remembers the last message he sent the night before – telling her how much he loves her and their family. That's the Ed she wants to believe in – that's the Ed she knows and loves.

Looking out the window to the greyest of days, Mel sees that the clouds sit low and heavy and while it doesn't appear to be raining just now, it's clear it has been recently, and will again soon. She wonders how Tilly will have managed with the sound of the rain battering off the roof of the caravan. Had she been warm enough? Had she been scared? After all, she'd seen her mother take her hand, bloodied and torn, out of the package yesterday and she must've seen the fear on Mel's face as the pain had kicked in. Mel had done her very best to hide how frightened and sore she was. With a concerned look on her face, Tilly had offered to go and get one of her beloved Gruffalo plasters from the first aid box and had looked absolutely crestfallen when Mel had told her she didn't think the plasters would be big enough.

'But Gruffalos are the biggest,' Tilly had said, her bottom lip trembling.

In pain, and worried about the sheer volume of blood running down her arm, Mel had found herself unable to comfort her daughter in the way she would have liked. It had taken every ounce of her self-control not to lose her cool and shout that Gruffalos were not real. She winces now when she thinks how close she had come to losing her temper. See, she thinks, Ed isn't the only one on his last nerve at the moment.

'Good morning!'

The same nurse who had tried to calm her last night pulls back the curtain from around the bed where Mel is still hiding.

'I'm finishing my shift soon. I just wanted to check in on you. You seemed to get a little sleep, at least?'

'I did,' Mel lies. She'll say whatever she has to if it gets her home as soon as possible. She's already feeling very vulnerable, having become so hysterical last night over the phone call. She doesn't want the nurse, or any other health professional, to know how unsettled she is. She doesn't want to come across as crazy.

'Do you think I'll be able to get home today?' Mel asks.

'It's hard to say,' the nurse tells her. 'Some of the consultants are more cautious than others and unfortunately, we had that run of high pressure last night when you were upset. But I've made notes on your file to that effect. You managed well overnight, and I can see this morning that things are looking under control, so hopefully...' She crosses her fingers and smiles at Mel. 'We don't tend to keep people in here longer than we need to. So take it easy, and hopefully I'll not see you later when I come back on shift.'

'Thank you,' Mel says, hoping against hope the nurse is right and she will be home with her family before long.

Mel is trying to spread a seemingly frozen pat of butter onto already cold toast when one of the labouring mothers from across the room speaks.

'I know you from somewhere,' she says, as she rocks her hips on a birthing ball. If she had to guess, Mel would put her in her late twenties. She clearly prides herself on her appearance. Despite her ongoing early labour, her hair is pulled back in a flawless French braid, and there is no other way to describe her eyebrows than being 'on fleek'. Her skin is glowing and free from the pregnancy breakouts that have plagued Mel. She is definitely not someone Mel has ever met before, which immediately makes her nervous. Thanks to her image being shared online and in a few newspapers, there is always the very real chance that the link will relate to the horror of last year.

'I don't think so.' Mel has decided that keeping her answers to a minimum in the hope of shutting down any conversation is probably the best approach. 'I'm new to the area.'

The other woman's brow wrinkles as she looks at Mel again. 'You are so familiar-looking though. Did you live here before maybe? Do you have family here you'd have been down visiting?'

Mel shakes her head. 'No family here. We just saw a house we fell in love with.' She smiles and shrugs her shoulders, turning her attention back to her toast and the unappetising cup of tea in front of her which now appears to have white dots of something – the best-case scenario being cream or milk maybe – floating to the top of it.

She hopes she has displayed exactly the right kind of body language to indicate that she is done talking and just wants to do her own thing. It seems, however, that her actions might have been too subtle to get the message across.

'I'm Kelly,' the woman says before Mel gets the chance to get out of bed and pull the curtains back around her bed. 'This is my first baby. Did I hear you say you already had a wee girl?'

Mel doesn't want to come across as rude, but she also doesn't want to answer. The more information she gives, the more she worries the penny will drop and Kelly will recognise exactly where she knows her from. She reminds herself to keep her answers short and sweet.

'I do.'

'Well, that's reassuring.' Kelly smiles.

'How's that?' Mel can't help but ask.

'Well, it can't be so bad if you're doing it a second time,' Kelly says, with a nervous smile that very quickly turns into a flurry of tears which she tries to wave away. 'I'm sorry. I'm just a little scared.'

'Mel here is the perfect person to help you then,' Lucie interjects, propped up on her pillows and looking less grey than the day before. 'She teaches that hypnotherapy in birth thing.'

As soon as Lucie says the words, Mel's blood runs cold. There is just something in her voice so different from when they last spoke, but it's something she recognises instantly. It's how people have been talking to her for the last year.

Or at least that's how the people who haven't crossed the street to avoid talking to her altogether have spoken. There's suspicion in it. Blame, even.

What little of the tea and toast she has managed to swallow now sours in her stomach. She can't even bring herself to glance over at Lucie because she knows in doing so she will see it confirmed in her eyes. But what can she do? It's not like she can start pleading with Lucie to say no more. Or like she can offer to talk to Lucie privately. Kelly, and the other labouring mother, are looking at them both expectantly. Mel wonders if Kelly is putting together the pieces of her own inner jigsaw puzzle – realising that's probably why she recognised Mel in the first place. Sure hasn't she been the talk of the town in every Facebook group from here to Carrickfergus, and every antenatal class and mother and baby group?

'Oh my God... are you *that* Mel?' Kelly asks, her eyes as wide as saucers, reminding Mel of Tilly and her exaggerated mannerisms.

'She is,' Lucie says, disgust dripping from every word. 'She told me her name and what she does yesterday, and it just rang a bell you know, so I googled her and sure enough… she's that doula woman who was there when the wee baby died.'

Mel's cheeks flame red with shame and embarrassment. She wants to start defending herself. She wants to fight her corner, but she just doesn't know if she has the strength. Not after the last few days. In truth, she's not sure she has the strength after the last year – during which she has learned that once people have made their mind up about her, there is very little she can say or do to change it.

Kelly takes a long look at Mel and seems to shrink away from her, but she doesn't speak. It's Lucie who continues to fire her salvo of shots. The same woman whom Mel had listened to yesterday as she cried and felt ill now looks at her as if she were the scum of the earth.

'Yesterday I was feeling really, really ill,' Lucie tells the room, 'and she was trying to tell me about her mumbo jumbo techniques and how they can make things easier and all – but they didn't make things easier for that wee baby. He died. I bet he wouldn't have if—'

'That was nothing to do with hypnobirthing,' Mel protests and she wants to scream that it had nothing to do with her. If Alice could accept that – could post it publicly – then surely these women could too. She considers showing them the post but she doesn't want to engage with them any more. She doesn't want to have to keep explaining herself. Nothing she says or does makes any difference – and clearly Alice's public apology hasn't made a difference either.

24

Ed is unusually quiet in the car on the drive back to the caravan and Mel is grateful for it.

Tilly of course more than makes up for Ed's silence by chattering incessantly about how loud the rain was last night and how much noise the builders are making. She lets slip that she heard one of the team using particularly colourful language – revelling in the opportunity to use the word 'fuck'. Mel tries not to react. She doesn't want to give her daughter cause to start using it as a weapon to get attention – good or bad.

'I think it's okay, 'cos he dropped a brick on his toe, and I think it was very sore so I would probably say "oh fuck" too, if it were me,' Tilly says earnestly. Ed just stares ahead.

Mel doesn't want to react to that either. Or more she doesn't have the energy to react to it. Not now. The last couple of days have drained her entirely. The last few hours have been particularly uncomfortable, waiting in a hospital ward with three women who were eyeing her up and down as if she were some sort of evil murderess. She had already decided she would sign herself out of the hospital if the doctors had said she should stay in. Although no doubt that would only have added more fuel to the fire.

She hasn't told Ed about her conversation with Kelly and Lucie, partially because she feels so absolutely humiliated, partially because Tilly is with them and, perhaps most significantly, as he will likely use it as an excuse to talk about Australia.

There's no denying there has been a shift in the atmosphere between them. Or maybe, she wonders, her paranoia is just in overdrive. It's hard not to feel as if the world is out to get her right now.

The sight of the 'Happy Birthday' balloon bobbing in the breeze as they arrive back at the house sets Mel on edge. She wants to get a pair of scissors and rip the damn thing to pieces. 'I thought you took everything down?' she asks.

'I took the bear down, but Tilly asked me to leave the balloon up.'

'No, Daddy. I wanted the balloon to play with it, but you said, "It's not a toy, Tilly."' She mimics her father's voice impressively well, while Mel glares at her husband.

Ed shrugs his shoulders. 'I thought it was a compromise of sorts. I didn't want her to go looking for it afterwards. And maybe, just maybe, it is a genuine memorial of some kind. We can't rule out the possibility it was something innocent.'

'I can rule that out right now,' she tells him, lifting her bandaged hand from her lap so he can see it clearly.

'Let's not have this conversation.' He nods towards the back seat where Tilly is already unstrapping her seat belt and making for the door.

'Mummy, I'm going to splash in the puddles!' she grins, pulling at the handle.

'Before you freak out,' Ed says, 'Tilly put on her new wellies and her messy play joggers before we left the house, so I think we can allow a little jump. What do you think?'

'Why not? A muddy child is a happy child.'

Tilly grins as if she's just been given all the sweets in the world, and climbs out of the car. She wastes no time in jumping right into the centre of a puddle.

'Mel, look, before we go inside, I need to tell you something.' Ed's voice is low and serious.

Her stomach immediately knots.

'You know how I moved the bear into the house so that Tilly wouldn't get to it?' he asks.

'Yes, and I thought you'd take the balloon down too.' She's unable to keep the barb to herself.

'Mel...' he sighs, clearly exasperated. 'We don't have to go over that again, do we? I've explained myself. Anyway... the bear. When I went into the house this morning, it wasn't where I'd left it. I asked the lads, and no one seemed to know anything. Fergus had a word with them and the only thing they can think of it is that one of them cleared it out into the skip along with the other kitchen waste yesterday evening. I could swear I saw it there last night after they left, but that would mean it just vanished and... well...' he trails off.

'Things don't just vanish. Not in deserted farmhouses in the back end of nowhere.'

'Exactly.'

A prickle of fear runs up her spine. Who could've taken it? It's hardly a desirable object. Why would anyone want it? Unless, she thinks, someone wants to hide what they've done. There's no way now for her to prove that her injury was definitely caused by the bear and not, as everyone and her mother tries to make her believe, by some sharp piece of metal jutting from the rusting gate.

Could the person who left it outside their home in the first place have come back for it? An image of a stranger dressed in black creeping into their house and poking about until they found the bear makes her feel queasy. But how on earth would that person know where Ed had put the bear in the first place? She shakes her head, annoyed that her paranoia is getting the better of her. There's bound to be a more reasonable explanation.

'Did you check the skip?' she asks. 'In case it simply *was* one of the builders clearing up. If that's what happened, then surely it will still be there.'

'The skip that's full to bursting with building materials? No, I didn't. No more than a cursory glance anyway. We didn't need both of us ending up out of action thanks to war wounds.'

It's a fair point. Even if she does desperately want some proof that she's not completely losing her mind.

'Did you at least get the security cameras sorted?' Mel asks him, remembering how he'd told her last night that he was going to do it this morning.

Ed looks down at the steering wheel, avoiding eye contact. 'I haven't quite got round to it, with everything that has been happening, and Tilly was very clingy and…'

She can't help but sigh loudly, frustrated now not only by the missing bear but also by the lack of urgency in improving their security. His inaction in this regard is so at odds with the belief that Alice is still waging a campaign – and not only that, it's getting more serious. So serious in fact that he thinks this might be the perfect time to up sticks.

'There is a lot to do here.' He sounds exasperated. 'I said I'd get round to it, and I'll get round to it.'

'I don't understand you,' she snaps, while trying to keep her face inexpressive. She doesn't want Tilly to look back at them sitting in the car and see their voices contorted in an argument.

'Well ditto,' he says, his voice tight. 'We spend a year being destroyed by Alice Munroe and then all she has to do is post a stupid letter on the internet and all is forgiven? Have you forgotten all those fake accounts she has used? All the lies she has told? Our lives are never going to be normal again. We are going to be looking over our shoulders for the rest of our days for as far as I can see – if the flowers to your parents' house, and this little roadside gift don't prove that, then I don't know what will. But still you refuse to believe now, just because she's pregnant again, that Alice would be capable of such things. The same Alice who has been perfectly capable when it came to making our lives hell and forcing us to leave our home? Come on, Mel! You're a smart woman! Aren't you?'

Mel doesn't recognise this version of her husband. This angry man who seems to regard her as being ridiculously naive – who sounds so patronising and disappointed in her. She doesn't answer him, unable to think of what to say that won't just start her crying. But it seems Ed isn't finished talking anyway.

'And yes, I'm sorry. I haven't put the security cameras up yet but I've been minding our daughter, and dealing with work, and the builders, and my pregnant wife who has high blood pressure – and I'm scared too, Mel.'

They both sit for a moment watching Tilly who, oblivious to the serious subjects being discussed just feet from her, is just living her very best life jumping in and out of puddles, covering her wellies in thick, brown mud and squealing with delight as the cold water splashes so high it splatters her hands and face.

'We invested so much to come here,' Ed says, his voice quieter now. 'We've poured everything into this house – into relocating my business here. Every penny of our savings is being held in reserve for this project and I think we'll eat through it – and probably more. The cost of materials is still soaring even with paring back, it's going to be a struggle. And I've still been okay with those challenges. I'd be okay with losing our savings if it meant we were safe and happy. But if you still don't *feel* safe, if we *aren't* safe here, then we might as well have pissed that money up the wall.'

'I didn't realise…' Mel stutters. She knows this has been a big investment, but she didn't realise just how close to the financial wire they were creeping.

'I didn't want to tell you because you've enough to worry about,' he says. 'And it's only money, in the grand scheme of things. What does it matter compared with our security? I thought we were leaving all that nastiness behind. We'd tighten our belts for a while but we wouldn't even mind because we'd be here, in this beautiful place, with our family, and it would all come good. But it's not coming good, is it? I turned down a project today. A good project. It would require me to be on site at a build for at least a month. How am I supposed to feel okay with leaving you behind with two small children when this madness is happening? And when you allow someone who caused so much hurt and damage to our family back in your life? It just feels like it's never going to stop.'

Words stick in Mel's throat. She hadn't realised Ed had turned down a project. That he felt he couldn't leave her and the children to go and work, as he would have done in the past. That he has his own wounds from what has happened over the course of the last year.

They fall into silence again. Mel's afraid to say the wrong thing. Maybe Ed thinks he already has.

'It's probably the case that one of the lads lifted it and threw it out not knowing what it was, and then was too scared to own up when I asked them,' he says after a moment. 'If it means that much to you, then I'll go looking in the skip later.'

'You don't have to,' she says, trying to show him she's been listening and knowing it is unlikely to be of any use to anyone any more. It will have been so contaminated that it would have no evidential value. And maybe Ed is right. Maybe she has been too quick to trust Alice again – so desperate for things to be okay that she has ignored obvious warning signs. At the same time, the small voice in her head asks her if she can really trust Ed, or does he have that big Australian ulterior motive driving him?

The reality is, she thinks, that she can't trust anyone but herself. Not for any of it. Someone is trying to scare her, and they are succeeding. They are trying to destroy her sense of calm, and they are succeeding. She just doesn't know if it's Alice, Ed or some unknown foe or foes. Or perhaps it's a combination of all of the above.

Just as if the universe were trying to prove that point, a shadow crosses the side of the car, followed by a loud bang on her window. Mel reaches for Ed's hand, forgetting for a moment that her own is injured. She winces as her hand finds his, but doesn't allow herself to focus on the pain shooting up her arm. She is looking for Tilly. Staring straight at the giant puddle where, just seconds ago, her daughter had been jumping around and having the time of her life. Instant dread hits her like a hammer – the thought of Alice outside Tilly's nursery trying to entice her away comes to her mind.

She tries to call out for Tilly, but fear binds her voice tight inside her throat. Where is her daughter? How can she have just disappeared from their view?

Another bang jolts her into action. She screeches her daughter's name, her panic building. 'TILLY!' Her voice breaks through this time as her free hand scrambles for the door handle to push whoever is standing there away and get out of the car to find her daughter.

25

The feeling of not being able to breathe but needing to move is as exhausting as it is overwhelming. Mel sucks in what little air she can in unsatisfying gasps as she pushes the car door open and tries to stand on wobbling legs.

She's aware of Ed's voice, but it's just noise. She doesn't have any energy to try and focus on it while she's searching for her baby.

Even though her vision is blurring and her head is spinning, she's aware of vague colours and shapes around her, and she wills her brain to sort through them and discard anything which couldn't possibly be Tilly as quickly as possible. The dark shape to her side – the figure who was pounding on the window of the car seems to have taken a step back.

Across the yard she can make out the tall, wide frame of whom she guesses to be Fergus, followed by a couple of smaller, thinner shapes – the bright yellow glare from their hi-vis jackets hurting her eyes.

The sound of the world around her melts away until all she can hear is herself gulping at the air, and the thud of her heart.

'TILLY!' she shouts again, as hot tears start to run down her face. This is too much, she thinks. These never-ending threats and worries.

While a part of her registers this for what it is – a panic attack – she cannot stop the voice in her head, the one that had told her she was just being paranoid, but who is now screaming that maybe, this time, it will be different. Maybe this is the time her heart will actually stop beating, She will suffocate, or hyper-ventilate so much that she will faint, fall and hurt herself.

Mel feels a hand grab onto her arm and her very nerve endings react with such a ferocious anger that she immediately wrenches free.

She doesn't want to see anything or anyone who is not Tilly. It's all too much. All of it. She wants to scream into the void that she didn't do anything wrong. She doesn't deserve to be tortured like this. She doesn't deserve to worry that some sort of vengeful presence will tear her children from her. She is tired of living in fear of retribution for something she didn't do.

'Mel?' A voice. Ed, she thinks. Her Ed.

'Are you okay, pet?' Another voice, one that is vaguely famil-iar, comes at her between gasps for air. She can't understand why they're both so calm, when Tilly is gone.

Her hands are reaching for her daughter, grasping at the air around her like a child playing blind man's buff, just hoping to land on what she needs.

Images, awful images, swirl through her mind. Things she has seen and wishes she hadn't. Things she fears are yet to come. Tilly cold and pale. Her own arms empty as well as her womb. And people pointing, whispering, *I know who you are.*

I know what you did.

Mel's vision tunnels in front of her as the lack of sufficient air to her lungs bends her double and her body slackens with fear and grief and—

'Mummy! Mummy! What's wrong? What's wrong with you, why are you crying?' A child's touch – a small, warm hand taking Mel's in hers – and fear immediately releases its grip on her, allowing her to swallow a deep, wonderful lungful of air, and the world to start to come into focus again. As it does, Mel pulls her daughter close to her. Tilly looks up at her, still bewildered and looking more than a little frightened.

'Why were you shouting, Mummy? I was just over there!' Tilly says, pointing to the small flower bed by the side of the house, where a cluster of daffodils is dancing in the breeze. 'I was going to get the flowers for you and my baby brother,' she adds, her brow crinkled with concern. Guilt washes over Mel as she realises Tilly must think she is being scolded and that her mum is angry with her. How can she explain to her daughter that she was just scared without giving Tilly cause to be scared too? There's no suitable way to explain to a four-year-old what's happening in Mel's head. There's no nice way to tell her about everything that has happened without putting fear and sadness into her innocent, precious little mind. And Mel doesn't want to do that. She doesn't want to hurt her like that.

'I was just being a silly sausage,' Mel says. 'I couldn't see you for just a second and I was a little scared that you had run away to join the circus.' She forces a lightness into her voice as if this were all just one big game and not their entire lives.

Tilly looks as if she were sizing her up before saying, in a very matter-of-fact way, 'You are very, very silly. Girls who are only four don't be in the circus!'

'I know!' Mel tells her with a squeeze and for those briefest of moments, she feels as if they are alone in their safe little bubble – until, that is, she remembers the bang on the window that set her panic off. Doing her very best to continue to appear outwardly calm, she looks around the yard and is shocked to see that the person standing by the car is not some angry thug or stealthy assassin, but Sheila Quigg, face sheet-white, clearly quite taken aback by what she has just witnessed.

'I… I didn't mean to give you such a fright,' she stutters. 'My Barney's always telling me I've neither style nor grace about me and don't know my own strength. I'm not one for being delicate and ladylike.' Mel looks at her short, dumpy frame, the wiry strands of white hair that point in a multitude of directions, and her weather-worn face. She looks like a woman who has worked hard all her life and not had much time or need for refinement. 'It was him who saw the commotion yesterday when he was driving down to the bottom fields. Said it looked like you were in a bad way and then there was me, worrying about the babby and how your man there would be coping if you were laid up in the hospital and so I thought I'd bring down something for you all.'

That's when Mel notices she is carrying a well-worn pot. 'It's nothing fancy, now. Just a good oul stew. Perfect for days like this. I didn't mean to give you a scare.'

Mel wants to fold in on herself with embarrassment at frightening an old lady. It's bad enough, she thinks, that she has acted like a lunatic in front of Ed and Tilly, not to mention Fergus and his men, but now she's gone and put the fear of God in her elderly neighbour who was, it seems, only trying to do them another act of kindness. Guilt doesn't so much as wash over her as threaten to knock her to the ground. Mel is trying her best to find the right thing to say but she just stands, her mouth open and her brain tired and still fighting the after-effects of the adrenaline surge that just powered its way through her body.

'Sheila,' Ed says, taking the pot from their neighbour. 'This is so very, very kind of you. Hard to beat a good stew, especially after a busy day. This will go down a treat for dinner tonight.' He lifts the lid off the pot and peaks inside; one eyebrow raises and he nods in approval. 'This looks perfect. As good as your bacon and cabbage! I'd nearly heat it up and have it now.'

Ed has such wonderful warmth and charm that Sheila starts to blush and comes over all schoolgirlish. As she flutters her eyelashes at him and breaks into a shy smile, Mel can see the echoes of the beautiful young woman she must have been in her earlier days. Perhaps before farming and child-rearing took the lifeblood from her.

'Yes,' Mel adds. 'It really is very kind indeed and it's so thoughtful of you to call in and check on us.' She wants to leave it at that. As much as she appreciates the gesture, she just wants some time in her own space with her family. She wants Sheila to say it was no problem at all, and then say goodbye before heading on her way back up the hill in her worn wellies, but she also knows that's unlikely to happen, especially as she had already made herself at home in their caravan before now.

Before she can say anything, Ed is inviting Sheila in. 'We can't have you heading back up that hill without so much as a cup of tea to warm you up first. Now, we don't have anything as nice as those delicious biscuits you bake, so you'll have to make do with chocolate digestives, if that's okay with you?'

'I never say no to a chocolate digestive,' Sheila says with a smile before Ed leads her towards the caravan door, Tilly skipping behind, well aware she'll get a chocolate biscuit out of this situation too.

It doesn't take long for Mel to start to feel a little claustrophobic once they are all inside.

'You look tired, dear,' Sheila says. 'You need to keep off your feet. Keep you and that babby of yours nice and safe. You're awfully pale. Have you had your iron checked? Now sit down there, and me and this good man of yours will make your tea.'

Mel does as she's told even though it feels weird to follow the instruction of someone she doesn't really know in her own place. How can it be that Sheila looks more at home here than she does? Mel watches as the older woman takes off her coat and hangs it on the back of a chair, having already pulled off her muddy boots and left them by the door. Tilly is sitting down at the table and has started scribbling furiously in one of her art books – coat and wellies still on. When Sheila reminds her this is a place for indoor clothes, she jumps to attention without so much as word of fuss and takes them off.

Mel watches this scene, and her husband pulling mugs from the cupboards and dropping teabags into them. Her hand throbs as if to remind her it's still injured, so she raises it slightly and rests it against her body.

'That's an impressive bandage,' Sheila says as she sits down opposite her. 'Was that what started the commotion then? Barney said it looked like you'd hurt your hand. Blood everywhere, he said. But he's not a nosey man so he didn't want to stay and gawp yesterday. I'm his opposite – nosey as the day is long – so I have no problem asking what happened,' Sheila says with a laugh.

'Ach, it's just a cut,' Mel tells her. 'Deep enough, you know, but I'll live. The hospital kept me in as a precaution because my blood pressure was a little high, but all good. Home now to rest, thank God.'

'And rest you must,' Sheila fusses. 'Let your man here do all the running about.'

'Oh, she lets me do that already,' Ed gives her a cheeky wink. Mel forces a smile on her face.

'Well, don't forget, we're just up the road if you need

anything. Neighbours need to watch out for one another,' Sheila says. 'That's the way it's always been around here and I know it's not easy raising wee ones. Takes a village and all that, so never you be afraid to knock on my door.' She gives another warm smile and there is a sincerity in her words that Mel wants to hang on to but just can't. It's hard to trust anyone these days.

'Here you go, Sheila,' Ed says, handing her a mug of tea. 'Now just let me go bring over those biscuits.'

'You're very kind,' she tells him. 'This looks like a great cup of tea all the same.'

'Well, I'm told I make a decent cup.' He passes her the plate of biscuits before sitting down beside Tilly. 'Tell me this, was there a bad accident or something along this stretch of road in the past? Maybe a fatality? Around this time of year?'

'Oh good God, no. Not in my memory anyway. Thankfully we're a bit far off the beaten track for boy racers and the like. We don't get much traffic at all if truth be told. Why do you ask? Is it something to do with that balloon bobbing about out there? I wondered if that baby of yours had made an early appearance.'

'The baby is still safe and sound where he should be,' Ed says. 'As you've no doubt noticed. But, yes, it is about the balloon. It just appeared yesterday, along with a teddy bear tied to the gate. Mel here went to look at it, and see if there was a card or anything, and that's when she cut her hand. Probably on the rusty old nails on the gate, so unfortunately the bear got soiled but we wondered...'

On one level Mel appreciates that her husband isn't spilling all their family problems, but she feels her ire rising that he is playing it all down. She knows it was no rusty nail on the gate that sliced into her hand... doesn't she?

'Dear God,' Sheila exclaims. 'Well, I'll tell you this much, I've thought that gate was in a bad old way before. No maintenance you see, and that's when the rust sets in. If it gets bad enough it can be as sharp as a knife. Dirty too. Nasty old business. You poor thing. But no, I don't recall there being any road accidents here. There's definitely never been any kind of a memorial left there in my time. Now that is strange. It makes no sense to me.'

'Nor to us,' Ed says amiably, and again Mel feels conflicted between vindication that she had been right, but also fear as to what that means.

'Although...' Sheila says, pausing, her brow wrinkling as she tries to pull something from her memory. 'All that being said, there is a bit of story here...'

'A story?' Ed asks. 'Where's here?'

'This house but... but you know it's most likely just nonsense. I don't believe in such things myself but my Barney... well, he might tell you different.'

Mel wishes the older woman would just get to whatever point she is trying to make, but she doesn't want to snap. She hasn't painted herself in the best light as it is without making things worse.

'I probably shouldn't say more,' Sheila says. 'I'm conscious of there being little ears in the room...' She nods her head towards Tilly.

'Tilly, love,' Mel says. 'Would you like to watch a little YouTube on Daddy's iPad?'

Tilly's face lights up at the prospect and she grins. 'Yes please, Mummy!'

Mel is already reaching for the iPad and the bright pink children's earphones that Tilly uses with it. 'Here, pet, let me get this going for you and then why don't you take it through to your room and watch it with your teddies?'

Tilly doesn't need to be told twice. She jumps down from her chair and takes the precious iPad from Mel before running through to her room.

'I think the little ears will be busy for a while now,' Mel says with a smile. 'What is it you were going to say?'

Sheila shifts in her seat, getting comfortable. 'Well, as I said, I'm not sure that I believe this but there's a story that has gone around these parts. That there was a wee boy who died in your house there. Years ago, mind. Before my time. I think it was maybe the twenties or the thirties. I'd have to ask Barney. He'd know the story better seeing as he has lived here all his life and his family before him.'

Mel looks to Ed whose expression says it all. He does not believe Sheila. He has never believed in such 'nonsense'. She shoots him a warning glance not to be rude and to at least listen to what Sheila has to say.

'The wee lad, only a baby himself, crawled off and was found face down in the stream a wee bit later. They say the wain haunts this place and you can hear him crying at night sometimes.' Sheila's eyes are wide, her voice solemn and stern as she relays this eerie tale. 'I believe there are some people – people who love spooky stories and the like – who like to scare themselves stupid by coming out here to visit. We had to chase young ones out of this house before more than once – when it was lying unsold. You know what young ones are like – get a story in their head about a place being haunted and then you find them crawling all over it making videos for that YouTuber or whatever it's called. I suppose those wee gifts could be something to do with that but... sure, I wouldn't know. I'd be more likely to think any crying heard is the foxes or feral cats around here more than any sort of ghostly baby.'

Mel isn't sure what to think. She has never considered herself to be particularly superstitious or a believer in ghosts or the afterlife, but still a chill runs down her spine. Another poor, dead baby. She can't bear it.

'So, Ed...' Sheila's voice is bright as she changes the subject. 'Is that for Edward, or Edwin, or Eddie?'

'Just Ed will do,' he says back with a smile. Ed Davison could charm the birds from the trees.

'Your wife here is a bit of a dark horse. Plays her cards close to her chest. What brings you over to God's country then?' Sheila doesn't break eye contact as she slurps from her teacup. Clearly her nosey side is back, Mel thinks, before chiding herself for being so uncharitable. This is an older woman who is offering them support at a time when support is thin on the ground.

'Ah, well, we just fancied a change,' Ed tells her. 'And you get more bang for your buck over here. This house, in this area, just seemed too good an opportunity to turn down. Sure, isn't it just gorgeous? How could anyone resist wanting to live here? Although maybe we'd have thought different if we'd known about the house's sad past.'

Sheila gives her head a little shake. 'Honestly, I wouldn't give that story a moment's thought. Sure, every house that's been up a while has a story attached to it. No doubt many of them have been embellished over time. You can take it from me that this is a great place to live. And a great place to raise children – letting them have the run of the fields and the woods and having their lungs filled with fresh, clean air.' She shrugs. 'Nothing would make me happier than to see my grandchildren grow up around here and enjoy that same freedom. But life doesn't always turn out the way we'd like, does it?'

There's an underlying sadness in her voice as she speaks, and Mel can't help but feel a little sorry for this woman who so clearly longs to have her family around her. Sheila isn't one to mope for long though and quickly switches back to using her cheery voice. 'Well, fair play to you both taking this place on. It's a lot of work all the same,' she says. 'Especially with the two wee ones to be looking after.'

'Not at all. Sure we've a great team of builders doing the heavy lifting so Mel here can focus on the children,' Ed replies breezily, offering Sheila another biscuit.

'That's a vocation in itself. Child-rearing.' Sheila gives Mel the full head-to-toe scan before she speaks. 'And your name,' she says, 'is that short for Melanie?'

'Melissa,' Mel replies. 'But no one calls me that except my parents when I'm in trouble.' There's something in the way Sheila reacts to this that makes Mel feel uneasy. She can't quite put her finger on why. It's just a momentary change in her expression – so quick that Mel isn't even 100 per cent sure it happened. It's more likely, she thinks, that her body is just on high alert, perceiving every last thing as a threat.

'So how long have you lived around these parts yourself?' Ed asks, and Mel feels an immediate relief that the focus has been taken away from her.

'Ach, a brave while,' she says. 'My Barney was born up in the house we live in now. He's never lived anywhere else and wouldn't want to. That farm has been in his family for generations. There'll be no moving him out of that house until the day they come and carry him out in a box. If they'd let him, he'd be happy to be stuffed and left to sit on his favourite armchair till the house falls down around him.' She laughs, then takes a bite of her biscuit before washing it down with another slurp of her tea.

'Anyway, Barney and me, we're just two grumpy old goats doing the same thing day in and day out. It's not very lively around here and that suits us just fine. Having new neighbours is enough excitement for us. Well, especially now we know that you aren't here to turn the house into some sort of monstrosity of a newbuild, or stick a couple of yurts out the back. We don't want a lock of yuppies arriving every weekend for a bit of country living. We're happy it's just the pair of ye, and the babies too, of course,' she says. 'It's always nice to have babies around. So tell me this, Ed, what do you work at that allows you to shift over the country so easily?'

Forty-five minutes and another cup of tea later, Sheila waves as she heads for the sagging balloon at the gate and turns left to walk back up the hill to her farm, having refused the offer of a lift because she wants to keep her 'old bones moving'.

'She'd be a good hire for the Spanish Inquisition if it were still going,' Ed jokes as he tidies up. 'She's a way of wheedling information out of people. I think she stopped just short of asking for our PIN numbers.'

'It's just PIN,' Mel says absent-mindedly – her mind racing as she tries to figure out just what it is about Sheila that makes her feel uneasy. Or maybe, as Ed keeps reminding her, she just has an overactive imagination.

'What do you mean?' Ed asks.

'It's just PIN, no need for "number" after it. The letters themselves stand for "Personal Identification Number" so saying "number" after it makes it become "Personal Identification Number Number", which makes no sense...'

She's talking but she's not really thinking about what she's saying. All she can think about is Sheila and why she has a feeling she's not a person to be trusted either.

26

'You're incredibly on edge,' Ed says that evening after Tilly has gone to bed. They have been watching TV together, but Mel has been like a cat on a hot tin roof – fidgeting and unable to get comfortable and even less able to concentrate.

'There's a lot to be on edge about.'

'Maybe, but you need to try and find some way to relax. It's not good for the baby, or for you for that matter. Here, why don't you let me give you a foot rub? Take your mind off it for a bit. All these problems will still be waiting for us in the morning.'

'I'm not sure it's something I can just switch on and off,' she tells him, although she does rest her swollen feet in his lap and lets him start to massage them. It's far from the sensual experience such intimacy used to be – her bandaged, swollen, and pregnant in a mobile home, terrified at every creak and clatter from outside.

He sighs. 'We need to think of a way to get through this,' he says, his tone gentle and caring, just like the Ed she has known all these years. 'You're making yourself unwell with the worry.

Tilly and I feel like we're walking on eggshells around you all the time. I'm not saying that to make you feel bad, or guilty...'

'Then why are you saying it? Did we not discuss this earlier? Was that not enough? I know it's stressful, Ed. I know it's not good for any of us.'

'Your reaction today when Sheila knocked on the car window... it was a bit extreme,' he says, and no doubt he'd tell her he was only concerned for her well-being, but she can't help but hear his judgement and frustration.

'I was startled by Sheila banging on the window of the car.' Mel feels her hackles rise as her defences kick in. 'And I couldn't see Tilly. Of course that panicked me. This is a building site, Ed. Not a playground. Anything could happen to her.'

'I knew where she was. I'd have told you – in fact I *tried* to tell you – but you were too far gone to take in what I was saying. You were already out of the car giving Sheila a heart attack. God knows what she thought of it all. It's not as if we haven't given her enough to gossip about already.'

Mel tears up at the frustration in his voice.

'I'm sorry,' she stutters, already knowing that nothing will stop the tears that are about to fall.

Ed sighs again and runs his hand through his hair. 'And I'm sorry too. If I'm being honest, I'm under pressure and I'm not handling it the best.'

'Please,' she begs him. 'Please let's not talk about Australia. Not tonight. We can talk tomorrow if you want. Or soon. I just don't have the emotional bandwidth to talk about it now. Love, if you could see inside my head right now, you'd see what a mess it is.'

Mel doesn't want to cry even though she has never been afraid to let her guard down in front of Ed before. He has been her safe space from almost as soon as they first met. She doesn't like that doubt now exists between them. That she no longer feels she has 100 per cent trust in him.

'Okay. We won't talk about it. Not tonight. But we do have to talk about it. All of it, at some stage. I'm not sure I'm prepared to just sit and wait for the next big disaster to hit – the next bouquet of flowers, the next poisoned messages online or whatever else might happen. Because I think we both know something else is going to happen. This isn't going away.'

They sit in silence for a bit. Mel doesn't know how long. Her feet are still resting on Ed's lap but he has stopped rubbing them. They are both just staring at the TV, not seeing or caring what is on the screen.

When Ed's phone bursts into life, Emma's name flashing up on the screen, he reaches immediately for it. 'I'll take this in the bedroom so I don't disturb you,' he says, answering the call with a very cheery 'hello'. 'You're up and at 'em early this morning!' Ed says as he walks out of the room.

Mel has never before felt uneasy when Ed has been talking with his twin. She has known from the very start of their relationship that the siblings maintain a close bond despite the miles between them. It isn't like Mel isn't fond of Emma – the pair had gotten along great since they first met when Ed took her for an extended holiday to Australia, back when she was still working as a teacher and got to enjoy the summer break.

Emma had even been a bridesmaid at their wedding and is Tilly's godmother. Up until now, she hadn't given Mel any reason not to like her. But things have changed. Mel wonders how much Ed's renewed passion about moving to Australia is of his own making and how much of it is being fuelled by Emma and her ever positive look at life.

There's no doubt, Mel thinks, that she is being talked about now. Ed will be sharing his woes – telling his sister how he thinks his wife is naive and how things are only getting more and more stressful. Her face blazes with the heat at the very thought. She wants to scream that she's doing her best and she and Ed had both agreed, a very long time ago, that they would stay in Northern Ireland to be near her parents.

She really wishes she were near her mother now. Wishes her mum could pamper her and help her with the tasks that are harder to do with just one hand. Wishes her Daddy could make her feel secure in the way only a father can. At the same time she knows she does not want to bring her troubles to her parents' door ever again. The flowers had been bad enough. The look on her mother's face as she spoke about them would haunt Mel for the rest of her days. She'll never forgive herself for causing her parents such distress.

Defeated and exhausted, she longs to go to bed. Even if it is the uncomfortable double in that pokey little bedroom. Of course, Ed is still in there. She can hear the low hum of his voice as he chats animatedly with his sister. Hopefully, Mel thinks, they won't talk for too long and then she can put this awful day behind her and get some sleep.

The documentary is just coming to an end, and Mel's eyes are growing increasingly heavy when her phone screen lights up. Glancing down, she sees Alice's name. Thankfully it's just a message. She doesn't think she would have the emotional or physical strength to have a conversation with Alice – or anyone else for that matter – just now.

The message is simple enough.

> Just checking how you are? The police never did call about the flowers.

She wonders for a second what her answer to Alice's question would be if she were to be completely honest. It would more than likely be that she is absolutely broken, in pain, scared and worried that far from saving her family, moving here was looking like it might just tear it apart.

But Alice isn't her friend, she remembers. She's not a person she can confide in any more. And although she might want to believe that her apology had been genuine, and that she truly wants to make sure that she is okay, Mel knows that she can't really trust the other woman and she doesn't have the energy to pretend any more.

Not tonight anyway.

Leaving the message on 'read', she switches off the TV and wanders through to the bedroom. She's too exhausted to even think about brushing her teeth, so she just climbs under the covers, hoping that will be enough to give Ed the none-too-subtle hint that she needs to go to sleep.

'Yes, I promise you,' Ed says down the phone. 'We're going to talk about it. And I'll make sure to tell Mel about the schools.' He laughs just as Mel feels tears prick at her eyes. 'Yeah, sure. Send them over. It can't hurt to look,' he adds. 'No promises mind, Ems. This is our home, so don't get your hopes up too high.'

There's a pause as Emma answers, not loud enough for Mel to hear what she's saying.

'Yes, I know, sis. Look, I promise you, we're being very careful. I love you very much.'

He says his goodbyes and ends the call. Mel lies as still as she can, keeping her breath slow and steady and her eyes closed tight so that it looks like she is asleep. She doesn't have the energy to deal with Ed or to discuss the conversation he has just had with his sister.

Mel knows she doesn't want to move to the other side of the world, but she's starting to think she might not have a choice. Not if she wants to save her sanity, and her family.

27

35 WEEKS + 1 DAY

Mel is the kind of tired you feel deep in your bones. The kind that encompasses your mental and emotional self as well as your physical self. What little sleep she did manage to get last night was plagued with nightmares.

She lost count of the number of times she got up needing to pee – the baby now seemingly delighted to be using her bladder as a trampoline. For the occasional five minutes in which her bladder had been empty, she had to contend with the throbbing pain in her hand. Paracetamol could only do so much to ease the discomfort and that 'so much' was even less than inadequate.

Most disruptive of all though was the constant overthinking. Life was not supposed to be this complicated, she thought as she had tossed and turned in the dark. Not that long ago, in the grand scheme of things, her life had been beautifully simple. She probably had taken all that for granted to an extent but, she thinks, at least she did appreciate a lot of it. She'd loved her job. Adored her husband. Would walk through heaven and hell for her daughter. She'd felt so very positive about the future – delighted to be living her dream life.

'It's understandable you're feeling down, love,' her mother says over the phone as Mel tries to stretch out her back on the gym ball she bought to help prepare for labour. 'You've an awful lot on your shoulders. My goodness, any one of the things you're dealing with would be enough to send a person over the edge. The house, the baby, all that nasty Alice business. Have you heard from her since at all? We've not heard a word more here.'

'I heard from her yesterday. She sent a message just to check in on me. But I was too exhausted to reply. It had been a long day and it's not like I even had a good night's sleep in the hospital...'

As soon as the word is out of her mouth she knows she has made a huge mistake. The decision not to tell her parents about the incident with the bear and her subsequent admission had been deliberate. Mel hadn't been sure how much more worry her mother could take and yet here she was piling worry on top of worry.

'Hospital? What's this about hospital?' her mother says, her voice shrill. Mel can hear her father asking what's going on in the background and she has to make a quick decision on just how much to tell them.

'It was nothing, Mum,' she lies. 'My blood pressure was a wee bit up and they just wanted to keep me under observation to check on the baby. All is good. They only kept me the one night.' She won't tell her mother about her hand injury. Certainly not today. And she absolutely won't tell her any theory about the teddy bear being left by one of Alice's supporters. She'll mould that story to one more palatable to her parents when the time comes. Maybe tell them it was a memorial and it was the rusty gate that had done the damage.

'You're not lying to me and still in the hospital? The baby is okay? Isn't he?'

'I'm at home, Mum. Here, I'll prove it. I'll just call Tilly. She's out in the yard with her daddy.' Tilly is always a welcome distraction for her grandparents.

'Tills! Granny and Grandad are on the phone! Come and say hello!' she calls and is rewarded with Tilly barrelling in the door like the human hurricane she is ten seconds later. She's wearing a child-size high-vis and safety hat – a present from Fergus when he arrived on site this morning.

'I'm very busy helping Daddy,' Tilly says breathlessly, running across and grabbing the phone before immediately launching into an in-depth chat with her granny. Thank God, Mel thinks, for four-year-olds.

'Mummy is resting 'cos my baby brother is being a rascal,' Tilly says. 'And her hand is still sore so she has to take it easy.'

Shit, Mel thinks. She didn't factor in her daughter telling her granny about her hand. There's another something she'll have to cover up.

'Tilly, I think Daddy is calling you. You better say goodbye to Granny and scoot!'

'Bye, Granny!' Tilly sing-songs without a moment's pause – handing the phone back over to Mel who is already preparing herself for the onslaught of yet more questions.

'It's nothing serious,' she lies as soon as the phone is to her ear. 'I cut my hand on some broken glass on the site. It's grand. I got a tetanus jab and everything. It's fine.'

'Are tetanus jabs safe when you're pregnant? You did tell them you're pregnant, didn't you?' her mother fusses.

'Yes, Mum. Tetanus jabs are perfectly safe when you're pregnant, but no I didn't tell them. I didn't need to. It's quite obvious at this stage!'

Her mother laughs just a little in response and it is so lovely to hear that sound after all the stress of the last few days. 'Your dad and I are thinking of taking a drive down to see you some- time soon. We might as well get a feel for this new place of yours sooner rather than later.'

'I'm afraid there's not much to see here, at the moment – certainly nothing that would impress you. It's a proper building site.' Even though Mel would dearly love her parents to come down to visit. 'It might be a bit more put together by the time this little one makes his appearance. The floors will be down again at least.'

'Are you sure you've not taken on too much?' her mother asks.

'Of course I'm sure,' Mel says, and it's another lie. She feels a knot in her back tighten and knows she needs to change posi- tion. She also knows she's very likely to make a very loud noise when she does so. 'Mum, this baby is making me need to wee again. I'd better go before I risk an accident. But I promise you I'm okay. We're all okay. I'll talk to you soon, I promise.'

'Okay, love,' her mother says. 'I'm on my way out anyway. Your dad and I are going to go out for some lunch. But promise me, darling, that you are taking proper care of yourself. You're under an incredible amount of stress and we worry about you.'

'I know, Mum. I worry about you too, you know.'

Mel ends the call wishing she could've told her mother not to worry and really have meant it. She wishes she could escape the worry herself, even just for a couple of hours, to slip into a long, peaceful sleep. She's starting to wonder if she will ever sleep properly again.

Against her better judgement she decides to look online and see what reaction there has been to Alice's post. Maybe, just maybe, she might find some clue in there as to who is behind the bear, the calls and the flowers. She also longs to know if Alice's words have had a positive effect that she just hasn't been able to see yet. If she can show Ed that the tide is turning, despite recent events, maybe it will help him settle into their life here.

She feels sick as she types her own name into Google and waits for the results to load. As she expects, the same vitriolic content is still online. There is a lengthy Reddit thread about Jacob's birth which pulls no punches and is loaded with insane conspiracy theories. She, according to the thread, is 'a sociopathic charlatan who likes playing God'. It's so off the wall but Mel can't help but keep reading.

She's pleased, however, to see a new thread. This time titled 'Alice Munroe apologises to doula'. Without wasting so much as a second she clicks the link.

MomOfThreeRascals: Well now – we have it. After all your conspiracy theories and hate on Mel Davidson, Alice Munroe has issued a massive apology and admitted that she had been lying. Haven't I said so much all along? Alice was, like, seventeen or eighteen days overdue? And she didn't see a doctor? And we were supposed to believe that was because of her doula? She destroyed that woman's life with her lies. I don't understand how Mel isn't suing her for everything she's got.

CrunchyMama: You know that it's okay to go overdue, don't you? A baby comes when it is ready. All those docs who force induction on mothers just want to pump you with hormones and chemical compounds to eject those babies from your uterus before they are good and ready. You don't think that chemicals cross the placenta? We're harming our babies and big pharma is making customers for life. If you ask me, the apology is just for show. I bet Mel has taken legal action or something to force her into apologising. The wording is very deliberate.

RealityBites: Oh, come on! Not everything is a big pharma conspiracy FGS! Studies have shown that the placenta can start to fail if you go that far overdue. That's way more likely to harm our babies. Just like Jacob. Wasn't that one of the factors in his death?

CrunchyMama: You don't believe everything a coroner says, do you? You don't think they're in the pocket of big pharma too?

MomOfThreeRascals: I think we're diluting the argument here, guys. This isn't about big pharma. This is about a mom going two and half weeks over and then blaming it all on her doula when it went wrong. The math wasn't mathing. It never was.

Big Bad Wolf: This is just my theory, but I have to agree with Crunchy Mama. That apology isn't genuine. You don't just get over the death of your baby. I'd say there's been some sort of settlement – probably out of court with an NDA. Sure hasn't Mel been run out of Carrickfergus? Rumour has it she's moved to the countryside. Her and her husband are doing some sort of big *Grand Designs* refurb of an old farmhouse. If you can afford to do something like that then money clearly isn't a problem. Typical of someone as arrogant as that char-latan, buying her way out of trouble, and waiting until the anniversary of Jacob's death is approaching to take advan-tage of a grieving mother is despicable.

Mel clicks on Big Bad Wolf's profile, wondering who this person is and where they are getting their information from. Yes, a lot of it was utter fiction but clearly, they knew some of the details. They knew she had moved to the countryside after all and was carrying out a renovation project. This was not information that was widely known, so it stands to reason that whoever is behind the account is someone who knows Mel and Ed to some extent.

The profile information doesn't provide many clues. What it does though is show that this person seems to be fixated on Mel and making sure she is punished for what happened. The account was only registered in June of last year and immediately started posting in the parenting threads about why people should not hire Mel. It hadn't taken long for this to morph into conspiracy theories which Big Bad Wolf seemed to enjoy sharing with anyone willing to listen, or read.

Her back aching and her head pounding again, Mel decides now might just be the time to try and get the nap she so desperately wants. Looking at the clock, she sees it's almost time for Tilly's daily nap. She could use this as an excuse to steal her daughter away and have a little sleep beside her. She figures she might as well make the most of it. God only knows how much longer she will get away with persuading Tilly to have a little afternoon snooze, and once the new baby arrives, her focus will be on him and not so much just on enjoying her daughter's proximity.

Ed is only too delighted to direct Tilly back inside. 'Fergus and I are going to head to the builders' yard,' he says. 'It's not the best place for a four-year-old to hang out.'

'Especially not a four-year-old as inquisitive as Tilly.' Mel smiles.

'Lock the door after I go out,' Ed tells her. 'Especially if you too are going to have a little sleep. I want to make sure you both stay safe.'

He kisses her gently on the forehead before bending to kiss Tilly in the same way. It's a rare moment of pure affection between them. These last days have been so strained, this gives her a little hope that he does indeed love her and their family.

Once in her bed, it doesn't take long for her, or Tilly, to fall asleep.

Mel slips into a dream where she is rocking her newborn baby boy as he sleeps soundly in her arms. She revels in the warmth of his skin, the softness of his downy hair and the way his hand curls around her finger. So small and so perfect. They are just mother and son, existing in their perfect little bubble. There is no sound except for their breathing together. There is no one to ask them questions, or tell her she's wrong to feel so at peace, or tell her she's naive to believe Alice. In fact Alice doesn't factor at all here. It is just about the two of them and their perfect bond. It's a message from her subconscious maybe that everything will be okay. As long as she has her family, she knows she will have everything that really matters.

They are together, curled on a soft chair and the only thing she can see – the only thing she wants to look at – is her beautiful boy. And he is beautiful, with long lashes and a button nose. His hair dark, just like his sister's was. She could quite happily stay in this reality forever.

Starting to sing 'Twinkle, Twinkle' to him, she watches as he shifts just a little bit, scrunching up and then stretching in that adorable way newborns do. She tells herself to enjoy every moment. This stage – the gorgeous, exhausting but wonderful newborn stage – does not last for long and it is always a blessing to be able to enjoy it. Especially now, in this sleepy safe bubble where there are no mystery flowers or gifts left at the gate. No cross words from Ed, or tearful pleas from her mother.

A soft jangling catches her attention and she looks to the window where a mobile made of stained glass tinkles gently in the breeze, casting its rainbow of colours around this unfamiliar room. The noise is so soothing, she thinks, until the breeze picks up and the once gentle jangle becomes percussive, loud and intrusive. Much too loud and no longer musical. In discordant notes, the pieces of glass, now shards, crash and smash against one another, sending jagged splinters through the air. She tries to protect her boy, tries to fold her body around him but the splinters slice through her – through skin, muscle and bone – and nothing she can do seems to stop them raining down on his beautiful, innocent face. When she glances at the window, she sees the mobile still hanging but blood drips from each shattered piece until it is everywhere, but she can't see where her son's wounds are. She can't see where to staunch the blood. The discordant notes crash together and become a twisted version of 'Twinkle, Twinkle', and she realises that to stop the glass raining down on them, she has stop the breeze blowing through the window. So she walks on broken glass, as the never-ending shards fly her baby piece by piece until she gets to the window and reaches out to pull it closed.

But there is a strange figure there. Dressed all in black. With dark eyes and long bony fingers. Terrifying, and silent. She watches, unable to move as it reaches towards her – no, not towards *her*, towards her baby – and as much as she tries to bat the figure away, she can't. Its fingers also glide and slice through her skin and grow longer and longer still, reaching for her precious boy. She opens her mouth to scream, but is silenced by the glass pieces showering into her mouth and down her throat.

And those long, grasping fingers peel her arms away from

her baby and claw him away from her. As they do, she reaches forward, desperate to save her son, and desperate to find out who this creature is. Who is behind it all. She grabs the cloaked figure's hood, trying to pull it from their face, but as she does so, as she thinks she's about to finally see the person who is making her life a living hell, a sharp pain pulls her from her sleep, leaving her gasping and sweating in the confines of the darkened bedroom.

28

Disorientated, on the verge of panic, it takes her a moment to ground herself and figure out what has just happened. The pain has eased, if it was ever there to begin with, and she feels the weight of her swollen stomach. Tilly, however – she realises with a thud – is no longer beside her.

Panic doesn't get a chance to set in, however, as she hears her daughter merrily chattering in the living room just feet away. Ed must be back, she realises, wondering just how long she has been asleep for.

Part of her wants to call Ed through to their room so she can ask him for a hug. No matter how strained things are between them, she still believes he loves her and she desperately wants to have him soothe her worries. Of all the bad dreams that have plagued her over the course of the last year, that was probably the most disturbing of all. She can't seem to stop the awful images of the dream from flittering on the edges of her consciousness.

It had all felt so real. She swears she could feel the figure's sharpened touch, smell its stale breath.

Pulling herself up to sitting and rubbing her tummy, Mel feels a wave of dizziness washing over her and immediately regrets sitting up so fast. Closing her eyes and taking a few deep breaths, she settles herself and the room stops spinning. 'I'm much too pregnant for this,' she mumbles as she pulls herself off the too-soft mattress and stands up, her back twinging. Could that have been the pain that woke her? Maybe it's time they get a firmer mattress too.

When her stomach rumbles, she realises she has barely eaten today. It's no wonder she's light-headed. She really does need to take better care of herself.

As soon as she opens the bedroom door she is met with the most delicious smell. Ed must be cooking, she thinks, instantly very grateful for the man she knows he still is.

But when she walks into the kitchen, expecting to see him at the hob so she can wrap her arms around his waist, she is shocked to find Sheila instead, stirring a large pot of what looks like vegetable soup. On the worktop there is a loaf of wheaten bread, partially wrapped in tinfoil. The spoils of an experienced home baker. Sheila looks like someone very much at home. She certainly looks as if she is much more comfortable in the caravan than Mel herself. Tilly is kneeling up on her chair at the table, slicing a carrot on a chopping-board with a recently sharpened paring knife. Mel instantly panics.

'Dear God, Tilly. Let me have that knife! It's much too sharp for you. You'll cut yourself to pieces!' There's more than a hint of hysteria in her voice but she feels her reaction is more than justified. Who on earth would give a four-year-old a paring knife?

'I'm just chopping carrots for the soup!' Tilly says. 'Sheila told me how to be careful.'

'I've been keeping an eye on her,' Sheila says. 'Children are capable of so much more than we give them credit for. I was helping my mother around the house from the day I could walk...' Sheila's tone is jovial but Mel is angry.

'You don't know her!' she says, using all her effort not to shout. 'She's only four. She should not have a sharp knife and how could you be keeping your eyes on her when you had your back to the table?' Mel has already taken the knife from her daughter, and is trying her hardest not to break down. This woman – this woman she doesn't know from Adam – has been supervising her child. Who on earth would leave a virtual stranger watching their child? And Sheila looks much too comfortable in a home that isn't hers. The way she busies herself around the kitchen, knows where everything is and is even wearing Mel's apron.

'What's all the fuss about?' Ed's voice as he walks in the door to the caravan stops her dead in her tracks.

'I think Mel here might be a little upset,' says Sheila, sounding wounded. 'The wee one was cutting some carrots for me. You know how we were all doing it yesterday? And I think Mel was worried she would do herself an injury.' Ed looks from Sheila to Mel as if expecting a response from the latter.

'I woke up and Tilly wasn't with me. I wasn't expecting there to be anyone else in the caravan, alone with Tilly. And I wasn't expecting our daughter to have a knife in her hand.'

'Miss Tilly let me in. She said her daddy was out and Mummy was sleeping,' Sheila says, wiping her hands on the apron. 'I didn't think it was particularly wise for her to have the run of the place, especially given everything that's gone this last wee while, so I decided to stay and let you have your sleep. God knows when the wee man comes along all thoughts of sleep will be gone for a while. We decided to make some soup to go with the bread I brought over. I'd brought down some fresh veg from the farmers' market, thinking it would save you running out to the shops. I didn't think it would be a problem to cook with Tilly. I was keeping a close eye. Better to teach them early so they've less chance of hurting themselves. My children were all cooking from they were no age.'

'Mummy!' Tilly exclaims before Mel has time to react to Sheila. 'I waked up ages ago. I helped Sheila 'cos she's says I'm the best helper and make the soup extra tasty.' She looks so proud of herself.

Mel glances to Ed, wondering why she's the only one who thinks it's not right to hand a four-year-old a sharp knife, but Ed's attention is on their daughter. 'You do, Tills. You are the best helper and I bet you did a great job.'

He turns his attention back to Mel. 'Isn't it so very kind of Sheila to come down with food for dinner again? She has us spoiled! And you want to taste that wheaten bread. It's unreal!'

'A family recipe,' Sheila says, although the wounded look has yet to leave her face. 'I can give you a copy if you want. Hard to beat some home-baked bread. I just thought it would help. You've been under so much strain and you know, sure what else have I to be doing with Barney out on the farm. I was just enjoying having happy faces to feed again, and this wee dote to chat with.'

'It's so yummy, Mummy,' Tilly explains. Meanwhile, the feeling Mel is being manipulated – by an old woman with no idea of personal boundaries – is back again. From near enough the moment they arrived, Sheila has been almost ever present. It's not that Mel's ungrateful, but she feels she can barely breathe. What kind of person comes into a person's home while they are napping and starts cooking a full meal with their child?

'You shouldn't have gone to the trouble,' Mel says to Sheila, knowing her tone is sour, but it has been a fucker of a few days and this has just been the last straw.

'Ach, nonsense. And sure, I feel sorry for you all down here trying to work in this wee kitchen.'

If Mel isn't mistaken, there's more than a hint of passive aggression in the older woman's voice. 'I'm always baking and it takes little to no effort to throw a little extra in the mixing bowl. And sure it's just a vegetable soup. Nothing fancy. All home-grown, mind.' Sheila smiles and turns back to the cooker, giving the pot another stir. 'Besides I had to come down and get my stew pot anyway.'

'It's very kind of you,' Mel tells her. 'Sure, I can take over now, so you don't have to hang about. You can get back up the road to that man of yours. I'm sure Ed would run you up in the car, save you the walk?' Mel is aware she has now progressed directly on to being rude but just wanting to be alone with her family in her own house.

Sheila stops stirring the soup momentarily before starting again, as if she hadn't just been told, in a roundabout way, that she is not welcome.

'Or feel free to eat here tonight, Sheila,' Ed offers. 'Since Barney is up in the fields. I wouldn't be sending you back up to be on your own. Especially not when you've been so generous. That's okay, Mel, isn't it?'

'Of course,' Mel replies, defeated. She suspects Ed knows she would rather the older woman not be there but that doesn't stop him ignoring her.

'I like it when Sheila stays for tea,' Tilly says. 'She tells good stories and jokes.'

'Ach, petal.' Sheila turns towards Tilly. 'You do my heart good, you know. I'd be proud to have a wee grandchild like you.'

'Mummy, Sheila says next year I can come and see the baby lambs in the fields. I wanted to go see them now, but I can't 'cos of my baby brother.' Tilly looks dejected.

'That's right,' Sheila adds. 'We can't go and see the wee lambs this year. Because we really wouldn't want anything bad to happen to the baby in your mummy's tummy, would we?'

There's something in the way she says it that makes Mel feel uneasy. She realises this is what her life has become – being suspicious of everyone, even her older neighbour who has done nothing except be nosey and prepare food for them.

Still, Sheila doesn't strike her as a clueless woman, and yet she is ignoring every sign Mel gives her that she is overstepping. And isn't it understandable at her stage of pregnancy, in the claustrophobic confines of this caravan, that Mel might want some space?

Suddenly she feels light-headed again. Maybe she's the unreasonable one in all this, she thinks to herself. Maybe she should just be grateful and sit down and eat the food that has been prepared for her.

She reaches for the worktop to steady herself.

'You okay, love?' Sheila asks, immediately at Mel's side, her bony fingers – long and thin like the creature's in Mel's dream – wrapping themselves around her arm to provide support.

Mel pulls away as if she has been burned, the memories of her nightmare haunting her. 'I'm fine,' she snaps far too brusquely, and she sees the wounding in their neighbour's eyes, just as she hears the disappointed way Ed says her name.

'Mel, there's no need.'

She feels as if she wants to crawl out of her own skin and escape from the caravan with its humid atmosphere, the bubble and hiss of the soup on the stove, the low hum of the TV and pitter-patter of rain on the roof.

'I'm... I'm sorry,' she stutters, knowing that if she were to storm out she would only upset Tilly. 'I'm not feeling myself. Just a little woozy. And achy. I don't think I've had enough to eat today. Or to drink for that matter.'

'Never you worry, pet,' Sheila says. 'It's hard work carrying a baby. Especially in those last weeks when the hormones are flying all over the shop. My Barney said I was like a fishwife when I was carrying ours – gulderin' all over the place if he so much as breathed wrong. And when I wasn't shouting, I was crying about something. Bloody hormones have a lot to be answering for!'

She reaches out to help steady Mel again but pulls back, as if afraid Mel might push her away a second time.

Flushed with embarrassment, Mel shuffles to the table and sits down, both overwhelmed and humiliated, while Tilly brings her a glass of water and Ed looks at her as if she were a total stranger to him.

29

---

35 WEEKS + 2 DAYS

Having such a deep nap during the day did Mel no favours in regard to getting a good night's sleep. Nor did being on edge and having to skirt round an increasingly frosty atmosphere between her and Ed.

After Sheila had gone home, refusing the offer of a lift because 'the walk would do her good', he had maintained a stony silence. Instead of taking his usual spot on the sofa beside her, he had said he was going into the bedroom to catch up on some work. Half an hour later she had heard the bathroom door close and the sound of the shower running. She'd done her best to ignore the feeling that something was very wrong by focusing on reading Tilly one of her favourite storybooks – the one she'd read to her ever since she was a tiny baby and much too young to understand what on earth she was talking about. Tilly had rested her head on her mother's tummy, earning a kick from her baby brother for her troubles, which thankfully she'd found hilarious. It was one perfect moment in a day that had been a complete horror and Mel wished she could hold on to it forever.

She'd expected Ed to come through to the living room after

his shower but he had simply gone back into the bedroom, closing the door behind him. She wondered what he was doing in there. Was he really catching up on work? Chasing another contract that he might actually be able to fulfil without having to worry about his wife and children? Or reworking the figures on the renovation? He'd yet to sit down with her to run through them so they could make the necessary revisions. Part of her wished he would, and the other was happy to put her head in the sand about it for another while. There is only so much stress a person can take. Or maybe he was searching through the property listings Emma had promised to send him.

Trying to distract herself from everything – and definitely wanting to avoid searching online again – Mel curled on the sofa and started watching a few episodes of *Schitt's Creek*, her comfort show. But not even Moira Rose could lift her spirits.

Now, at one in the morning, all she can think about is the awful mess her life is. Perfect moments, or even just okay moments, shouldn't be the exception and yet here she was with her husband mad at her, her parents in pieces, their neighbour offended at her rudeness, and unable to shake the very real, very terrifying thought that something very bad was about to happen.

Her back nips again and there's a dull ache in her pelvis, no doubt from all the walking she has done lately, and the lengthy car journeys. Braxton Hicks contractions have kicked in – a sure warning she has done too much – and she's still feeling woozy. It's no wonder though. Despite her hunger at teatime, she struggled to eat; shame and embarrassment robbed her of her appetite. She has just managed to eat a slice of Sheila's wheaten bread though. Tilly was right, she thinks. It is 'so yummy'.

Cradling a cup of decaffeinated tea, Mel, still feeling more than a little penned in from earlier, opens the door to the caravan, enjoying the feeling of the cool night air. It's dry and the sky is clear and glittered with stars. She takes a seat on one of two Adirondack chairs Ed has set up in front of the caravan. It's probably too cold to be outside just yet – she can see steam rise and swirl from her teacup illuminated by the soft light of the lamps inside the van. This place should be everything to them.

She can see the house, now gutted of its old kitchen and bathroom. A small excavator is abandoned at the rear of the building where it has been digging out the packed earth, ready for the foundations of their extension to be laid. In her mind's eye she can see how it will all come together. She can envisage how beautiful this place could be when it is all done. How they could build a tree-house for the children, and get a swing set. She can see her parents coming to visit and falling in love with the quiet location – close enough to the city but far enough to not be annoyed by the noise, lights and constant rush-rush of city life. It should be their perfect life but maybe she was living in cloud cuckoo land thinking she would get a happy-ever-after. Maybe she doesn't deserve one.

Still, it is silent in the yard save for the odd rustle of the leaves or creak as she shifts in her seat. She should feel completely at peace here in the stillness of the early morning but she doesn't. She's on edge. Or high alert. One ear listening for footsteps, or the sound of someone breathing nearby. Someone who might be creeping around their temporary home, or sneaking in and out of the shell of their house. Knocking on windows, leaving grim surprises. Those security cameras need to go up, she thinks, suddenly unwilling to wait any more for Ed to do it.

Back inside, she reads the instructions on the stick-up cameras and sets the batteries in each of the three devices to charge. Once they are up – and she fully intends for them to be up this morning – she tells herself she will feel a little safer.

Unable to do any more until the camera batteries are charged, and still feeling no closer to sleep, she lifts her phone and starts scrolling her social media accounts. She vows she won't look at the forums and gossip pages where she is likely to read something hurtful. Instead she starts to scroll reels on Instagram, watching videos of amateur comedy skits and silly animals. It's enough to stop her mind racing at least.

As her fingers hover, a notification pops up on her screen. An Instagram message from Alice.

ALICE

You awake? I can see your status.

MEL

Yeah. Can't sleep *sigh* #Pregnancyinsomnia

ALICE

I was worried. You didn't reply to my message.

MEL

Sorry. I've been a bit out of sorts. It's all getting to be a bit too much.

ALICE

Has more happened since the flowers?

Mel's not sure what to say. Surely if she trusts Alice as much as she says she does she should have no problem at all in telling her everything that has happened. Then again, she remembers – Alice is not her friend. Their truce is a fragile one and there is a lot of healing still to be done.

And maybe, just maybe, she doesn't actually trust Alice as much as she thought she did. At this precise moment she doesn't think she trusts anyone. She decides to play it all down a bit.

MEL

Just the same old nonsense. People and their theories.

ALICE

Do you want me to say something more? Tell people they have to stop? I never knew it was this bad.

Mel wants to take this at face value, but she knows it's not entirely true. Okay, there have not been funeral flowers sent before, or eerie memorials at her gate, but Alice must've known when she lost her business. That was within months of Jacob's death. She must know it was as a direct result of her smear campaign – the smear campaign Mel is trying so desperately hard to believe was just the action of a woman deep in grief.

MEL

Well, it wasn't this bad before. I mean, obviously I had to close the business and I got hateful messages sent through the site. But this is new. But no, I don't want you to say anything else. It would only stoke the fire. More people will say I'm bullying you into it, and the whole story will start circulating, and no doubt being embellished, all over again.

ALICE

God, this is awful. I'm sure that, like me, you just want to get on with your life and look forward to your baby being born. The last thing you need is stress.

MEL

Exactly. And things are stressed. Ed is on edge – he really wants us to emigrate away from this all. Go and live near his sister in Melbourne.

ALICE

Australia? Wow! That's a big move.

MEL

It is, and it's not one I really want to make, but maybe we have no choice. Things are just getting tougher here.

ALICE

Even down in your new house? I know you said there's a lot to do, but it sounds ideal.

MEL

Well it would be ideal, without everything else going on. Which is all just making Ed fixate more and more on Australia…

And that's how, despite her intention to keep Alice at a safe distance, Mel finds herself getting lost in a lengthy chat in the wee small hours of the morning. A conversation with a woman who may or may not be trying to ruin her life. A conversation that Ed would never forgive her for.

30

---

35 WEEKS + 6 DAYS

The following few days pass incident-free but not without a degree of tension.

Ed insists on still throwing Australia into the conversation and has gone so far as to send her on the listings of the houses from Emma. 'You said you would at least look at them,' he said. 'It doesn't commit us to anything.'

To keep the peace, Mel has reluctantly agreed. Yes, Emma's suggestions are gorgeous. She has even sent them a listing for a renovation project in that looks like it could be something really magnificent but, Mel thinks, Emma must have her head in the clouds when it comes to their financial status. Property in Melbourne is eye-wateringly expensive. Especially a good-sized family home with garden space. She doesn't understand why Ed is insisting she looks into something that is very clearly out of their price range – something that was out of their price range even before they had sunk every penny into their current home.

From what she can see they'd have to look at a rental in the first instance – certainly until they'd built their savings back up again.

There's no doubt though, it would make more financial sense to stay put. They'd stand to make a substantial loss on their investment if they pull out of this project now and God knows that while moving to Derry had been hard when she was pregnant, moving to Australia would be a nightmare with a newborn – but Ed doesn't seem ready or willing to have that conversation yet. He keeps urging her to 'think about it' and 'not to rule it out'.

Determined not to have an argument with him, Mel decides to adopt a solid 'let's not talk about it' approach to the whole thing. So long as things stay quiet, she figures that should be easy enough to maintain in the short-term anyway.

It's surprisingly easy, she finds, to not talk about things when their relationship still feels a little strained. It's not that they are arguing, as such. But something is definitely off-kilter between them. She feels as if she's always just a beat behind where she should be with him, and no matter how much she tries she can't seem to get her thoughts or feelings in sync with his.

It doesn't help her sense of peace that she is feeling an increasing amount of aches and pains, and according to her latest visit with Lindsey the midwife, the baby has now flipped 'the right way up' and his head has dropped a little.

This revelation shot fear through her heart as she realised she is terrified of giving birth. She is terrified and she supposes it's no wonder given her last experience of birth was Alice's. It would be naive to think she wouldn't hold on to some residual trauma from it all. But it wasn't something she felt she could chat to Lindsey about, scared that she would be judged again, so she has done what she would've told all her clients not to do and has bottled it up. Something she knows is not healthy in the long run.

'I wouldn't worry about going overdue,' Lindsey had told her. 'I don't think he's going to keep you waiting. That said, Mel, that blood pressure isn't behaving the best and there's some protein in your urine this time. When I tell you that you need to rest, I mean that you need to rest. Feet up as much as possible. Don't stand when you can sit. Don't sit when you can lie down. Try to lie on your left side to get the best flow of oxygen through the placenta. Monitor your headaches and if they seem to be getting worse at all then call me. If it's the weekend, call the hospital. And if you've any visual disturbances I want you to go straight to the maternity ward. Okay?'

Mel had nodded. She'd do what she was told to the very best of her ability.

Ironically, her one saving grace these last few days has been Alice and their late-night secret chats. She is trying to keep things on a fairly superficial level, but she has felt herself opening up more and more each night.

It's been so nice to have a female friend to talk to again. Actually just to have a friend she can talk to who doesn't seem to be sitting in judgement of her constantly. Again, the irony of that situation is one she is well aware of. But Alice has become someone she can share her pregnancy with, something she has missed since being excluded from the pregnancy support community forums that had once been such a lifeline to her. There was no way she could appear back there and take the chance of letting whoever Big Bad Wolf is know even one more detail about her life.

Alice has become someone she can talk to about the ins and outs of preparing for a new baby. Silly things maybe, but incredibly important to her. Last night they had spoken for the longest time on what car seat is best to buy. Alice had donated many of the baby items she had bought for Jacob in the aftermath of his death. She'd found them simply too painful to look at, but now, halfway into a subsequent pregnancy, she was starting to feel brave enough to look at what she would need this time round.

'I don't suppose you'd want to come up and go pram shopping with me?' Alice had asked, as they'd shared another quiet conversation in the wee hours.

'Is that not something Thomas wants to do with you?' Mel asked, exceptionally keen to not step on Thomas's toes. That last phone call she had with him, when he had accused her of 'hiding evidence', still weighed heavy on her mind.

There was a pause as she waited for a reply. 'Thomas is still grieving,' Alice said eventually. 'I think he's scared to acknowledge this baby. Obviously I'm still grieving too but I know we have to be practical. Can't have the wee mite arriving and having to sleep in a drawer!'

'It really must be very difficult,' Mel said. 'But please God this baby will go a very long way to healing both your hearts. You'll never forget Jacob of course, and nor would you want to. Maybe if I come up, if it's not too painful, we could go and visit his grave together? I'd like to say my goodbyes.'

There was another pause before Alice, clearly emotional, replied, 'I think I would like that very much.'

Now, in the cold light of day, Mel thinks she was probably a little foolish. She can hardly go tearing off to Carrickfergus pram shopping when she has been ordered to rest? It would be a madness and God alone knows there has been enough madness in her life.

She'll simply have to tell Alice that it would probably be best to wait until after the baby is born. Surely she will understand?

The decision made, Mel feels a little better. Everything will be easier once her baby is born and in her arms, she tells herself, and with every day that passes she is drawing closer and closer to that end point. That is what she has to focus on now. That and Tilly.

* * *

'Mummy. Will I still be your baby when my brother is here?' Tilly asks as they draw and colour in together at the kitchen table.

'Always, my darling. Even when you're a big grown-up girl with a baby of your own.' Mel is determined to reassure her daughter.

'And will we be able to play together when my baby brother is here? You and me?'

'Of course, my darling. I'll always want to play with you. Now, when your baby brother is very small and he needs changing and feeding and his back rubbed so he can get his wind up, then I might not be able to play with you right away. But there will be lots and lots of times when he is asleep in his cot or in his pram when we *can* play. And when he's bigger, he'll be able to play with you too.'

Tilly nods, taking in everything her mother is saying.

'And Sheila says she will play with me too,' Tilly tells her as she colours in a large section of blue sky on her drawing. 'She says I can come up to her house and we can do cooking and baking together and go and play on the farm with all the animals.'

Mel bristles. She's pretty sure Sheila should not be making plans with her daughter without discussing them with her and Ed first. She'll have to talk to Ed about it later. It might be better for him, and not her, to remind their neighbour that Tilly is only four and not old enough to make these decisions for herself.

'Maybe,' she replies to Tilly before lifting her stick figure drawing of a mummy, daddy, little girl and baby and showing it to her daughter. 'What do you think?'

'You did a good job, Mummy!' Tilly reaches across to give her mum a little kiss on the cheek.

'Thank you, baby.' Mel beams, pulling her daughter into a hug.

31

'I don't think she'll have meant anything by it,' Ed says as they tidy up after dinner. 'You know what's she's like. She's just a lonely old woman who wishes she had her grandchildren close to her and who, yes, might stick her nose in a little too far but she doesn't mean any harm. She has only ever helped.'

He hands Mel a wet plate which she dries and puts away in the cupboard.

'That may be the case, but we've only known her a matter of weeks and she's already inviting our four-year-old up to play in her house. That's not right, Ed. We don't know her that well and we don't know her husband at all. I don't think I'm being too cautious to say that we need to be careful with these things.'

'Of course not,' Ed replies. 'But chances are Sheila just didn't think, or said it one way and Tilly has interpreted it differently. I'm not sure our four-year-old falls into the category of reliable narrator.' He hands her another plate and flashes her a smile. The kind of cute conspiratorial smile that made her fall in love with him in the first place.

'That much is true,' Mel says. 'She has quite the imagination.'

'That reminds me, I know we haven't really spoken to her too much about it, and maybe we should've, but she mentioned the bear to me when I was putting her to bed last night. She said she was scared the man who left the bear would come and take her baby brother.'

Mel freezes. 'What? And you didn't tell me?'

'It went out of my mind.' He hands her another plate which she sits on the countertop without drying before turning to face him.

'Don't you think that's the kind of thing I would need to know about? Did you ask her why she thought that?' Mel feels her skin prickle again. She does not like this.

'I told her it wasn't a bad man who left the bear and that it was someone who made a mistake leaving a present for a baby. I didn't want to start asking more questions of her or putting notions in her head. I don't want her scared, Mel.'

'But don't you think it's unusual she said "bad man"?' Mel asks. 'Why would she say that?'

Ed shrugs. 'Because that's what people always say to children. "The bad man will come and get you if you're naughty." "Don't wander off in case the bad man gets you." That kind of thing. It's probably nothing more than that. And it's hardly a wonder she's a bit scared by it. She did see you get hurt and have to be whisked off to hospital. That would traumatise any child. I'm not sure asking her a hundred and one questions about it will have any other result other than to traumatise her more.'

'But maybe she saw something?' Mel says, lifting the plate again and drying it. 'Did you think of that?'

'And yeah, maybe Sheila is an evil crone from up the road

who wants to steal our child? Maybe she left the bear and the balloon?'

Ed's voice is mocking. Mel can take teasing and banter. She can't take this.

'You can be an asshole sometimes, Ed,' she says, throwing the drying cloth onto the counter-top. 'I need to rest.'

She hasn't taken more than two or three steps when there is a light knock on the caravan door before it pushes open and Sheila herself walks in, looking a little pale.

'I hope this isn't bad timing, Ed, you did say I could come on in any time?'

Mel glares at her husband. Why doesn't he just invite her to move in with them if he's so happy to give her free rein of the place? 'I was just doing a bit of clearing out in our attic and I found these books that I thought Tilly might like.' She holds up a plastic shopping back filled with well-loved children's books. 'But don't worry. I won't stay. I just thought it would be nice to drop them in. I noticed Tilly seemed to be reading the same two or three books over and over again and, well...'

Mel can't bring herself to speak. She is enraged at Ed, but also utterly mortified. The window in the small caravan kitchen is open and it's entirely likely Sheila may have heard Ed's evil crone comment.

She feels her face heat, shame course through her. Sheila looks to all intents and purposes as if she on the brink of tears. 'You don't have to go so fast,' Mel says.

'I think I do,' Sheila replies, her voice a little cold.

'At least let me drive you back up the hill,' Ed pleads, clearly having the same mortified thoughts Mel is.

'No. No. It's fine. The walk will do me good.' With that she turns and leaves, closing the door with a heavy hand.

'Fuck,' Mel swears. 'Do you think she heard us talking?'

'I'm going to go after her,' Ed says, drying his hands. 'I'll make this right.'

All Mel can think is that if she was concerned she had an enemy in Sheila before, she is now certain of it.

She doesn't have too much time to wallow in her self-pity though as her phone starts to ring, her mother's name popping up on the screen. Tempted as she is to ignore the call and allow herself some time to decompress, she is well aware of just how much her mother worries these days and she does not want to cause her any further distress.

Sitting down on the sofa, she answers the call. 'Hi, Mum. Everything's okay here. How are you?'

'Mel…' Her mother's voice is shaking. Mel's heart rate immediately soars.

'Yes, Mum. What is it? Are you okay? Is Daddy okay?' Even in asking the questions she knows she does not want to hear the answer if either of them are anything other than completely and totally okay.

'It's not us,' her mother says. 'But Mel, I need to talk to you. Are you sitting down?'

'Jesus, Mum. You're scaring me!' Mel says. 'Yes, I'm sitting down.'

'I didn't want to tell you this because of your blood pressure but you need to know. I just can't believe anyone could be so wicked.'

Mel's imagination is running wild. Has something else been delivered to her parents' house? Has someone done something to them?

'Mum! Please just tell me what it is!'

'I was out for a walk today with your daddy. Down by the marina. It was such a nice evening, Mel. Warm and just a lovely wee gentle breeze,' her mother says, as Mel wills her to just get to the point. Nothing in what she is saying sounds as if it is leading anywhere 'wicked'.

'Well. We were walking and then there she was. Bold as brass. Like butter wouldn't melt.'

'Who?' Mel asks, willing God to give her patience.

'That Alice creature! Chattering and laughing like she doesn't know what she's done!'

'Mum, you know Alice and I have reached a sort of truce. She's apologised and she's concentrating on her new baby. We don't have to be angry with her any more.' Mel decides it's probably best not to tell her mother about their plans to go pram shopping or to visit Jacob's grave. Her mother just wouldn't understand.

'Mel, you don't understand,' her mother says. 'You said she was pregnant again – well, if she's pregnant she has the flattest stomach of any pregnant woman I've ever seen in my life. Didn't you say she was halfway gone? Well, there she was out for a jog, in leggings and one of those crop top things that looks more like a bra if you ask me and Mel, she was definitely not pregnant.'

Mel can't quite process it. 'Are you sure it was Alice?' she asks – the only logical explanation being that this is a case of mistaken identity.

'Mel, my love. I will never forget that woman's face for as long as I live. It was her. And I'm telling you now, she is not pregnant. She's been lying to you.'

'But she had a bump?' Mel says, her mind racing. This can't be right. Why would Alice do this? Why would anyone do this? Unless, of course, her mother is right and Alice is truly, truly wicked. And if she has lied about this, and started rebuilding a friendship with Mel on the basis of that lie, then just what else is she capable of lying about? Just what else is she capable of doing?

32

Fear and shame mix with disbelief as Mel sits on the sofa trying to take in what her mother has just told her. Her stomach churns, the dinner she has not long ago finished eating threatening to come back up.

Alice, who had convinced her she was pregnant. Alice, whom she has spoken with in the wee small hours during these last few sleepless nights. Whom she has discussed prams with, and car seats and her baby names. Whose apology she believed with her whole heart. Whose explanation she believed as to why she was keeping her pregnancy under wraps. Whose swollen stomach she had seen in front of her that day in the coffee shop.

Maybe, despite her mother's conviction that she knows whom she saw and it was definitely Alice Munroe, there is some mistake. Her mother is wrong. Because the alternative is worse than anything else she has endured these last weeks and months.

Her hand instinctively cuddling her stomach, she thinks about the funeral flowers again. How there were only ever a limited number of people who would know the exact arrangement she had sent for Jacob's funeral. She wonders why she had been so eager to believe Alice when she seemed so shocked and upset at the news. Why she asserted again and again to her parents and to Ed that Alice couldn't have been the person behind them. Why she felt in her gut that Alice had been telling her the truth.

A bud of anger starts to form and grow in the pit of her stomach. This wasn't just a lie. This was a betrayal, and the only reason she can think even remotely plausible is that Alice had finally broken entirely and in breaking, had decided she hadn't made Mel's life hellish enough. She wants her broken too. She wants to steal her peace of mind, her new-found security in their new home and her marriage too if she can help it. And my God, Mel thinks, if it's all a lie, does that also mean she *was* trying to entice Tilly away that day at the day care? Alice knows where they live now. She has sent that card. Mel has discussed the renovation with her. Without realising, Mel has been feeding the woman who would do her the most damage in the world information to use against her. Every conversation they have had, no matter how seemingly banal, has given Alice more and more ammunition to add to her arsenal.

She thinks of this past week alone and how everything has ramped up again coinciding with Jacob's due date – how she had been only too eager to write this off as a coincidence. How could she have been so stupid?

The realisation that she has been tricked, and that she never knew Alice to begin with hits her like a slap to the face. Hands shaking, and heart thudding, she considers her next move.

Her immediate thought that she should call the police fades away as she realises that pretending to be pregnant is not something they will likely find interesting. There is no evidence of any direct threat. The bear is long gone, the skip long emptied – not that it would've contained any proof anyway. The call she had received in the hospital was anonymous. The Internet trolls no doubt untraceable, but what had they done anyway? In terms of the law they had only come up with wild theories and torn strips into her. It was nasty, yes. It was defamatory, certainly, but it was hardly going to result in an immediate police investigation. This, she realises, has all been plotted out very carefully with a degree of calculation that makes her blood run cold.

Part of her wants to call Alice. To scream and shout at her and ask her just what the fuck does she think she is doing, but isn't that exactly what Alice wants? Some sort of reaction? No doubt the other woman has been thriving off Mel's upset and discomfort these last few days, knowing all this time she has been, at best, making a fool of her and, at worst, watching the puzzle pieces of her plan fit into place.

Tears slide down Mel's cheeks, now ablaze with shame, as she thinks of how her mind has done gymnastics as she has tried to pin the blame on someone else. Even her beloved Ed, who maybe was just feeling the pressure as much as she was and was desperate to get away from it all. She had talked him down every time he had dared to criticise Alice these last few days. Maybe Ed knew the only way to get his wife out from under Alice's grasp was to get her as far away from here as possible.

She shakes her head, her mind scrambling to try and land on an alternative, innocent explanation for it all. Her phone still in her hand, she scrolls until she finds Alice's number and she's just about to press the call button, ready to unload her anger and hurt, when the door to the caravan opens and Ed walks back in, his expression grim.

33

Mel doesn't know how she's going to tell her husband what she has just discovered. It should be easy. They should be on each other's side without reservation, but instead they have been so divided these last few days.

'Did you catch up with Sheila?' she asks, knowing full well she is stalling but also swamped with guilt as to how short she has been with Ed, and Sheila too.

'Yes,' he says. 'She still refused a lift. Said she would be better walking the mood off her.'

'She was angry?' Mel asks.

'I suppose. More hurt. You were right. She did hear us through the window. Or more to the point, she heard me and the whole "evil crone" thing.' He looks utterly ashamed. 'She said she didn't mean to overstep her place and she was only trying to help. She thought that given we were away from family and living in chaos that she was doing a good turn. Said she should've listened to her Barney, who tells her she has a habit of getting over-invested in people's business.'

'Shit,' Mel says, guilt flooding her.

'She said she gets a wee bit carried away sometimes, especially when it comes to children, as her own grandchildren never come near the place. But she's got the message now.' He grimaces.

'What did you say?' Mel asks, aware she is only half listening. In her mind she is running through every conversation she had with Alice this past week, trying to work out if there were any clues to what was really going on.

'I told her that I was sorry. That we were sorry. That it's all been very stressful moving here – what with you pregnant and not keeping the best. I didn't want to tell her everything about what has happened this past year, but I did tell her we had an incident at the day care Tilly attended that left us both a bit shaken and concerned for her safety.'

Ed pulls a seat from behind the kitchen table and sits down before pinching the bridge of his nose and giving his head a shake. 'And yes, I know you're going to say that Alice has explained all that and it was innocent, but I had to think on my toes and...'

'Alice was lying,' Mel blurts, bracing herself for his reaction.

'What?' Ed asks, his brow crinkled.

'She's... she's not pregnant.'

'Sorry... what? How? How do you know?' Ed looks completely thrown.

'My mother just called. While you were out. Says she saw Alice down at the marina. Going for a run. She was wearing tight sports gear with a perfectly flat stomach.'

Mel braces herself for an explosive reaction from Ed. It's what she deserves. She expects every 'I told you so' in the book.

'Fuck,' he says, his eyes wide. 'Fuck, Mel. What are we going to do?'

'I don't know,' Mel replies, the threat of tears growing ever closer. 'I feel like it's not going to matter anyway. It's not like the police are going to listen. There's only my word for it that she said she was pregnant. They'll see her apology online and think we're being unreasonable. Or they'll just tell us to keep a diary again. Waiting until she says something directly threatening or does something to hurt us...'

'Restraining order,' Ed says. 'We can do that. Can't we? I'll get in touch with a solicitor tomorrow morning. See what our options are, legally speaking. We'll up the security. Maybe those cameras aren't enough. Maybe we'd be better to move off-+site altogether until the house is finished and secure?'

Mel wonders if he means Australia. At this precise moment, faced with the truth of what Alice is and what she has done, she thinks just maybe it's time to acquiesce to his long-held dream, even if the pain of leaving her parents would be devastating.

Her tears are more than just a threat now, she tries to wipe them away with the cuff of her well-worn cardigan. Ed moves a little closer and pulls her into a hug, allowing her to sob on his shoulder.

'I'm so sorry you've been let down like this,' he says, kissing the top of her forehead. 'I know how desperately you wanted her to be pregnant again. How much you have missed her.'

Mel thinks of how Alice had wanted her to come to Carrickfergus and go pram shopping with her. How much longer did she think she was going to get away with the lie? What was she planning to do when she had no baby to show off?

A chilling thought crosses Mel's mind. If Alice had tried to lure Tilly away in the past, what's to say she has no plan to try and get her hands on Mel's baby too? A woman who could send funeral flowers, and ghastly memorials, who could tell lie after lie online and who was still half mad with grief could be capable of anything at all.

34

36 WEEKS

Unsurprisingly, Mel has not slept yet again. But unlike the previous few nights she has not had Alice to keep her company. Not that Alice hasn't tried. There are a host of unanswered messages on Mel's phone as well as a series of missed calls.

The messages started off ordinarily. A simple 'How's things?' before slowly progressing through layers of curiosity to panic to those tinged with anger.

> Are you okay?
>
> You haven't gone to the hospital, have you?
>
> Is your blood pressure okay?
>
> I think I might have a UTI. The baby is using my bladder as a trampoline!
>
> Mel?
>
> Maybe you're sleeping? It's just I tried to call but there was no answer.

Oh God, Mel, please let me know you and the baby are okay? I'm getting worried here.

Answer your phone, please!

I can't help but fear the worst. This is like PTSD to last year, please, reply as soon as you see this!

This is cruel, Mel. You are being so very cruel. I thought better of you. Fuck you.

Sorry. I'm sorry for that last message. I'm just scared. I need to talk to you.

I can see you're reading these messages! What the fuck, Mel?

Ed had advised Mel not to answer and she was only too happy to take that advice. She didn't know what she would say to Alice in any instance. Everything they had spoken about since they reconnected had been a lie. Mel had no desire to keep fuelling that lie while they waited for Ed to get in touch with his solicitor.

'You could block her number,' Ed had said.

'Then she'd know immediately something was very wrong,' Mel had replied.

'By the look of those messages, she already knows. There's nothing she can say or do at this stage to make this any better.'

Immediately, Mel knows he is right, and she also knows that she no longer wants to jump every time her phone pings, nor does she want to keep reading the messages that are landing in. She doesn't want Alice to have any power over her at all.

'Okay,' she says. 'You're right. I'm going to block her number.' She does it there and then without thinking about it any further.

To her surprise, she feels an immense sense of relief to see the blocked icon beside Alice's name.

'I thought I'd call into the solicitor's,' Ed says as he bites into a slice of toast. 'Maybe you could come in with me? I doubt he'll be able to see me, but I figure if I explain the case face to face to the receptionist there might be a chance of plucking some heart-strings. I can emphasise how urgent it is. I figured we could take Tilly with us, maybe go and get some shopping after if you're up to it? Although I have to say, you look very tired.'

'I'm exhausted,' Mel says. 'I don't think I slept for more than half an hour at a time this morning.' She's also well aware her eyes are rimmed with red and swollen from the hours she spent crying. 'My head's lifting too.'

'Your blood pressure?' he asks, his eyes wide with concern.

'It could be, but I suppose it's more likely to be because I'm so tired.'

He raises one eyebrow.

'Okay, I know. To make us both feel better, I'll call the midwife or call in to have my blood pressure checked later. I was just thinking I'd get a little sleep first. Just an hour or two. Then I was thinking we could call up to see Sheila. I'll apologise to her. Explain what's happened. I feel really guilty about yesterday.'

She doesn't tell him about the aches and pains in her pelvis and back though, telling herself it's just from the old mattress, or from napping on the couch. After all, she still has over a month until she is due – but on the off-chance the midwife decides to admit her once again after her visit, Mel wants to make sure she gets as much rest as her body will allow her before all the disruption of a noisy ward.

Ed nods and pulls her into a hug, just in time for Tilly to come wandering into the kitchen carrying a now empty melamine plate.

'The toast was yummy, Mummy,' Tilly says. 'I think my tummy might like some more.'

'Maybe just a little bit.' Mel smiles, popping another slice of bread into the toaster.

'Hey, Tills,' Ed says. 'I have to do a few errands this morning and I think Mummy is very tired, and I really need a helper.'

'I'm a good helper!' Tilly squeals.

'I know, baby girl.' Ed smiles. 'And I thought you could help me choose some flowers for Sheila as a big thank you for making us all the yummy dinners!'

'Great idea, Daddy,' Tilly says. 'I'll go and get dressed.'

'Make sure you have your toast first!' Mel calls as the bread pops out of the toaster.

'My tummy is not hungry any more,' she says with a grin and runs out of the room.

* * *

'Are you sure you'll be okay?' Ed asks as he puts on his coat an hour later. 'The lads will be in the house if you need anything. But make sure to keep the door locked all the same.'

'I'll be fine,' Mel assures him. 'I'll be asleep before my head hits the pillow if how I feel right now is anything to go by.'

'And you've made an appointment to see the midwife this afternoon?' he asks.

'I have. Three o'clock, but she can see me earlier if this headache gets any worse.' Or, she thinks, if her back starts to hurt any more. But, no, she's sure this has to be a combination of Braxton Hicks and that damn mattress.

'You'll call me if anything worries you,' he says. 'We won't be too far away. I can be back quickly. I feel a little uneasy leaving you here on your own.'

'I'm not on my own,' Mel reassures him, and herself. Fergus and his builders are already working in the house. She can hear the whirr of the cement mixer and the tinny echo of their radio.

Tilly, dressed now and in her beloved wellie boots, runs across the room to her mum, and gives her tummy a big kiss. 'Baby brother! I used to live in there before you!' she says, and laughs.

'That's right, Tills, you did. When you were much, much smaller!' Mel tells her, wrapping her arms around her and pulling her into a big hug. In this moment, Mel can pretend everything is perfect. Maybe it's perfect enough for now – having Ed show her such care and affection. He hadn't reacted angrily as she'd expected last night – instead he has been the model of a good husband. Without that affection she's afraid she would be a complete wreck just now.

'Mummy?' Tilly says, gazing up at Mel with her brow furrowed. 'How did I get outside of your tummy?'

'I think that might be a question for another time,' Ed laughs. 'Shall we go, Tilly?'

'Can I get an ice cream?' she asks, all thoughts of birth forgotten.

'I think it might be a little early in the day for ice cream,' Ed says. 'But maybe we can get a McFlurry later after we take your mummy to see the midwife? Mummy might even want one too.'

'That would be lovely,' Mel tells him.

'I do love you,' Ed says, all of a sudden. 'You know that, don't you?'

It is so good to hear him say it and to feel as if he really means it – as if their marriage is what really matters to him.

'I love you too.'

He kisses her on the forehead. 'Get some sleep. Make the most of it before I bring Hurricane Tilly back.'

'I'm not a hurricane!' Tilly pouts, followed quickly with, 'What's a hurricane?' Mel can't help but laugh.

'I'll explain in the car,' Ed tells his daughter before turning back to give his wife one more look. 'Don't forget, if you need me back here, then please just call. We'll drop everything and come right back.'

'Will do,' she says before she locks the caravan door and heads for the bedroom.

Their bed might not be the best, but it's better than trying to get comfortable on the sofa, and at least the bedroom has blackout blinds. She kicks off her shoes and socks but doesn't get changed out of her joggers and sweater, not wanting to lose even one minute of precious sleeping time. It doesn't take long for her to drift off into a blissfully dreamless slumber.

* * *

She jumps awake, roused by the sound of persistent, urgent knocking on the door. Her first thought is that it must be Tilly and Ed, home already from their errands. She wonders how long she has been asleep for.

But no, it can't be Ed. Ed has a key. Whoever is banging on the door is thumping so hard Mel starts to worry that they might break through it. Fear immediately digs its claws into her. She realises that apart from the knocking, there is just silence. No sound of the mixer, or the radio, or the shout from one brickie to another. Immediately she feels very vulnerable.

With shaking hands, she reaches for her phone, ready to call 999 if she has to. Blinking, she unlocks its screen and the dark room in which she has been sleeping is illuminated. Her screen is littered with notifications – missed calls from a number she does not recognise. Immediately, she thinks of Alice – of how she doesn't put it past her to have a host of burner phones. Phones she will have used to troll and frighten. To use for her different identities. Maybe even for Big Bad Wolf. Mel should've known that not even blocking Alice would stop her getting in touch. She won't like that she has been found out and that she can no longer play with Mel's emotions.

The knocking on the door starts up again, louder this time, as if someone is trying to kick the door of the van in.

That's when she remembers the security cameras, which Ed finally put up. She knows she can check the app to see who exactly is on her doorstep. To her utter surprise, it's not Alice.

It's Thomas.

35

This doesn't make sense. Thomas? And there's no obvious sign of Alice with him. She feels immediately uneasy. There is another knock on the door, louder. Manic.

Her mind immediately jumping to the worst possible conclusion, she worries that in ignoring Alice, who is already obviously unstable, she has caused her to do something stupid. Something Thomas is now here to hold her account-able for.

'Mel!' she hears Thomas shouting. She doesn't want to open the door. She doesn't want to move. Where the hell have Fergus and the boys gone? They are supposed to be her protection. Mel looks at her phone. She dials Ed's number but it goes straight to voicemail. She swears.

Looking at her phone again, she tries to work out what she should do. She could call the police, maybe? But has no idea what she would say. She doubts 'A man I know is knocking on my door' would get the response she wants.

'Mel!' Thomas calls again. 'Mel, I need to talk to you.' His voice doesn't sound angry. If anything, it sounds desperate. 'Alice is missing. I know she's been talking to you again. Do you have any idea where she might be?'

He sounds so worried – his voice with the same desperate, pleading tone she remembers from this time last year. He must be seriously worried if he has driven all the way across the country to speak to her. Poor Thomas, she thinks. He is living this nightmare too.

'I'm on my way,' she calls, padding through to the living room. When she opens the door, she is shocked at the shadow of a man who is standing in front of her. Thomas looks wretched. He has lost weight, his eyes are bloodshot and he is in desperate need of a shave. There's a slight tremor in his voice when he asks if he can come in.

'I didn't know what else to do,' he says as she invites him in and leads him to the sofa. 'I didn't know where else to go. Her phone is going straight to voicemail. No one seems to have seen her.'

'Do you want me to try and call her?' Mel asks, taking her phone from her pocket. Maybe if she unblocked Alice she could try and call her.

'There's no point,' Thomas says firmly. 'I've been trying all morning. A few of our friends have too. Everyone is just going straight to voicemail. You know as well as I do that she never ever switches her phone off. She's been so irrational coming up to Jacob's birthday,' Thomas says. 'Really manic. I thought things were settling down again with her, you know. We were finding our way through it. But she started posting online again. Posting the vilest things. Posting about you... You must have seen it.'

'I have.' Mel is aware that Thomas's eyes keep flicking from her face to her stomach and back again. She's suddenly very self-conscious of her bump – very conscious of what she has and what Thomas has lost.

'She's not well,' he says. 'I'm afraid of what she will do. To herself, never mind others. I'm desperate, Mel. I wouldn't come to see you if I weren't. I'm so ashamed of how I treated you last year.'

'Last year you were in shock,' Mel tells him. 'You were in pain. But I'm sorry, Thomas, I don't know where she is or what she is doing. I have been getting calls from this number though? Maybe you know it?' She shows her phone screen to Thomas who sags when he sees it.

'That's my number. I was trying to call you to see if you'd heard from her. When was the last time you spoke?'

'The early hours of yesterday morning,' she says, still standing as Thomas sits down and surveys the caravan – his eyes darting around it.

'How did she seem?'

Mel knows she owes it to Thomas to handle this as sensitively as possible. 'She seemed okay. Upbeat if anything. But, Thomas, do you know she had told me she was pregnant? More than halfway gone. She came to see me and she even had a bump.'

His eyes widen. 'No.' His voice breaks. 'I didn't know that. Not at all. I'm... I'm so sorry. Why on earth would she do that?'

'I was hoping you'd be able to tell me,' Mel says.

He shakes his head slowly. 'I wish I could. Shit, this is serious.'

Mel notices his hands are shaking. 'Can I get you a cup of tea? Or coffee? Something to steady your nerves?'

'Tea,' Thomas says. 'That would be great. I got straight in the car. I woke this morning and just had a feeling something bad was going to happen today. Deep in my gut. I tried every number... I...' He breaks down. 'I can't lose her. I can't lose anyone else.'

Mel gets up to the make the tea, biting the inside of her cheek as a twinge, stronger than the ones she was having last night, tightens her stomach. This is the last thing she needs right now.

She fills the kettle and switches it on. Maybe she should cross the room and offer him a hug, try to console him in some way. But despite his obvious distress, she can't get past the memory of how he had shouted at her down the phone a year ago. She feels heart sorry for him but given the events of the last year, she doesn't trust him.

'This place is a little cramped, isn't it?' He looks around the room, his whole demeanour changing. He sounds calm now. All trace of upset gone. 'How are you going to manage here with a new baby?'

'It'll only be for a short time. The builders are really getting ahead with the work.'

'But they're not here today,' Thomas says.

'They must've just nipped out for supplies. They were here before and I'm expecting them back imminently.'

'And where is Ed? And Tilly? I'd love to see them again. Since I've come all this way.'

'They had to go run a few errands, you know. Supermarket, few other things. Tilly's a daddy's girl. Always loves to be with him and I thought it would be the perfect time for me to get a sleep.'

Thomas nods. Mel feels the very hairs on the back of her neck prickling. She glances at the clock on the wall trying to work out how long it will be until Ed is home. Okay, she tells herself, it has been about ninety minutes since Ed and Tilly left. She has no idea how much longer they will be.

'That's a shame he's not here. It would've been nice to chat to him. Maybe he could tell me all his plans for this place? I'd love to see the plans.'

If Mel finds it strange that he is suddenly chatting very amiably, and no longer seems to be bothered about where Alice might be, she says nothing. She just keeps herself busy making the tea and putting some biscuits out on a plate.

'I'm sure he would love to show you. He's very excited about it.'

'And this place? This location – it's special, isn't it? The perfect place to raise children, I'd think.'

The topic of children makes her feel uncomfortable – guilty maybe. She tells herself she is being silly. It's natural to talk about children – especially with her heavily pregnant right in front of him. Especially since children were at the heart of the relationship between them in the first place.

'Yes, it is. We're looking forward to it. Lots of fresh air and places to explore.'

'Why don't you give me a little tour?' Thomas asks.

'Ach, it's little more than a mud bath at the moment. I'm not sure there's much to show you.'

'There's all this beautiful countryside,' he says. 'Sure isn't that enough?'

'I suppose.' She scoops the tea bags out of the cups and tosses them in the sink. She's rewarded by another twinge across her back.

'Ooooof,' she groans, unable to hold it in. She tries rocking back on her heels to trying to stretch her back, but nothing eases the pain. *Please*, she thinks, *this can't be labour. Not now and here in this company.*

36

'Are you okay?' Thomas asks.

'Yeah,' Mel says, grateful to feel the pain in her tummy subside. 'I think I just over-stretched. Keep forgetting I have this bloody bump in the way. You'd think it would be impossible to forget but still...' She smiles.

Thomas's eyes go straight to Mel's heavily swollen stomach and back to her face. He smiles but it doesn't reach his eyes. 'Why don't you sit down and I'll make the tea?'

'It's nearly done now,' Mel says, 'I think I have it under control.'

'Okay, if you're sure,' Thomas says. ''You shouldn't be over-doing it. Although I bet that's impossible, living in a place like this. It's very brave of you, taking on this project. I admire that. It must be stressful though. Don't they say moving house is one of the most stressful things you can do? And you're combining that with moving across the country and doing a renovation. Definitely brave, or very foolish. One of the two.' Thomas gives a sharp laugh. 'If I were lucky enough to live here, with my little happy family, life all perfect, I suppose I'd feel it was all worth it. But we don't all get choices about how our lives play out, do we?'

The tone of his voice chills Mel to the very bone.

'Just a drop of milk for me,' Thomas says, a smile back on his face as if everything were normal. As if he weren't switching from being distraught over his missing wife, to talking about cups of tea, to making barbed comments about Mel's new home.

'Yeah, I remember.' Mel glances again at the clock which seems to be moving so slowly it might as well be in reverse. 'You take your tea fairly weak, don't you? Ed has become a full builder's brew man...'

'Yeah, not too strong,' Thomas says. 'And then you can show me round the site when we're done? Since Ed doesn't seem to be anywhere near.'

'Yeah, sure.' Mel turns to stir the tea.

'Here, let me help you with that,' Thomas says from directly behind her. Mel jumps, not having realised he had crept up behind her.

'Jesus Christ! I didn't hear you come across the room. You scared the heart out of me.'

Thomas moves just a little too close for it to be comfortable.

'Ah now, sure it's only me! I'm not scary.' He's close enough that she can smell the staleness of his breath. 'Sure we're friends. We've shared so much. I'm hardly going to cause any harm to you... or your baby.' He reaches out his hand to touch Mel's stomach and she cannot stop herself from recoiling – the image of the strange man in her nightmare flashing into her head. With his long, bony fingers and an air of malice – just like Thomas right now.

'Jesus Christ, Mel!' Thomas says, his voice mocking Mel's from just a minute ago. 'You're very jumpy today. Are you actually scared of me?'

'Of course not,' Mel lies, feeling her heart racing. She's not sure what the fuck is going on here but she just wants him to go. And now.

'Thomas, you know, Ed will be back any minute now and we have to go out to an appointment. It's a lot later in the day than I thought it was. I don't think I have time for tea after all. If I hear anything from Alice, anything at all, I will call you right away. Maybe you'd be better back at home in case she comes back.'

The lies trip easily from Mel's tongue. She hopes they work. She doesn't know what she will do if they don't.

'Is the appointment with the midwife? Is it about your contractions?' he asks.

'What contractions?' Mel tries to hide her growing panic from her voice.

'Sorry... I meant surges. Isn't that the mumbo jumbo you asked us to say last year? Just as long as it distracted us from what was going wrong.'

She wills herself to sound calm even though she feels anything but. 'Contractions or surges – it doesn't matter. I'm not having any. I'm not due for ages yet.'

'But babies come when they are ready to come.' Thomas smiles. 'You know that. This isn't your first rodeo, after all. You've done this before. You've seen so many babies come into the world. That must be really magical. I can't wait to be present at a birth that doesn't end in silence.' His voice is even – completely lacking in emotion. Mel thinks that's more terrifying than if he were screaming and shouting.

'Why don't you sit down?' Thomas nods towards the table. 'I'll carry this tea over.' Mel does exactly what she is told, a growing feeling of desperation in the very pit of her stomach.

Thomas takes his time, even when he sits himself down and

brings his mug to his lips; it feels to Mel that he is in slow motion. He is relishing this.

'I'll tell you a secret.' He pauses. 'I don't really care about Alice. That's not why I'm here.'

'I don't want to fight with you, Thomas. If you need to tell me I'm evil, or twisted, or a murderer, do it. I've heard it all this year already.'

'Are you trying to make me feel sorry for you?' he asks. 'Because that's not going to happen. You don't get to be the victim here. What is it with you women? Always claiming the victimhood as if no one else was hurt? As if I didn't lose my son?'

'I'm very sorry for your loss. I will always be sorry for your loss, but I still want you to leave now. You're making me feel uncomfortable.'

Thomas gives her a pitying look. 'Well, we couldn't have you feeling uncomfortable now, could we? But if you want me to leave then I'm more than happy to leave.'

She sags with relief.

'As long as you come with me.'

37

Mel is confused. She doesn't know what it is he wants from her but she does know that the very last thing she wants to do is go anywhere with Thomas Munroe.

'This is such a beautiful part of the world. So remote and quiet. And it's warm too, just as it was when Jacob was born. Alice and I always used to talk about that, you know, how we couldn't wait to take our baby out in his pram or in a sling for long walks – hikes through the forest. That kind of thing. There has to be some lovely walks around here? All those fields and the hills and the trees...'

'I don't want to go with you,' Mel says, too scared to think of any other excuse. And there's no way she wants to go for a walk. She knows that her aches and pains might well be signs of an early labour kicking in, and she is now sure Thomas has noticed that too, no matter she has tried to hide it. She doesn't want to do anything to speed the process. And that's without saying the absolute last place she would feel safe right now is walking along deserted country lanes with a man who so clearly detests her and wants her to experience some of the pain he has.

'A bit of fresh air will wake you up!' Thomas says. 'And walking is great for pregnant women, isn't it? Do you remember it was just like this the day Alice went into labour with Jacob? You and she went for a walk along the shoreline? You told me it would do her good, would help move things along. I remember her coming back, all red-faced and sweaty, stopping to breathe through a contraction – sorry, a surge.'

Mel just nods, as she bites on her inner cheek to stop herself from gasping as the grip of another pain wrapped its way around her pelvis.

'There are so many things we won't ever know,' Thomas says. 'Like, if she'd rested then instead, like you want to rest now, would Jacob have been okay?'

'There's no reason at all to believe that going for a walk had anything to with what happened to Jacob.'

'To his death,' Thomas says, coldly. 'It wasn't just "what happened to Jacob". That's all everyone ever says. No one just says it like it is. He died. Alice didn't give birth to—'

'—she did give birth!' Mel protests. 'She brought him into the world.'

Thomas raises his hand to silence her.

'She didn't give birth. She gave him death. Our baby died. He's fucking dead!' he shouts. 'And I'll never forgive either of you for it. When I say I don't care about Alice, I mean it from the bottom of my heart. Do you think I could stay with her after what happened? She pushed for her alternative birth. She told me it would be okay. And you? You encouraged it! And both of you now carry on as if nothing ever happened.'

'You've no idea,' she bites back. 'As if nothing ever happened? My life has been destroyed. Alice has destroyed it. And that is not the action of someone carrying on as if nothing ever happened. Thomas, she was pretending to be pregnant! Are you two in on this together? Is this some sort of sick revenge scheme?'

He snorts, pushes his seat backwards and stands up. 'I've told you before. I don't give a damn about Alice or what she has been up to. She's as dead to me as our son is. Now, Mel, I think we should get on with our walk now. Come on! No time like the present.'

'Thomas, I'm not going to do that. I'm staying here and keeping my baby safe.'

'No,' he says. 'No, you're wrong there. You're coming with me.'

Mel knows, more than she has ever known anything in her entire life, that Thomas is not asking her. She doesn't have a choice in this. Her phone is back on the worktop in the kitchen and she can't even reach it. Not even to slip it into her pocket. If she could just grab it while she's getting ready then maybe, she thinks, she can pocket dial Ed, or send him a message and let him know what is happening.

'Okay,' Mel says. 'I'll just go and get my shoes and socks.'

Thomas glances down at Mel's bare feet and shakes his head. 'No. No I think we need to go now, before the weather changes. I mean what if it rains?'

'I can't go without shoes!' Mel protests.

'Oh for fuck's sake,' Thomas grumbles, looking around the room and spotting the wellies by the door. 'Put those on!' he barks.

'I need socks.'

He looks at Mel as if she has just asked him for a million dollars, instead of making a very reasonable request to wear a pair of socks.

'Come on! You don't need socks! We need to go. Come on, Mel. Just tell yourself it's not uncomfortable. You know all about hypnosis. Hypnotise yourself so you feel as if you're wearing a pair of fluffy slippers.'

'Thomas,' Mel says, thinking she really needs to try and regain control of this conversation, 'I'm starting to think these are more than just Braxton Hicks so I really do want to stay here. At least until Ed gets back.'

She hopes her admission will knock some sense into him.

'We've been through this,' he replies without so much as blinking. 'It moves things along. Keep moving! It will help get the baby into position. So we really, really should go, and *now*.'

'I really don't think—'

'Now!' Any hint of softness is gone from his face. He looks manic, and absolutely determined to get his way.

Mel pulls on the boots and reaches for her jacket. This much Thomas allows. 'I'll just grab my phone,' Mel chances.

'You don't need your phone,' Thomas says. 'I have mine. If we need anything, I'll make the call.' With that, he opens the door to the caravan and nudges Mel towards it.

'Think of my baby,' she pleads. 'I already have high blood pressure. If I am going into labour, then I need to go to the hospital. Thomas, please!'

'I *am* thinking of your baby. And the way I see it, is that you owe me, Mel.'

He follows her out of the caravan, slamming the door behind him. 'Let's go. And don't even think about running,' he says.

It's only then Mel notices he has lifted one of the knives from the caravan, and it is poking out from the sleeve of his jacket.

38

'Where are we going?' Mel asks, trying to stem the rising panic in her chest as they reach the gatepost where the balloon, partially deflated and sorry-looking as it sinks closer to the ground, is still tied.

Thomas doesn't answer. For a moment he seems lost in his own world – a world where his baby should be preparing to celebrate his first birthday.

'He deserved much more than that,' he says, ignoring Mel's question. He nods his head towards the gate 'I wanted to make sure you remembered him. That you were forced to think about what should've been.'

'I always think about him,' Mel says.

'Not enough. Not every moment of every day so that you can't sleep. You can't function. I wanted you to feel some of that. I wanted you to be marked by it forever.'

'My hand...'

'A big enough cut to leave a scar. Just as I'd hoped.'

'And what if Tilly had got to the bear first? What if she had opened it?' Anger nips at Mel and she has to hold it in, afraid to antagonise him further but also so very, very angry that her child could've been marked for life.

Thomas just shrugs and says nothing. It's clear he doesn't care. It's naive for Mel to think he cares about anything or anyone bar his own thirst for revenge just now.

'Let's walk. This way,' he says, and the pair start walking away from the house and farther along the country road and away from the likelihood of passing traffic.

'Do you know what I was looking forward to most?' he asks. 'When Alice was pregnant with Jacob? Did I tell you how much I was looking forward to just being recognised as a dad? I was going to 100 per cent lean into the smug dad aesthetic,' he says. 'I was going to prove just how good a parent I could be. How valuable a father figure is. That we're not all useless lumps who don't know how to change nappies. I just couldn't wait to have him with me all the time – but where I could see him and feel the warmth of his tiny body against mine. You know that newborn scrunch? Where they are all curled up on your chest? I just wanted that so much. Alice and I would talk about it. Laugh that we'd forever be fighting for a turn. I wanted the skin on skin contact as much as Alice did. She'd had him for nine months and I figured it was my turn. People don't think fathers can love their children as much as mothers, but I loved him. I still love him. I wanted to carry him in a sling – to feel our hearts beating together. To know that at any time I could just bend my head and give him a gentle little kiss on his warm head.'

'You'd have made a great father,' Mel says, trying to mollify him before wincing as her stomach starts to tighten again. She forces herself to stay silent. She doesn't want Thomas to know she's in pain and scared. She's worried that if she does, he will enjoy it a little too much. He seems to be getting off on it. He would just revel in how vulnerable she is. 'You owe me, Mel,'

Thomas had said. Mel wonders, what exactly did he mean by that? Just how far is he planning to take this?

'The thing is,' Thomas keeps his gaze forward, 'I never got to do that. I only got to hold him for the briefest of times and he was already gone. His wee body was already growing cold. I never got to live that dream.'

Mel breathes in and out slowly as her body continues to prepare itself for birth. When she knows she can speak again without giving her state away, she tells Thomas she can't imagine how horrible that must've been. 'You've endured something no parent should ever have to endure,' Mel says, and she means every word of it. 'It's not right. It goes against the order of things for a father to be forced to bury his child.'

Thomas lets out a single, gut-wrenching sob before sucking air back into his lungs. Such a wail of grief is always hard to hear. Coming from a man, it threatens to tear her heart from her chest. Mel cannot help but feel desperately sorry for him despite everything that he is putting her through.

'I know there is absolutely nothing that can make up for the loss of Jacob,' Mel says, 'but there's nothing to say you won't have another child. One that will help you heal.'

'But it won't be him. And it won't be with Alice. All those years hoping and planning to be left back at the start? With nothing? No son. No wife? At my age.' He walks on, faster, calling her to hurry up.

'I'm doing my best,' Mel gasps, feeling the growing pressure in her pelvis of her baby getting ready for birth. She tries to force herself to speed up. But her chest is tight and her head is light. She closes her eyes for just a moment, hoping that when she opens them again the light-headed feeling will have passed. Instead, she struggles to focus, white dots floating in front of her eyes and her head aching. She knows this is likely to mean her blood pressure is climbing and now she is not just scared. She is terrified. For herself. And for her baby.

'Thomas, please,' she begs. 'I don't feel too good.'

He takes her in, looking her up and down. 'You'll be fine.' He walks on while Mel has to stop and catch her breath, before releasing a small groan as her stomach tightens once again.

'This is exciting. Everything seems to be happening today!'

'Thomas, please. Let's go back to the caravan. We can talk there. You can say everything you need to say and I promise you I will listen. I'll listen for as long as you need me to.' She doesn't want to beg but she will.

Her heart is thumping in her chest now, the feeling of dread growing with every second. She has broken out in a sweat, and every muscle in her body aches. She wants to sit down on the ground and refuse to move. But she remembers the knife and that this man is completely unhinged – more than she ever believed Alice to be – and she is afraid of what he might do with it.

'We are not going back. We'll keep going. That's what you have to do with grief, you see. You have to keep going. There's no way to stop it, or pause it. There's no way to go around or run through it. You just have to endure it. And it doesn't matter if someone else is grieving too. It's different for everyone. Alice got to carry him. She got to feel like a mother. She got to own that title, you know.'

'You're still a father. You'll always be a father,' Mel says, trying to keep the tremor from her voice and sound as sympathetic as possible. 'There's nothing to stop you from owning that title. You are Jacob's daddy.'

'But it's not enough,' he howls. 'I'm a father, but I don't have a baby. And it hurts every moment of every day.'

'I'm sorry,' Mel stammers. 'I can't imagine the pain.'

'Exactly,' he says, speeding up again, urging Mel to keep up with him. 'You don't know. You walked away that night and you never had to deal with it. With the consequences.'

Mel wants to scream that she did not walk away. She has been pushed. Shut out. And she did not just slip back into her life with no consequences. But she knows in her heart it will only enrage him further, and she can't risk doing that.

'You're right. I'm sorry,' Mel says.

He sniffs. 'You say that, but you also say it wasn't your fault. You say you did nothing wrong. So, you're not sorry at all.'

Mel wants to defend herself, but Thomas is beyond listening. He's beyond thinking rationally.

'You get it all,' he continues. 'A new start. A lovely new house in the countryside. A partner who loves you. Your wee girl. And a baby. A baby boy of all things. And what do I have?'

Mel says nothing. She wants to let Thomas rant, hoping he will shout and scream until his anger is spent.

'What do I have, Mel?' he asks again, coming to a sudden stop and looking Mel directly in the eye. 'Tell me. I want you to tell me. What do I have? What was I left with?'

Mel doesn't want to answer. There's nothing she can say that will make this situation any better.

'Come on, Mel. You're a smart woman. What was I left with?' Thomas asks, pain etched across his face. He steps towards Mel, invading her personal space, the knife now uncomfortably close to her tummy. Thomas wants an answer. He wants one now and Mel doesn't know what to do. She doesn't know how to get away from this.

'No one ever thinks of the father,' he says, his breath warm on her face.

As she opens her mouth to offer another inadequate apology, a pain, sharper this time, bends her double and she feels a pop deep inside, followed by a steady stream of warm liquid running down between her legs.

Her waters have gone.

She can't hide the pain, or the fear, from her face – nor can she hide the darkening of her jogging bottoms as liquid floods them. Her fear is turning to panic and she looks at Thomas, desperate to connect with him. Mel knows Thomas is in pain and is made desperate with grief. She knows though, he's not a monster. Surely he won't want to hurt Mel's baby.

Will he?

39

'Walk!' Thomas orders as Mel straightens up, gasping as she tries to regulate her breathing. She has no doubt her baby is coming, and by the looks of things, he's not going to take his time like his big sister did. Woozy and desperate for the chance to sit down and catch her breath, Mel stalls.

But Thomas's expression remains cold. 'I said "walk"!'

'Thomas, please. My waters have just broken. We need to go back to the caravan!'

'Moving about helps to progress labour,' he parrots again. 'You'll be fine.'

Mel takes a few steps, aware of the now trickling water that she knows will continue through labour. 'I don't feel too good,' she says, 'Please. I just want to go home and get Ed and go to the hospital.'

Thomas shakes his head. 'No. I don't think so.'

He grabs Mel's hand, squeezing it tightly, and hauls her forward. Mel prays for a car or lorry to pass by. She might have half a chance of signalling at them in some way, or maybe they will notice how distressed she is.

With a wave of despair, Mel realises more than likely they'll just think they've seen a couple out for a walk and think little of it. If they see the wet markings on her joggers they'll probably do their best to pretend they didn't. Maybe they'll mention to someone later in conversation that they saw a woman who had wet herself walking the country roads. People don't like to intervene. They're usually too busy getting on with their own lives or thinking about their own worries.

Thomas is muttering now, his voice low, and Mel can't make out what's he's saying over the thumping of her own heart and the heaviness of her breathing.

'Thomas,' she pleads.

'Stop it!' He glares back at her. 'I have to think. I have to get it right this time.'

'What are you doing?' Mel asks. 'What are your plans?'

He shakes his head and continues his indecipherable mumbling.

'We moved away because we didn't want to make it harder for you,' Mel tells him. It's not a total lie. They wanted to be away from Carrickfergus and the chance of bumping into Alice and Thomas again before the baby was born. Mel didn't want them to see her growing stomach. More than that she did not want them to see the baby. She knew it would be unbearably painful for them and she knew – or feared – it would just lead to Alice kicking off her hate campaign again. Mel had wanted to put as much distance between them as possible, but she had been focusing on the wrong parent all this time.

'I don't think you did a great job of that,' he says, sarcasm dripping from his tongue.

'I know. I know. I fucked up!' Mel cries, wishing she were in South Yarra now worrying about how to make their rental payment, while watching Tilly play in the pool with her cousins. 'Where are we going? Please tell me!'

'Shut up and walk!' Thomas shouts, tugging extra forcefully on Mel's hand so that she stumbles and falls to her knees. She tries but fails to stop herself from falling farther forward and onto her stomach.

'Oh, for fuck's sake!' Thomas exclaims as Mel tries to process the pain in her knees, and the burning in her bandaged hand which she instinctively used to try and break her fall. A searing pain and the slow seeping of red through the white of the bandage tells her she's managed to open the wound.

'Get up!' he yells.

Mel just wants to curl up in a ball and hug her stomach – do whatever she can to protect it, protect her baby.

'Now, Mel!' he shouts, bending down over her. 'Get up now or so help me I will hurt you. Don't think I won't.' The tip of the knife jabs at Mel's back and she slowly starts to get up, pain radiating in her back and through her middle. She no longer knows if it's a contraction or Thomas driving the damn knife into her.

Sobbing loudly, she gets to her feet.

'Don't worry,' he says, voice light again. 'I don't think we've too much further to go.'

Grabbing Mel's hand again, he pulls her forward. He even keeps Mel walking when another contraction starts up, refusing to allow her the chance to simply breathe her way through it. Mel still has no idea what his endgame is, but she no longer believes they are going to turn and walk back home at any stage.

As they reach the brow of the hill, she sees a cluster of outbuildings, some small, and a large steel-framed barn a short distance away. Hope lifts her heart that it could be Sheila's farmhouse. She is their nearest neighbour, after all. Mel remembers that Sheila has warned them of a dog that runs up to say hello.

That might be enough to distract Thomas to gain the upper hand.

If Mel can just get to the house and put the barrier of a door between them, she, and her baby, have a chance. She can call the police. And an ambulance. There has to be a way. But as they get closer, the yard looks deserted and there's no sign of a house, and as they get closer still it becomes clear this site is abandoned.

The stone buildings are ramshackle – their roofs sagging. There are weeds climbing around the door-frames and peeking out through shattered windows, crumbling mortar, and anywhere they have been able to gain purchase. There are no animals milling about. No cluck of chickens, nor barking dogs. No farm machinery. A wall to the back of the yard is partially collapsed, spewing its aged stones over the muddy ground. The barn might look more modern from a distance but as they approach, it doesn't seem to be in any better condition. Rust climbs the sides of the structure in autumnal-coloured fronds, burning like acid through the corrugated steel.

'I can't go any farther,' Mel sobs, her legs buckling again. Her headache is severe now and she empties the contents of her stomach on the muddy ground. 'I can't,' she repeats, sobbing.

Thomas drags Mel to her feet and across to the old barn. Mel knows it's a bad idea to go inside the barn – that being out of the view of any possible passers-by will be a very bad thing indeed, even if she feels she doesn't have the strength to take just one more step.

Didn't Sheila say she only lived a mile away, surely she must be nearby now? She could push herself on, she supposes.

'Ah! Here we go!' Thomas exclaims, dashing Mel's hopes as he pushes the large door partially open. It emits a deafening screech of tin on rusty tin. 'Get in,' he shouts, pushing Mel into the dark, dank barn before following her in. Mel is grateful at least to be able to keep to her feet – especially when she notices the sludge-covered concrete flooring just as her nose is assaulted by the stench of decay and animal faeces. She startles as something – too large to be a mouse and too small to be a cat – scurries in front of her, sending her flailing backwards until Thomas breaks her fall and pushes her back to standing.

'Oh for goodness' sake, Mel. It's just a rat. It will be more scared of you than you are of it,' he says as he fishes his phone from his pocket and switches on the flashlight, surveying the barn. In the shadows, Mel can see mounds of rotted hay, some sacks spilling God knows what onto the ground which is floored with mouse droppings. In one corner there sits a rusty camping chair, long past its best, and some tarpaulin sheeting. Empty cider bottles and cigarette packets litter the space, a shoddy graffiti tag in red spray paint on the wall. This place has been used as a drinking den but by the looks of it, not recently.

'It's not ideal here,' Thomas adds, 'but it will do.'

'For what?' Mel asks, fearing his answer but needing to know what she is up against.

'For a baby to be born,' Thomas says with a broad smile. 'A barn was good enough for Jesus. Or a stable? Was it a stable? Still, close enough.' He is back to being composed but Mel finds that more frightening than any degree of shouting.

'I can't have the baby here,' Mel says, desperate to connect with Thomas's sense of humanity. 'It's filthy. We don't have anything we might need. And my blood pressure...'

'You'll be fine,' he says dismissively, his eyes darting around the space. 'You've been through countless births before. You know what to do, don't you? And I can support you through it.

You know, return the favour. There's a beautiful symmetry to it. And then, I promise you, I will leave you all alone. As soon as Jacob gets here safe and sound.'

40

'Jacob'. Thomas has just said Jacob. That's when the full horror of the situation hits Mel. She'd suspected it would be bad, but her mind had not allowed her to go to a place where Thomas believes Jacob is about to be reborn.

'This isn't Jac—'

Thomas raises a hand to silence her. 'I said you owe me and you do. You know it yourself. That's why you came back looking for Alice. You knew you owed us,' he says as he pushes Mel towards the back of the barn where what remains of a bale of hay is clumped against the wall. He starts to kick the hay around, sending a flurry of mice scurrying from it and back into the shadows. 'Sit,' he orders.

Mel sobs, her skin crawling, her stomach turning. 'I don't want to.'

He just shakes his head. 'You can cry first, then sit down. Or just sit down and save yourself the trouble of a sore head from all the snivelling.'

As another contraction starts to build, Mel sits, her legs shaking and her body overcome by the growing pain in her pelvis. She can feel her baby move down, opening her cervix, getting ready to be born. She's relieved to find the hay isn't soaked through, even if she can feel its cold dampness seeping into her clothes.

Thomas looks around again and spots an old plastic milk crate which he turns upside down and takes a seat on. 'Don't be afraid, Mel. It's not good for labour, or the baby. I'm here to support you through it.'

'Thomas, please. You can do whatever you want to me. If you really think I'm even partially to blame for what happened with Jacob. But don't put my baby in danger. He doesn't deserve this.'

Thomas shakes his head. 'I'm not going to hurt the baby. I have everything ready for him at home, you know. The nursery. The pram. The baby carrier. Alice told me to donate them. Get rid of them in whatever way I saw fit, as if it were just her decision to make. As if my grief didn't deserve consideration. Thankfully my mother was only too happy to let me keep them in her house. She understands my grief. He was her first grandchild, you know. It broke her that she never got to know him. So don't worry. The baby will be fine. He has the best of everything waiting for him and a granny that will love him as much as I will.'

Mel shifts, to try and get comfortable – her wet joggers are now cooling and sticky against her legs.

'You're not well,' she tells him, shaking her head. 'You need help.'

He snorts. 'Tell me something I don't know. How is anyone supposed to come through what I did and be *well*? We don't all just brush these things off and opt for a brand-new start. We're not all lucky. Although you camping out in a caravan was a surprise. I wasn't sure what to think when I came down to hang the balloon and saw it. You scared me a wee bit with that.'

Mel pauses for a moment, lost in her own thoughts, while she tries and fails to think of a way to get out of this mess.

'I was worried you'd hear me,' he says, breaking the silence. 'I mean, caravans aren't really soundproof. I was afraid you'd hear my feet on the gravel or something. Let me tell you, my heart was in my throat waiting for the lights to come on and you or Ed to appear at the door. But neither of you did. I was even able to have a little nosey around the site. It's a nice house – or it will be when it's done. I'm not sure I'd have opted for such a big project but sure we're all different, aren't we? I considered trying the door to the caravan, maybe popping in to say hello to Tilly... but then I decided that would be taking things too far. I'd be asking for trouble with that, wouldn't I? So I just peeked in the window...' He drifts off. She shudders thinking how close this man had been to Tilly while she and Ed had been lying fast asleep nearby and none the wiser.

'I wasn't going to come back after that, you know,' he says.

'So, you didn't call me? Let a baby cry down the phone?' I ask.

He looks at her, eyes wide in shock. 'Oh God no. I wouldn't do that. I'm not cruel, Mel. That's really more the kind of thing Alice would do. She wanted to make your life more difficult. She shared your number around. She blackened your name. That was all her. I supported her, of course. You deserved it, but then she grew a conscience and wanted to back off. Hmmmm.' He thinks. 'I wasn't going to let all that good work go to waste. She'd made sure a lot of people knew how to get under your skin. They were very good at it. I might've encouraged some people to call you – but no. I didn't do it myself.'

'And you were behind the bear and balloon, and the flowers at my parents'?'

'I thought that was a nice touch. I knew you'd immediately blame Alice,' he says.

Mel gasps as another contraction starts, sending another gush of liquid from between her legs.

'I suppose we'd better start timing those, though I'd put money on it that they're getting closer together,' he says.

And stronger too, Mel thinks, but says nothing, instead just focusing on trying to breathe her way through the pain.

He looks around the barn, his leg jiggling up and down with nerves. 'You don't even realise I would've left it at that,' he says. 'But then I heard it's all a smoke show, isn't it? This perfect life you've built for yourself here? It's far from it. Your husband has money worries. He wants to move. You don't have the energy to look after Tilly, never mind another child, and the gaslighting that goes on in your marriage? My, my, that's impressive.'

'How the hell do you know anything about my marriage?' she asks. 'You don't know us. Not the real us. What has Alice been telling you, because I can assure you, she is not telling you the truth.'

He shakes his head, taps the side of his nose. 'That'll be my wee secret for now.'

Anger rises in Mel along with the strength of her contraction. 'You're mad.'

'And you can't bring yourself to admit I'm telling the truth. I bet you are secretly so grateful to me right now. Once Jacob is in my arms, the score will be even. It will be all done,' he says. 'You can walk away from Ed – you and your daughter can build your new life and he can fuck off to Australia where he clearly wants to be. Without you.'

He glances at his phone screen, then stands up and claps his hands together. 'You know we should probably check that your waters are clear. We both know the dangers that come with meconium. I don't want to take any chances.'

'Thomas,' Mel says as she tries to process what has just been said to her. 'We're in a filthy, deserted barn and you're telling me you don't want to take any chances? Please, if you're serious about it, if you're really not a cruel person who would hurt an innocent child, then please let's call for an ambulance. There's time to get help.'

'No,' he says, 'I have to be able to hold him first. You know that. Bonding is so important right from the start.'

Mel shakes her head. 'This isn't Jacob,' she hisses through gritted teeth as another wave of pain lands on top of the last.

He laughs. 'See! Just as I said. You can't admit it because you don't want your perfect little facade to falter, but I know you know it's true. It's fate. Jacob is coming back to me and if we don't do it here, someone will take him from me and I'm not going to let that happen. Not again. Do you know how much effort we've gone to just to keep an eye on you? To make sure we have our timing just right? You don't even realise how lucky you are. You've gone into labour. We were starting to think it would have to be a Caesarean and to be honest, I'm not sure that would've ended at all well for you.'

'It's not Jacob!' Mel shouts, knowing it's pointless. She is not arguing with a sane person. This man has completely lost his hold on reality. Still, she will say it again and again until it sinks in. 'This is not your baby.'

A sharp slap to her right cheek leaves her dazed.

'You don't speak,' he says. 'You don't speak again. You focus on your job.'

He's pacing now, agitated, and Mel can see the knife glinting from the bottom of his sleeve. He walks to the door of the barn and looks outside before coming back.

'Who are you waiting for?' she asks.

'What?'

'You've walked to that door and looked outside. Is someone coming? Is it Alice?' Mel asks, as it strikes her he had been talking about a 'we' as he mentioned a Caesarean – the thought of which is too horrific to contemplate.

'It doesn't matter,' he says, but he is clearly on edge.

Mel doesn't know what she can do. All she knows, right now, is that this hurts. Her insides feel as if they are being twisted and torn apart, and everything about this feels wrong. It's too fast. It's too intense. Her stomach is churning and her head is spinning. Before she knows it, she is vomiting again from the pain of another contraction. She can't sit any longer – the pressure is growing too strong and the pain in her back is too much. She clambers forward onto all fours, groaning as the contraction peaks. She is scared. She is not in control. Everything is wrong. The pressure in her pelvis is now matched by pressure in her head – a headache like no other.

'Please, Thomas,' she begs. 'I don't feel right. Something is wrong. What if he's in distress?'

'Quiet,' Thomas says, pacing and mumbling to himself, walking back to the barn door and swearing.

'What if he gets stuck? Like Jacob? What if we lose him?' she says, her own fear growing.

He stops pacing and looks at Mel. 'You said "we",' he says. 'You can say it now. He's my baby.'

'How can I give him to you if we can't get him here safely?' Mel groans through gritted teeth, aware that this lie might be her only chance of getting her and her son through this. 'That's all that matters, isn't it? Getting your baby here safe?'

Thomas crouches down beside Mel, brushing her hair from her now sweat-soaked face. 'My baby,' he whispers. 'My son.'

'Your baby,' Mel says before another pain takes her voice from her.

'Okay,' he says, standing up. 'Okay. You're right. We need to get him here safely.'

He pulls his phone from his pocket once more, holds it up and scrolls at the screen. 'Fuck! No signal,' he swears and Mel lets out an anguished sob.

'Where is she?' Thomas shouts as he makes his way to the rusty door, punching at the screen with his fingers. Mel is too far gone at this stage to wonder who the 'she' is. She's quickly losing her grasp on consciousness, the pain in her head growing.

Through blurring eyes she can see Thomas's frustration growing as he waves the phone above his head trying to catch a signal. She's about to shout to him to go outside and try, it's not like she's in any fit state to run away. But all she can do is cry out in pain, then fear as she watches him hurl the phone onto the concrete floor in frustration, stomping on it in anger.

'Damn thing. There's no time,' he says, rushing back to Mel. 'We have to do it. Just you and me. We can do it.'

And as Mel feels the weight of her baby's head start to make its way down into the birth canal, she knows she has no choice but to push.

41

Slick with sweat now, her legs shaking uncontrollably, the urge to push takes over Mel's body.

'Help me!' she calls to Thomas as she tries to peel off sodden joggers and underwear. There is no time nor energy for embarrassment now. The baby is coming and it doesn't care if she is in danger. It doesn't care that this man is the only person there to help.

When another surge comes, hot on the heels of the last, Mel, on all fours, pushes down into her pelvis with all her might and puts what little energy she has left into expelling her baby into the world, even though she doesn't want to. She wants him to stay safe with her. Attached to her. Where she can protect him. But this is a primal force, beyond her control.

She has reached the stage of childbirth where her body's natural reflexes have taken over and are forcing her to keep pushing through the burning pain of another contraction as she feels her baby's head starting to crown.

'I see him,' Thomas sobs, pulling off his jacket and then his hoodie. 'I see his head.'

Fear swamps Mel. Fear and grief. She can't bear the thought of Thomas claiming him. She is scared of what he will do to her once she is past her usefulness to him. 'I... I can't...' she screams, feeling as if her soul is being ripped from her body.

'You can,' Thomas tells her. 'You're doing it.'

These are echoes of words she said to Alice. Words she has said to every woman she has had the pleasure of supporting. They should be soothing but they are not. Not this time. Not coming from his mouth.

Mel's head is now pounding with a pain so severe it eclipses the pain of birth. She's scared. She wants to scream to the world that she is scared. She wants to cry out for her own mother. But when she tries, all that comes out is a guttural cry as another contraction forces her to keep going. Her head, she thinks, will combust under this pressure.

Instinctively, she reaches her hand down between her legs and can feel his soft, downy hair, wet and warm. She sobs as her body releases him into a world where it can no longer keep him safe.

Rocking back onto her legs, her head too heavy and racked with pain, Mel tries to reach for him and guide him to her chest, but Thomas is already sobbing and wrapping him in his hoodie, even though the baby is still attached to her.

As her body shivers violently, she opens her eyes to see Thomas sawing at the umbilical cord with the knife he had been carrying. Bile rises in her throat. Mel knows that in a minute or two he will have taken her baby from her entirely and carried him away. And no one knows Mel is here. That she is here and feels like she is going to pass out. In this moment, that feels like it would be a blessed relief, but she knows she can't abandon her baby.

Try as she might though, she cannot find the strength or the break from pain to reach for him.

'Please, Thomas,' she begs, her voice sounding pathetic.

'I'm sorry,' he says, never taking his eyes from the mewling baby in his arms as he gets to his feet, turns away from her and starts walking towards the door. Mel doesn't know if the apology was meant for her or for the baby.

But the door screeches open before he can reach it.

Her heart lifts when, silhouetted against the doorway, she can make out the familiar shape of Sheila. Help is here and she will make everything better.

She opens her mouth to call out to her neighbour but just as she does, she hears Sheila herself speak.

'Dear Jesus, Thomas! What have you done?'

And just like that, nothing makes sense again.

'It's Jacob,' she hears Thomas say. 'She was too far gone to get as far as your house. We had to stop here. We'd no choice. What kept you? We needed you,' Thomas sobs as he cradles the newborn infant.

'He sounds fit and well to me, but Thomas, what have you done with that poor girl?' Mel watches in disbelief as Sheila approaches her and crouches down beside her. 'It wasn't meant to be like this,' she says. 'I'm sorry you've been through this. But my son deserves to be a father. I deserve to be a granny and you know I will be a good one. You've seen how I am with little Tilly.'

'I need help,' Mel says, shivering violently now. 'Please, Sheila. Please, help me. Tilly needs me and so does the baby.'

'Tilly will be perfectly fine with her daddy and he'll probably get the chance to follow his dreams now that he doesn't have you holding him back,' Sheila says, stroking her hair as the full horror of the situation becomes all too clear.

'Please,' Mel begs. 'I won't tell anyone. I promise.'

'I don't think so, dear. We've already gone to too much trouble to get to this point. We're not about to throw that all away now. I'm sure you understand. A mother would do anything for her son. Anything at all.'

Sheila stands to leave, turning away from Mel who, try as she might, cannot pull herself to sitting, never mind standing. She watches, helpless, as Sheila Quigg – or the woman who identified herself as Sheila Quigg – wraps her arm around her son's shoulders and leads him from the barn.

The sharp screech of the barn door as they pull it closed, plunging her once again into darkness, feels like the clanging of a cell door.

Her baby is gone. And with it, her hope. All that is left is the cold of this place wrapping itself around her, and the pain in her head. She knows she should get up. That she should use what little strength she has to try and leave but she can't. She's too tired. Too sore. Too cold. She just wants to sleep. To slip away from it all, even though she knows she may never wake up.

As her eyelids begin to flutter closed and just as she starts to surrender to unconsciousness, there is a deafening blast of sirens, the flashing of blue lights and there are voices everywhere. The barn door screeches open again, bringing with it a blast of cold air. Indistinct shouting, crying and orders being barked, but it's too fuzzy now for Mel to make sense of. She just wants to close her eyes to escape the searing pain in her head.

She feels a hand take hers, and she tries to pull away, terrified it is Thomas or Sheila or the man in black from her nightmares come to take her away for good.

'Mel, Mel! Stay awake. It's going to be okay. You stay with us, okay? Your baby is safe. He's going to be fine. We need you to be fine too. Oh Mel, I'm so sorry,' a strangely familiar voice says, but it's not enough to keep her in the room.

The voice fades, followed by the distorted sounds of men shouting instructions. 'She's fitting!' a voice calls out. There are hands on her body, a blanket, a cannula, but she feels none of it. She has drifted away.

42

TWO DAYS OLD

The crisp white linen, stiff with starch, feels cool on Mel's skin. She is so very tired – the effort of showering and changing into fresh pyjamas has been intense. But she's had Ed to help her, while her mother held Teddy and rocked him gently to sleep. And while she is exhausted from the effort of something as simple as washing her hair, she feels so much better for it. Even though she has washed before, she can't get the smell of the barn from her nostrils. Ed tells her she's wrong. There's no smell, but she swears it lingers.

Or it did until now – now she smells fresh and clean – *feels* fresh and clean. She is back in bed and resting, her blood pressure still being monitored two days after everything went so badly wrong.

The doctors have told her she is lucky to have been found when she was, her blood pressure being worryingly high and having had several seizures both in the barn and in the ambulance as she was blue-lighted to hospital.

Postpartum preeclampsia can be fatal, they've told her. Ed said he'd known she would be okay when Mel had joked with the doctors that she could have done without the extra trauma of thinking about a brush with death. 'Giving birth in a barn with a seriously disturbed person was bad enough,' she'd told them.

It's something she knows she will have to process in time but for now she wants to focus on the positive. She is here and so is Teddy. They are here and they are well. And a mother would do anything – endure anything – for her child.

He is the most beautiful creature, a perfect echo of his big sister. Mel feels so very blessed. She knows it could've been so different.

It would've been so different had it not been for Alice, of all people. Alice who had tried so desperately to get in touch with Mel on the phone. Who had been so worried that she had contacted Mel's mother to see if the baby had been born, only to have strips torn off her for her cruelty.

Alice who had sobbed, humiliated. She hadn't wanted to be cruel. She just wanted to relive, even as fantasy, what it had been like to be pregnant. Who had felt so lonely without her friend, and without her son, that she had clung to make-believe. She hadn't intended to take it so far but it had been so nice to pretend everything was okay. To talk about her marriage as if it hadn't exploded. To pretend there was a baby bouncing on her bladder and that she was able to consider buying a new pram. Her entire being still ached for Jacob and this time of year was brutally hard but still, she had not intended to hurt Mel. She knows she has hurt her enough. More than enough.

There is no way she could have known what sick game Thomas and his mother already had in play. How Thomas, enraged by Mel and Ed's escape across the country to start all over again, had hatched a plan with his mother that helped him feel he had avenged his son. It had been easy for Sheila to rent a house close to the Davisons' new home. She just had to be vague about it when she spoke to them. Always refuse a lift. Insert herself into their lives so much that they never had the chance to come looking for her. She was able to keep a very close eye on what exactly was going on in that household. To witness the strains and pressures they were under and convince herself that their baby boy would be better off with a father who adored him – and a granny who would spoil him with home-cooking and storybooks.

Still, it was never meant to be as brutal as it turned out to be. Sheila could not have predicted that Mel would develop high blood pressure, or that she would overhear Ed calling her a crone. Mocking her behind her back. That had hurt. It had hurt and enraged her, and it was then she had told Thomas it was time to take action.

The plan was certainly not for Mel to give birth in a barn. They had not expected her to go into labour. It was all supposed to be a lot more controlled and sanitised but things had gone wrong, as they often did for Thomas.

Just as they were enacting their plan, and Mel's mother was telling Alice that her daughter knew she wasn't pregnant, Alice was deciding the only way to make it good was to visit Mel herself. Talk it out – the truth, the whole truth and nothing but the truth.

Her heart had almost stopped when, driving towards the Davisons' house, she had spotted Thomas's car. She'd felt, in her soul, that something was wrong. Very wrong. And this was only confirmed when she checked his location on her phone – something they had not quite got around to stopping – and saw that he was at the caravan.

That she was able to track him as he led Mel up towards the barn was a stroke of luck. Maybe she should have intervened sooner but she didn't want to endanger Mel or the baby by making Thomas angry.

Thankfully she was to intervene just in time – the emergency services arriving not a moment too late to retrieve the baby and save his mother.

Mel doubts she will ever be able to thank Alice enough. But she does know there is a whole lot of healing that needs to happen on all sides. Healing that will require them to talk and share and work together. Ed and Mel have their own journey to go on. But for now, they have their baby, and with the threats against them gone, the desire to leave the country has also decreased. It remains something they will talk about, at another time. For now, they will work on their future, and their dream house, together. Ed has taken on the big project that will keep him away from home but Mel doesn't mind. She's very much going to enjoy being spoiled by her parents while Ed is away. It will be nice for them all to be home together in Carrickfergus.

'Do you want him over now?' her mother asks, standing up and carrying a sleeping Teddy to Mel. Once he is safely in her arms again, she feels complete. This little boy is so loved, and so very special. Mel doesn't think she will ever stop being completely enthralled by him.

As she breathes in her son's baby smell, she hears the unmistakable noise of a four-year-old who is running down the hospital corridor towards her room. She is chatting to her grandad who chatters back with such joy in his voice that Mel's heart swells.

She grins as her little girl runs into her room and straight for her hospital bed, clambering up to see her mummy and Teddy, while Mel's father walks in behind her, smiling broadly.

'You're looking much better,' he says. 'More like yourself. I'm glad to see it. There's a bit more colour in your face.'

'I'm feeling a lot better today, Daddy,' Mel reassures him as he walks towards her, kisses the tips of her fingers and touches Teddy's forehead.

'He's a wee dote,' he declares. 'Nice rosy cheeks too. He'll be a great fella altogether. Like his grandad!'

As she hands her baby to her father, and the rest of her family sit around her bed, she thinks of just how precious life, and family, can be – and how easily it can all be lost.

She'll be holding on tight now though. Forever. And she won't take a moment for granted.

* * *

MORE FROM CLAIRE ALLAN

Another book from Claire Allan, *The Affair*, is available to order now here:

https://mybook.to/TheAffairBackAd

ACKNOWLEDGEMENTS

Writing a book requires many, many hours of solitude and the space to disappear into your own imagination for days at a time. This book was no different but without the support of a small army of people, it never would have seen the light of day.

My first word of thanks goes to my editor Rachel Faulkner-Willcocks for her unending patience, invaluable advice and ability to help transform a half-baked first draft into the book you read today. Not only do I admire Rachel's ability to help me tease out a story, but also her drive to push me out of my comfort zone at times. That is, after all, where the magic happens – according to David Bowie. Rachel's understanding when the curve balls were thrown in my direction is also greatly appreciated.

Thanks to all at Boldwood Books, including the many faces behind the scenes who work constantly to put our books in front of readers. Thanks to the marketing, sales and production teams, with special nods to Claire, Jenna and Ben who were so very helpful. Thanks to copy-editor Sandra Ferguson for her keen eye and Christina Curtis for her proofreading skills. And, of course, thanks to Amanda Ridout, the indefatigable woman at the helm!

As always I have to offer my thanks to my agent Ger Nichol who, twenty-one books in, continues to be a cheerleader and shoulder to cry on when necessary. I can't imagine finding my way through this business without her by my side.

Thanks also to Hannah at The Rights People for overseeing

my foreign rights sales and pushing my books out further into the world.

Thanks to the book bloggers, reviewers and booksellers who make this job possible. It's a competitive world out there and this writer appreciates your support. Special thanks to Lesley Price at Bridge Books, Dromore, who is a one-woman hand-selling machine. Thanks to the many members of her book club who have come to listen to me blether on about books a few times now and who are genuinely the loveliest people.

Thanks to all my readers – especially those who have stuck with me through thick and thin and everything in between. I see you and I appreciate you more than you can know.

I want to give a special mention here to Jodi Harte, a very lovely woman who brought her niece – the amazing Emma – along to my book-signing. Emma entertained us all and I am sure this young lady has a long and successful career as a writer waiting for her in the future. Dear Emma, the character of Emma in this book is named after you.

To my writer friends – especially those who give unfailingly of their time and friendship. With special love and appreciation this year for John Marrs, Emma Heatherington and, as always, my soul sister in writing, Fionnuala Kearney.

To those real life friends and family who have supported me and accepted that my mind is often wandering to imaginary places – I thank you. It's been an intense writing year and I have often been too busy to step away from my desk – and you still are friends with me and I appreciate that! Thanks especially to Julie-Anne, Marie-Louise, Fiona, Erin, Catherine and Bernie for staying in touch. Thanks to Serena for the continued laughs and solidarity.

Thanks to my parents, whom I love with my entire heart, my sisters Lisa and Emma, my brother Peter – along with their assorted spouses and offspring – both human and furry! Thanks to my husband for a room to write in and for listening to my long explanations of how publishing works. Thanks to my amazing kids – Joe and Luka. I am so proud of you both every single day in life. You make me laugh and you make me think of the world in a different way. You both also make me broke – but I forgive you.

Thanks to the staff at EDIT, including Janice and Martine who have moved on. You are incredible human beings.

She can't read, but I'll thank my best furry girl Izzy as well. One of four animals in our household, she is my soul-pet and my constant reminder that hugs help.

Finally, thanks to each and every one of you who picks up this book and gives it a chance. Without readers, a writer is nothing. Thank you.

ABOUT THE AUTHOR

Claire Allan is the internationally bestselling author of several psychological thrillers, including *Her Name Was Rose*. Boldwood publish her women's fiction under the name Freya Kennedy and will continue to publish her thrillers.

Sign up to Claire Allan's mailing list here for news, competitions and updates on future books.

Visit Claire's website: www.claireallan.com

Follow Claire on social media:

facebook.com/claireallanauthor

x.com/claireallan

instagram.com/claireallan_author

bookbub.com/authors/claire-allan

THE
Murder
LIST

THE MURDER LIST IS A NEWSLETTER DEDICATED TO SPINE-CHILLING FICTION AND GRIPPING PAGE-TURNERS!

SIGN UP TO MAKE SURE YOU'RE ON OUR HIT LIST FOR EXCLUSIVE DEALS, AUTHOR CONTENT, AND COMPETITIONS.

SIGN UP TO OUR NEWSLETTER

BIT.LY/THEMURDERLISTNEWS

Boldwood

Boldwood Books is an award-winning fiction publishing company seeking out the best stories from around the world.

Find out more at www.boldwoodbooks.com

Join our reader community for brilliant books, competitions and offers!

Follow us
@BoldwoodBooks
@TheBoldBookClub

Sign up to our weekly deals newsletter

https://bit.ly/BoldwoodBNewsletter

www.ingramcontent.com/pod-product-compliance
Ingram Content Group UK Ltd.
Pitfield, Milton Keynes, MK11 3LW, UK
UKHW020634070225
454767UK00001BA/17